PHILIP EDWARD THOMAS, eldest son of Welsh parents, was born in 1878 in London. He was educated at Battersea Grammar School, St Paul's and Lincoln College, Oxford, where he married Helen, daughter of James Ashcroft Noble, who had encouraged the publication of his early nature essays and *The Woodland Life* (1897). At first an active, poorly paid journalist-reviewer (especially for the *Daily Chronicle* and then *The Bookman*), he soon left London for Kent (1901–6) until he finally settled near Petersfield close to Bedales School. There his elder children (Merfyn and Bronwen) were pupils and his wife often taught in the kindergarten until his third child (Myfanwy) was born. Many country books, including *Oxford* (1903), *Beautiful Wales* (1905), *The South Country* (1909), *In Pursuit of Spring* (1914) were followed by seven literary studies, especially on *Richard Jefferies* (1909), *Maeterlinck* (1911), *Pater* (1913) and *Keats* (1916). These were interspersed with the tales in *Rest and Unrest* (1910) and *Light and Twilight* (1911) and a novel, *The Happy-Go-Lucky Morgans* (1914).

As his critical standing rose and his earnings fell, for two years before 1914 he seemed an uncertain, irresolute wanderer. Much encouraged by Robert Frost, Edward Garnett and a Civil List grant, he suddenly turned to poetry in November 1914. He enlisted in the Artists' Rifles the following July, was commissioned in November 1916, embarked for France with the 244 Siege Battery RGA in January 1917 and was killed at an Observation Post near Arras on Easter Day 1917. Posthumous works included *Poems* by 'Edward Easterway' (1917), *A Literary Pilgrim in England* (1917), *Cloud Castle and other Papers* (1922), *The Last Sheaf* (1928) and *The Childhood of Edward Thomas* (1938). The publication of his *Collected Poems* (1920) confirmed his reputation as one of the finest poets of the early twentieth century.

R. George Thomas was educated at University College

Cardiff and, after war service in Iceland, India and the Far East, he returned there and eventually became Professor of English Language and Literature, a post he held until 1980. A Fellow of his old college and a founder member of the Welsh Academy, he has written numerous books and articles. He edited the standard *The Collected Poems of Edward Thomas* (1978) and is author of the definitive biography *Edward Thomas: A Portrait* (1985). He is currently completing the *Selected Letters of Edward Thomas* (with Professor A.J. Smith) for O.U.P.

EDWARD THOMAS

The Pilgrim and Other Tales

Selected with an Introduction by
R. George Thomas

J.M. Dent & Sons Ltd
London
Charles E. Tuttle Co. Inc.,
Rutland, Vermont
EVERYMAN'S LIBRARY

Made in Great Britain by
The Guernsey Press Co. Ltd, Guernsey, C.I. for
J. M. Dent & Sons Ltd
91 Clapham High Street, London SW4 7TA
and
Charles E Tuttle Co., Inc.
28 South Main Street, Rutland, Vermont 05701
U.S.A.

First published in Everyman's Library 1991

British Library Cataloguing-in-Publication Data
for this title is available upon request

ISBN 0460 870831

Everyman's Library
Reg. U.S. Patent Office

Typeset at The Spartan Press Ltd,
Lymington, Hants

Contents

Introduction

Three quarters of this selection was written between 1909 and October 1911 (the exceptions are *Morgan* (1913), *Seven Tramps* (1903), and all the sketches from *The Last Sheaf*, apart from *The Friend of the Blackbird*). They mark a critical staging post in Edward Thomas's slow evolution as a writer. At seventeen or eighteen he was a *belle-lettre* journalist and Paterian essayist. After three years at Lincoln College, Oxford, he frequently inserted carefully polished 'prose poems' into a series of nature and topographical books while he was establishing a formidable reputation as an independent reviewer, especially of poetry.

Between 1912 and 1914 there followed a period of falling readership for his books and complete personal uncertainty during which many of his best critical-biographical studies were published. Suddenly, late in 1914, when the onset of war seemed to have closed all doors on a reflective writer, his poems began to flow and continued until he left for France and his death near Arras on Easter Monday 1917. Since then his reputation as a poet has continued to grow, especially so since the 1960s. His poems seem to reflect the social, spiritual, and intellectual needs and concerns of a younger generation. But the puzzle remains: why did it take so long for Thomas to discover the appropriate medium for what he had to say of permanent value to his potential readers? As W.H. Hudson divined in a letter to Edward Garnett[1] in December 1913:

[1] Edward Garnett (1868-1936) was an influential publisher's reader and critic who became an adviser to many of the most important writers of the period. He was married to Constance Garnett (translator of Tolstoy) and was father of David Garnett.

Thomas is essentially a poet, one would say of a Celtic kind . . .
I should say that in his nature books and fiction he leaves all
there's best in him unexpressed . . . I believe that if Thomas had
the courage or the opportunity to follow his own genius he
could do better things than these. You noticed probably in
reading [*The Happy-Go-Lucky Morgans*] that every person
described in it . . . are one and all just Edward Thomas. A poet
trying to write prose fiction often does this.

It is his ability to confront the dream world of the poetic
imagination with the ordinary world of practical decisions that
gives the tales and sketches in this selection their distinctive and
challenging quality.

Thomas was not quite the hampered prose writer that Hudson
suggests. As a lad, exploring the commons around the ever-
expanding suburbs of South London, and thirty years later as a
soldier in training, he had remained a seasoned trespasser who
persistently followed his own path. The original writing of the
two volumes *Rest and Unrest* and *Light and Twilight*, despite
their liberal, ironic titles, brought him deep personal satisfaction,
if little financial reward. This was for him a particularly happy
stretch of writing that certainly extended from January 1909 until
September 1910. In December 1908 he had abandoned the
superficially attractive post of Assistant Secretary to a new Royal
Commission on Welsh Monuments and had decided to continue
earning a living as a journalist and writer. Previously he had relied
heavily on multiple reviewing for his staple modest income and
had relieved this 'unskilled labour' by the regular submission of
short sketches (nature articles, reveries, and extracts of personal
statements from his various commissioned works), to a variety of
weeklies and monthlies. With the constant support of Edward
Garnett, Duckworth published three collections of these sketches
in their *Roadmender Series*. *Rest and Unrest* (1910) and *Light
and Twilight* (1911) belong to this period and his satisfaction is
shown in his letters:

I have been writing not reviews, not commissioned books, not
landscapes, stories etc. Since the beginning of the year I have
had an extraordinary energy in writing and have done nothing
else and only been to town for one day . . . I don't know what
these sketches will turn out to be. For I have been too busy to

copy them, except one or two that are short. Most are unfit for the papers and magazines by being too unpleasant, or too fanciful, or too quiet. (To Gordon Bottomley[2], 13 February 1909)

Here is nearly ¼ of the year gone and I seem to have been sitting close up to the fire all the time writing all sorts of things which you shall see some day only I don't like to trouble you with M.S. and the typescript is being thrust upon editors. I have done a great deal at first under a real impulse but latterly (the long frost having quite undermined me) by force of daily custom as much as anything. I can do almost anything if once I can start doing it every day at a certain hour. And as reviewing has been scarce I have had few interruptions. I feel sure it is better work or in a better direction than all but the best of the old but it is even less profitable and quite impossible to palm off on a publisher as part of a guinea guide book. (To Bottomley, 15 March 1909)

I am glad you found things to like in the little book. It is too small a selection from the things I have been doing to be quite fair to me. Also it is my own selection . . . I think I agree with your preferences – also in what you say of note books. But I shall not burn them I expect. Only I shall certainly use them less and less as I get more of an eye for subjects. Among my bad habits was that of looking through my old note books of scenery etc. in order to get a subject or mood suggested to me. I now use the note books more and more exclusively for the details of things conceived independently. Also I am casting about for subjects which will compel me to depend upon what I am – memory included but in a due subsidiary place. I think of Welsh legends. As to modern subjects I can do little with more than one character and that one is sure to be a ghost (of a pretty woman or nice old man) or else myself. (To Bottomley, 12 October 1909)

I don't think I should offer the proposed book to any other publisher yet. So far as I know no other would give me £10 for it, and Dent might be willing to give something less than he did

[2] Gordon Bottomley (1874-1948), a bank clerk who later became a prolific and highly-acclaimed poet, writing epic as well as lyric poetry, and poetic drama. He was a life-long friend to Edward Thomas and later Robert Frost.

for *The South Country* if we try a little later. It looks very much as if I had got to the point where I have been tried and found wanting and must look forward to publishing occasionally a book for the usual 1000 readers and getting 7 copies free in return, depending on reviewing for what is called a living. (To his literary agent, Cazenove, 26 December 1909)

After the publication of *Rest and Unrest* in February 1910 and the confirmation of his wife Helen's pregnancy with their third child, Thomas decided to replace complete reliance on reviewing by the writing of commissioned books of a more literary kind. 'Very rashly but yet necessarily,' he informed Bottomley in March, 'I have undertaken to produce three books in the next twelve months. One is practically written. The other two books are (1) on Maeterlinck and (2) on Women and Poets.' He tackled the second book first and worked faster than he needed 'in a kind of suppressed panic', he told Bottomley. 'I am sick at having to do it but I believe I am justified in not doing as well as possible a piece of work I never could do really well with my powers. That is provided I do not harm my ability to do other things more natural to me. The slightest of these you have seen in *The Nation* etc.' These latter 'more natural things' refer to some of the smaller sketches in this selection.

Commentators on Edward Thomas's poetry have missed the significance of the decisions he took at this time. Boosted by the excess of energy and confidence that produced these tales and sketches, he decided deliberately to substitute uncongenial critical-biographical bookmaking for routine reviewing as his staple source of income. This led to many hurried tasks that did not sell despite favourable reviews, until he began to believe that his work was undervalued. He left Steep for longer periods in order to be nearer London and to pick up casual journalism, even while his quality as a leading critic of contemporary poetry was being more firmly established. Eventually he gave up his fine, specially-built house on the hill above Steep for a cheap semi-detached workman's cottage in Steep village; there he soon found it impossible to work except up at his hill-top study which he had retained as almost a grace-and-favour residence from his friend Geoffrey Lupton – and there his poetry was first begun in late 1914.

One of his worst bouts of severe depression developed in the autumn of 1912 and, for eighteen months afterwards, he walked or wandered or worked as a paying guest away from home – but always with regular visits to his family at Steep – in a fiercely severe attempt to understand his own nature, his past, his compulsive urge to write, and what he really had to say to others. He had begun the insistent quest for those 'living, social words' which he declared to be absent from the style of the still fashionable Walter Pater. Throughout this period, when he was consulting the Jungian analyst Godwin Baynes, he never ceased to work at his books, articles, short stories and sketches. As usual, he met all his deadlines promptly and included, in sections of all this work, the opinions, attitudes, and ruminations that chart the progress of a better understanding of himself, and prepare the way for the sudden emergence of his poetry.

Edward Thomas, as man and writer, does not fit easily into readymade categories despite the wide range of memoirs recorded by his numerous friends. Plagued by occasional bouts of severe melancholy and, on one occasion, suspected (even by his wife) of the suicidal tendency described in *The Attempt*, he was sought after as a walking companion by a wide variety of men – writers, civil servants, naturalists, a parson-poet, business man, men of private means, artists, musicians, dramatists, countrymen and close relations. They all recall his gift of acute observation, coupled with bouts of silence broken by occasional discussions in exquisite, thoughtful language on a variety of topics. Others recall his gift for singing songs of all kinds – popular, folksy, or vulgar – and his love of good ale, good tobacco in clay pipes, and tavern meals. He himself was puzzled, on his long tramps or cycle rides, that the people he met casually didn't know how to place him. He wasn't a gentleman, he wasn't a bohemian artist, he wasn't a naturalist – he was something in between these recognizable types. One suspects he was delighted with the ambiguous station so accorded him. He was happiest observing from the outside: it left him free to observe and record for future use all that he saw and heard. (Ironically, he met his death in France at the advanced Observation Post of his Artillery battery in the early morning of a successful offensive.) On one point all the memorialists agree – even the subaltern who shared his O.P.: from adolescence he was dedicated to the vocation of a writer. This avocation first emerged as he escaped from his South London suburban home into the commons and woods of the surrounding Surrey countryside. His youthful articles about them were published in a variety of papers.

For the remaining twenty-one years of his life he felt more at home in rural South England, although he spent parts of his working life in search of literary-journalist employment in London. Eventually, he would leave the intellectual stimulus he had sought in luncheon and teatime gatherings – or in evenings spent at the homes of a curious range of friends – and return to his succession of rural homes and the complete solitude he always demanded for his commissioned work. And then, invariably, he would set off on interminable walks that were the natural accompaniments of the long hours at his desk. This dual nature has obviously determined the titles of some of his most personal prose. (His own suggestion for the collection published posthumously as *Cloud Castle* was *Thick and Clear*.) He pondered and admired the instinctive songs of birds that rarely departed from their effective true statement: and he desired for his own writing that it should be in 'a language not to be betrayed.' He seemed to hold in equipoise and simultaneously both sides of any experience that gripped his attention.

Edward Thomas frequently played down his gift for sustained thought although he knew quite early, before he attended St Paul's School, that he had 'a way with languages and dictionaries'. Throughout his life he preferred the company of artists to that of the many advocates of tough intellectual argument in luncheon gatherings and Fleet Street offices. On one of his Cambridge visits he felt distinctly ill at ease with some of Rupert Brookes' friends: he was genuinely on securer ground with James Guthrie, W.H. Davies, Conrad and De la Mare, with William Morris's disciple the craftsman Geoffrey Lupton, with the untypical Edward Garnett, or the wide-ranging W.H. Hudson. Within the private bounds of his own created fictional world, he gravitated towards the adopted figure of the peasant Dad Uzzell – or at least to one part of him – rather than towards the intellectual, Comtean,[3] progressive, overcombative world of public debate and social action in which his own father

---

[3] Auguste Comte (1798-1857). French philosopher whose ideas on the development of human knowledge laid the foundations for the study of sociology. Thomas's father was a great advocate and writer on Comtean philosophy.

flourished. It would be foolish to accept Thomas's declared inability to conceptualize at his own face value, but somehow, as sections of *The South Country* and *Maurice Maeterlinck* clearly show, he had learned to distrust wholehearted reliance on the processes of ratiocination alone (a distrust clearly revealed in many parts of this selection). For Thomas kept himself – as far as possible – outside the groups and causes and cliques that were the hallmark of the English literary scene between Edward VII's accession to the throne and the Great War. His own concerned interests moved consistently around definite topics, scenes, and attitudes. This selection represents them all without tendentious bias: the dream world, eminently so in *A Sportsman's Tale*; the harsh plight and treatment of social misfits in *Seven Tramps* or *Hawthornden* or *A Group of Statuary*; the limited freedom of escapees from a modern industrial world (*In the Crowd at Goodwood*, *Morgan*, and *The Friend of the Blackbird*); the conflicts inherent within the creative writer's temperament in an uncongenial epoch (The Pilgrim, *The Stile*, and *The End of the Day*); the trained reporter's impartial, sympathetic eye in *A Third Class Carriage*, *Tipperary*, *Sunday Afternoon*, or *Mothers and Sons*. There still remains an undercurrent of idealized, often legendary portraits of women of almost Pre-Raphaelite provenance and a constantly charged depiction of tensions within clearly observed family relationships. The range and quality of these concerns can be matched repeatedly in the Thomas note books preserved in the New York Public Library; in my judgement, they are also vividly present in his one hundred and fortyfour poems.

The Welsh tales in this selection confirm the special role of this happy year of writing (1909) as a bridging period in the poet's evolution. Reading them, one moves into a world that lies hesitatingly between the borders of dreams and workaday experience, between a semi-idealized Edwardian prose and the flexible yet more concrete idiom of modern poetry. Here he recalls the long vacations from school and university that were spent with his father's family in the Pontardulais area, where his lifelong friendship with the Welsh bard and theologian, Gwili, first began. This younger Thomas emerges clearly from two studies of Welsh characters in his *Beautiful Wales* (1905). One is of Llewellyn the Bard:

I think that he likes men truly because they remind him of something he has read or dreamed, or because they make him dream. In a world where things are passing, he loves best things which, having past and having left a ghost of fame behind, can live for ever in minds like his . . . He sees the world as a commonwealth of angels and men and beasts and herbs . . . After all, in matters of the spirit, men are all engaged in colloquies with themselves. Some of them are overheard, and they are all poets. It is his fortune that he is not overheard, at least by me.

There is another study of Morgan Rhys, bard and tinplater, whose so-called matter-of-factness in combination with a rich imagination is 'perhaps a Welsh characteristic':

Along with his love of poetry went a curious study of appearance and illusion. He has never tired of considering them; of trying to elucidate the impressionism of the eyes and the other senses; of trying to know what there was in a tree or face or flower which many measurements, scientific descriptions, photographs, even pictures did not exhaust.

Often in his long solitary walks, Morgan Rhys

stepped over the edge of the world and saw the gods leaning from the stars among the clouds, and perhaps the loneliness that followed appalled him . . . For these days flew fast. And so he tried to fortify himself by mingling with the life of everyday in the village, where his reputation was for generosity, hard drinking, and perfect latitude of speech. But he could not live both lives . . . He began to shrink not only from all men but from all outward experience, and to live, as only too easily he could, upon his own fantasy.

On the evidence of Thomas's large 1903 book of notes for *Beautiful Wales* (preserved in the Colbeck Collection in Vancouver) and many letters to Gordon Bottomley, these Welsh character studies were based exclusively on himself, his own father, their many relations in Wales and the two bards Watcyn Wyn and Gwili. These affectionate, confessional portraits offer many clues to his happy self-absorption in writing *Rest and Unrest* and *Light and Twilight*. His inclusion of many 'prose poems' in his nature and travel books had gained only critical acclaim. Gradually publishers rejected his outlined proposals for new books because they were 'too vague'. He was a successful reviewer and knew the constraints under which literary reviewers had to work, but he complained frequently in his letters that even the most favourable reviews missed completely what his books were about. By recalling his earlier Welsh experiences he appeared to find a suitable form for a neglected side of his nature that demanded acute personal reflections far removed from the topic immediately before him. Some shorter tales – like *The Stile*, *The Fountain* and *The End of a Day* – confirm that this highly competent reviewer and scrupulous travel-book writer was equally determined to record his solitary excursions into the world of reverie and waking dreams. He seemed always to walk the tightrope between the competing claims of tenuous speculation and precise observation, exactly as Morgan Rhys had done in the period 1902-3. His correspondence with his agent (preserved in Durham University) suggests that he hoped that his freedom in writing these tales would lead to a wider audience and a more lucrative market. When these hopes failed, and despite the perceptive qualities at the centre of all his critical biographies written between 1911 and 1914, his acute depression increased and he turned further inward into himself. This is the false trail of the unfinished, unpublished 'Fiction', the suburban novel *The Happy-Go-Lucky Morgans*, the posthumously published *Childhood of Edward Thomas*, and the 'Other Man' episodes in his last travel book, *In Pursuit of Spring*, which caused Robert Frost to insist that Thomas should abandon his attempts to write novels or travel books full of 'prose poems' and to devote all his time to poetry – a counsel that Thomas immediately rejected.

Fortunately, Thomas himself had then emerged from an eighteen-month period of intense self-examination with a clearer view of his own gifts as a journalist reporter and had learned to forge for himself a style that was finely attuned to combine the velleities of his inner vision with a clearheaded perception of life around him.[4] To this self-cleansing we owe the combination of clearly-etched studies and unquestioned sensitivity to the plight of others that marks most of the tales and reports in the two posthumous collections drawn upon for this selection. It was no surprise to discover that in November 1914, Thomas at first

[4] See in particular the article 'How I Began' in *The Last Sheaf*.

began to write two short prose passages that were quickly turned into such poems as *Up in the Wind* and *Old Man*. In 1914 too, his staple income had been assured by a modest grant from The Literary Fund, itself a public confirmation of the esteem in which the literary establishment had regarded himself and his work.

Edward Thomas's best prose accords readily with the plangent concerns of the later twentieth-century reader. Always aware of his own roots, he inevitably describes his characters within their total environment. In his innumerable reviews, as in his literary studies, he responded directly to writers with a quasi-mystical sense of the union between all created things. Alert to the complex nature of the human personality, he can still apprehend the simpler unifying qualities of shared human experience. For him, despite his many bouts of acute depression, the essential quality of successful living was not based on cultivated eccentricity or slavish conformity, but on a humble, alert acceptance of things as they are. This was a hard lesson for a writer whose earliest devotion was to the works of Shelley and Blake. Tied by his profession to Edwardian literary London, and surrounded by the friendship of the best successful writers of his day, he chose to write about the simple, the unaffected, the artless, and the independently free people he encountered (and sought out perhaps) in his long tours of the South of England on bicycle and foot. Wales, like Cornwall and Wiltshire, became a potent evocative symbol in all his writing for the things that endure because of their direct links with an ancient, almost pre-historic, natural way of life. This too was the touchstone he applied in his appreciation of other men's writings (W. H. Davies, Conrad, Masefield, Synge, Yeats, and Frost), and it becomes the hallmark of his own verse.

He had a natural ease as a prosewriter and critic. Having decided in Oxford that poetry and prose were no longer distinguishable, he experimented endlessly with prose-poems even as he was moving slowly towards his declared ideal manner of writing that could catch the echo of his thought. He did not cease the search, as his letters from France, to Frost and others, show quite clearly. His poetry has still to be accepted for what it imperfectly was at the time of his death, only thirty months after it began: a search for a medium of fidelity of statement, a quest for an angle of vision that glimpsed 'eternity' in a grain of sand or a shaft of light, a patient pursuit of one's true self, however fragmented, through all its accidental, shifting metamorphoses. Eventually, his writing, like his deliberate choice of soldiering in France, was an act of complete affirmation in the oneness of experience in this world only, when reduced to its simplest yet most abiding terms. Two extracts, fourteen years apart, best illustrate the quest:

> It is the peculiar boon of the woods, that in them we can be most truly ourselves; we yield unconsciously and slowly, but not undelighted, to the power of the wood, and become as children under it, and we gain such a supreme content, that once more we weave the daisy chains, and let our spirits again leap with the song of the lark. ('Mighty Harmonies', a newspaper article in 1897)

> I had learned that I am something which no fortune can touch, whether I be soon to die or long years away . . . but I shall go on, something that is here and there like the wind, something unconquerable, something not to be separated from the dark earth and the light sky, a strong citizen of infinity and eternity. (*The Stile*, 1911)

Llanishen, Cardiff   R. George Thomas

SELECT BIBLIOGRAPHY

[Wherever possible the first edition of each item is followed by the most recent edition available to present-day readers]

Significant Prose Works by Edward Thomas

Oxford, painted by John Fulleylove, R.I., described by Edward Thomas, 1903. Revised, 1922. Hutchinson pbk, 1983.

Beautiful Wales, painted by Robert Fowler, described by Edward Thomas, 1905. 2nd edn, *Wales*, 1924. O.U.P. pbk, 1981.

The Heart of England, with 48 coloured illustrations by H. L. Richardson, 1906 and 1909. With a foreword and 3 wood engravings by Eric Fitch Daglish, 1932, 1934.

Richard Jefferies, His Life and Work, 1909. Ed. Roland Gant, Faber pbk, 1978.

The South Country (in The Heart of England Series), 1909. With an introduction by Helen Thomas (The Aldine Library, no. 12), 1932 and Everyman's Library pbk, 1984.

Rest and Unrest (The Roadmender Series), 1910.

Light and Twilight, 1911.

Algernon Charles Swinburne, 1912.

George Borrow, The Man and His Books, 1912.

The Country (Batsford Fellowship Books), 1913.

The Icknield Way, 1913, 1916, 1929. Wildwood House pbk, 1980.

The Happy-Go-Lucky Morgans [A Suburban Novel], 1913. Webb and Bower pbk, 1983.

Walter Pater, A Critical Study, 1913.

In Pursuit of Spring, 1914. Wildwood House pbk, 1981.

Keats (Jack's The People's Books), 1916, 1926.
A Literary Pilgrim in England, 1917; (The Traveller's Library), 1928. O.U.P. pbk, 1980.
The Last Sheaf, Essays by Edward Thomas, Foreword by Thomas Seccombe, 1928.
The Childhood of Edward Thomas, a fragment of autobiography with a preface by Julian Thomas, 1938. With a preface by Roland Gant and Thomas's War Diary, Faber pbk, 1983.

Books about Edward Thomas

Biographical Works

Thomas, Helen. *As it Was* and *World without End*, 1935. Faber pbk, 1972.
Farjeon, Eleanor. *Edward Thomas: The Last Four Years*, 1958. O.U.P. pbk, 1979.
Thomas, Helen. *Time and Again*, 1978.
Thomas, R. George. *Edward Thomas* (Writers of Wales), Cardiff, 1972.
Thomas, Myfanwy. *One of These Fine Days*, 1982.
Thomas, R. George. *Edward Thomas: A Portrait*, Oxford, 1985. O.U.P. pbk, 1987.

Critical Works

Coombes, H. *Edward Thomas: A Critical Survey*, 1956.
Cooke, William. *Edward Thomas: A Critical Biography*, 1970.
Marsh, Jan. *Edward Thomas: A Poet for his Country*, 1978.
Motion, Andrew. *The Poetry of Edward Thomas*, 1980.
The Art of Edward Thomas. Edited and introduced by Jonathan Barker, Poetry Wales Press, 1987.

Rest and Unrest

(1910)

The First of Spring

Alice Lacking had reached an age when already one man had confided in her his admiration for one of her friends scarcely younger than herself, one of those friends who already called her a dear old thing. In comment she allowed herself one of those faintly twitching smiles which seems to most people exquisitely tender, resigned, and sweet. Though but thirty-one years old she was one of the goddesses of twilight, pensive – restful – dim; at least, she gave others rest. She was tall but stooped; her hair was black and noticeable only for its sharp edge against her pale face, which was bony and a little askew; her dark eyes were ardent, and constantly rebelling against the tired expression which her white eyelids tended to give by slipping down. She talked little, but most of all when younger women and much younger men chanced to speak to her of poetry. A young wife suddenly thoughtful, with one child and a hunting husband who drank, would come to her with Browning's 'Parting at Morning'; and Alice would look into her eyes . . . and explain . . . in a comforting way: the young wife would look back and press her child to her breast and give a glance of perhaps melancholy discontent that the unmarried Alice should be so wise and then lastly smile with faint self-approval, as much as to say, 'At least, she cannot know everything': and Alice would caress the child. Perhaps she gave such women a faint thirst for revenge, and their way was to remark, during a whole ten years, how extraordinary it was that no man had insisted on marrying her; it was taken for granted she would be fastidious, reluctant.

For a year Alice was seriously ill. She became so much paler and her smile so much more painful in its sweetness that everyone was sorry, albeit pitiful. She kept more to her bees now and talked less than ever. She walked alone as she had always liked to do. Every week she repeated the same three or four walks several times, often the same twice a day, though laughing at herself and vowing not to do so again. Wet or fine she walked, apparently with indifference, except that her eyes were brightest in rain; both soft and stinging rain made her sing. She looked forward to the spring as to a great certain good, enjoyed all its tortuous approaches and withdrawings, yes, every one, so that the healthy fortunate men and women who went about bluffly complaining that it was too cold or too warm or too windy or too wet had throughout February and March at least one consolation, that they could joke at the expense of Alice who professed to like each separate day and its ways; and after hearing the opinion from one clever man they all agreed that she must be a pessimist at heart, or she could never be so different from them all, plain fox-hunting or agricultural or do-nothing people, optimists, of course.

Spring really seemed to have come on the twenty-seventh of March as Alice stepped out of the house and saw, though it was only two hours after sunrise, the single yellow crocuses pressed flat by the kisses of the sun, and one broad cluster of the same flowers – that could not open so wide because their petals touched – glowing as brightly as if there, at the foot of the oldest oak, the marriage of sun and earth had been consummated and was now giving birth to a child as glorious as the sun himself and also lowly and meek as earth, the mother. Beyond the edge of the garden was the hollow vale of grey-green grass, and dark woods each slightly lifted up on a gentle hillock, and water shining between, and jackdaws playing half a mile high, so far away that they were no bigger than flies and sometimes invisible, and yet their joy as clear as if it were crying out in her brain. The vale was bounded by naked, undulating hills and, above them, sunny white haze and, above that, layers of rounded white cloud melting below into the haze and behind into the blue that was almost white.

The grass was not yet green, the woods were still dark, but that could not postpone the spring. The river shone in the vale, the white roads on the opposite hills; but that did not make the spring. She knew it was spring by a grey cart horse that went by straining at a load: three brass bells tinkled and glittered between his ears and three behind his neck; his brow carried a brass crescent and four others hung before his chest; and there were scarlet ribbons about his head. There was spring in the smoke lying in a hundred white vertebrae motionless behind the rapid locomotive in the vale. There was spring in the crowing of a cock, in the silence that followed, in the crunch of distant wheels on the drying road, in the voice of the horse whinnying in his dark stall, in the childish blue of the sky between the pure white flocks at the zenith. Two girls, Alice's neighbours, dark bold girls, with deep voices, who raced about the countryside, kept poultry and dressed with an untidiness which all ridiculed and envied, rushed by; one said, 'We're going to play tennis this afternoon, and let the lawn go hang,' and the other, 'Come and look at our March chickens': and in them also there was spring. But without these things there was a something in the landscape which made her forget that it had looked haggard yesterday, haggard and drenched, hardly consenting to live; a something in the mist of love faintly enveloping the vale, not to be heard, seen, touched, tasted or even smelt, that told her it was spring; and with this inner certainty she descended the hill from her gate almost without using eyes and ears.

The steep road was disused, dry as a bone, but lumpy and hard, its unbroken flints polished like iron. Alice went down faster than she wished, and half way down she paused, already hot and fatigued. The weather which filled her with a desire to do more than she had ever done before, left her at the same time as weak as a child and on the edge of inexplicable tears. She went in under the unfenced trees at the side of the road, and sat down upon a trunk that lay mossy among a thousand wide open yellow flowers of celandine. Through the trees she could see the valley again, spread out at the foot of the hill which the road descended. She looked at it without seeing it. She half-closed her eyes to keep out the dazzle of the celandines. Her flesh, her brain, her nature, was sopped in spring like bread in wine. Her shoulders drooped forward, her neck bent, her hands supported themselves on the fallen tree, her legs changed their position slowly as if arranging themselves for sleep. She seemed to be dissolving in the languid air, her mortal flesh quivering as it acknowledged the spiritual things. Two bright chaffinches fighting and chirrupping as they chased one another swiftly through the air took her breath away. Nothing could have been more intimately and exquisitely pleasant than the first moments as she sat down, if it had not been that something in her mind rebelled, was discontented, tremulous, unhappy, and that not on account of any thought left in it from the remote or immediate past, but only, as far as she knew, because along with the surrender to the deep, rich, calm flood of spring came again an aspiration as in former springs, a desire as deep as her nature, a strong but vague and wordless desire to be something other than she was, to do something other than she was doing or had ever done – an unsatisfied desire, a worship without a skilled priest, nay! without a god even.

The laugh of a woodpecker awakened her; in her mood it was as if the laugh was her own but none the less surprising; she rose and went on down the hill. The trees on the side away from the valley were dark as if winter hid there yet, but the hazels filled the dark air with yellow and orange catkins as with vibrating dancing flowers. Alice lifted a hand as if to catch one of the loosest and ripest of the catkins, but it hung high and her hand fell again to her side. She started to run, but her limbs were unwilling, and she blushed at the ungainly failure as if she might have been seen. She walked slowly, looking down at the road and shutting out all thought, remaining only just aware that but a feeble crust covered over and kept down the seething in her mind. Before reaching the bottom she again sat down and gazed over the oak tops of a little wood, waiting and not quite unconsciously expecting that covering crust to break, perhaps helping herself to break it. And as she sat motionless the notes of a travelling organ, played in the garden of one of the houses hidden behind the oaks, rose up to her ears. It was a too slowly played tune, heavy to sickness with insincere emotion. Unembodied, uncontrolled by any passion or personality in the composer or the performer, the notes were floating about the world in a loose haze that might presently fade altogether, or on the other hand take some human shape by entering a human ear. Alice frowned and yet at the same time gave to the music just that shape which it desired in order to live and work its proper enchantment. It entered her spirit and she heard the organ with her ears no longer. The old Italian with one hand in his pocket and the other on the organ handle was playing one tune in the far-off garden, a different one in Alice.

To the sound of that music was painted and sung and spoken a tale beginning when she was eleven.

She saw herself a bright-cheeked girl, even then too thin, her eyes much larger than now, with a mane of heavy curling hair clipped short at her shoulders because it was too heavy. She wore a dress of green and yellow, as green and yellow as a furze bush that is half flowers. She was sitting curled up in a big arm-chair by an open window. It was June and not yet dawn, and all the house was asleep except the Irish terrier who was barking at her to come out again. But on her knee she had a book; it was open, and she was writing in it; and half of the book was full. She had got up early every morning that summer to write. And what she was writing was poetry – poetry in stanzas of four lines, irregular in length and accent, but rhymed alternately. She was happy. She was not unhappy now, or had not been a moment before; and in the feeling that possessed her while this picture stayed it would be impossible to divide pleasure from sadness, and both were pure and profound. She tried to remember some of the verses. They were about an oak tree. Grown-up people had told her they were not a mere senseless echo of some grown-up poet's emotion or words, as a precocious child's verses often are, but really seemed to shadow forth the child's impression of the life in the big Briareus tree with its strange silences and strange voices. For an instant she felt herself standing under the tree as a child, but she knew that she dreamed and in an instant, all was gone. The pictures ceased while she remembered simply the bliss which she had in those days not recognized. Then through that solemn haze of emotion many scenes reassembled again – a few people, rooms, gardens, fields, and streets, shadowy and precise, and strange too because all, animate and inanimate, were equally alive – like shapes moving or still, seen through softly drifting rain. Clearest of all was that child that had been herself, a bold, strong, original child – it could not be denied – passing through that large many-coloured world as if she had been the spirit of it all. Words were spoken, little words surviving like poems out of the ruins of a life; actions were performed. Books appeared, distinct passages, the very language often, and then also the pictures they had called up in that early time. Everything had given way to her in that year and the one that followed. The world was made for her, it was hers. How confidently she went about! what joy, what power! And she carried with her a secret – her personality, her self, what made her the equal of all men and things, even in a sense their superior, since she grasped them and did not feel herself grasped by them, not yet. She and her mother possessed the world. Her golden-haired mother she saw in one attitude always, seated, curved graciously forward, head slightly bowed, but eyes raised and fixed upon nothing of this world, unconscious that the child beside her was watching her through the hair which her fingers were tangling amorously; she also had her secret, a mighty mother she seemed, greatest of all the things that had life on earth, who yet had nothing to do but to love Alice who on her part had nothing to do but to give her occasions for love, for love and forgiveness. A greater painter than Titian had painted those people and those days. In their veins ran gold of June, and all about them was poured an equal holy light. It was to last and she was to live for ever. She had heard the word, and the meaning, of death, only to resolve that it was not in her destiny: she was even sure that no one with whom she was linked by any close bonds could pass away; upon everything was a seal of everlastingness.

Then a schoolroom, many books, grey books, books that rasped the hand and the soul, that were quite other than that fair world. Several of the years that followed were cut off, she knew not where or how, from those when she wrote poems: she wrote no more. She remembered other children, numbers of them, who were not as those of the earlier time, but as if they had come out of the grey books with which they were linked. She read the books and listened to men and women who explained them and asked her questions. She forgot continually, but was praised for what she retained, was given prizes and talked about in her own hearing as a clever child. She lost her secret; her mother had taken her own away and died. She still enjoyed many things but not as before; she had a sense of something postponed; the next day or perhaps the next the veil would be lifted that had fallen insidiously, a veil of huge, dim, unintelligible things, of mere greyness, having nothing to do with life but acquiesced in as in a disease, like which it brought its own opiate.

The veil was lifted, but underneath were not the colours of the regretted time; there was pain, weariness, misery, ending in illness from overwork. As she lay in bed she looked back as she was doing now. The weakness, silence, and solitude, the independence of the sick room, seemed about to restore the old time through the tears she wept quietly and long in thinking of the grey shameful years. Her window looked out upon the country and the spring, upon a shallow river rippling under alders, between meadows that rose gently up from it to the steep wooded hill which closed the view and shut out all of the sky, except a narrow indigo band against the dark trees and the firm snowy bases of the freshest white clouds she had ever seen. The alders had been lately cut to within two feet of the earth and their sharp gashed stems, moistened by rains, were orange; at their feet were primroses so numerous that she could see them as far as where the river wound out of sight. At the edge of the high woods, which were of pine and very dark, she could see shining almost white the breasts of the two missel-thrushes whose songs she heard, and of a wood-pigeon that had been there since dawn. Within the wood there was one bent silvery birch that seemed to her every time she looked at it to be a lost princess just about to run away from that immense dark host of pines. The sun burnished the white clouds, the grass now green for the first time in the year, the ripples at the curves of the river, and the breasts of the three birds. The missel-thrushes had repeated their wild sweet song over and over since she awoke. There was only one other sound and that was of the bees which she knew must be at the crocuses out of sight under her window. The air was moist, cold, pellucid and so pure that as the bees passed her window she thought she could smell their fragrant burdens. She was happy, or she was going to be very happy; she was expecting something which never appeared, and she thought she wanted someone to be near her. She called out but when someone came she knew there was no one she was willing to have; she sent for a doll she had not seen for three years and fell asleep with it before the missel-thrushes had ceased. That night she was ill again and near death.

Thinking now of the years of crawling convalescence, the arrested development, the slight curvature of the spine, the drooping eyelid (as if in that narrow room the prostrate child had been through all womanhood), thinking of the isolation, of the childless echoing house where she had rested a long bitter rest, of the little country town's one winding broad street – a flock of sheep pressed in between the high grey houses of melancholy stone, very silent – that passed at either end quite suddenly into the purest country of slow rivers and gradual hills, thinking of things almost of yesterday, Alice became fully awake and conscious of the organ music, and tried to put it away from her, but failed. Several times she dipped her fingers into the wet grass and bathed her eyes. Then she stood up straight, for a moment even on tiptoe, slowly let her head fall back, fully extended her arms with outstretched fingers, and drew in a long breath as if drawing in, with prayer and confidence, all the sweetness and strength of the air, and, afraid of the involuntary sigh of the expiration, began to walk rapidly down the hill.

She did not stop until she came to a cottage at the border of a green. The children had rooted out a bat and ball and some stumps, and with coats off were playing cricket for the first time in the year. She went round to the back of the cottage where a woman of equal massiness and agility was washing clothes in the open air, the hard white linen and the loose froth mimicking the heavy and the lighter clouds in the blue sky.

'Good morning, Mrs Appleyard,' said Alice.

'Good morning, miss,' replied the cloud-maker.

'What shall I do? play cricket with the boys or help you?'

'Won't you sit down, miss? 'Tis weariful weather. I feel myself as if I could sleep for a week. Still, 'tis beautiful weather, too.'

'Yes,' said Alice, lost for the moment in following Mrs Appleyard's magnificent energy, presently adding, 'How is the baby?'

'Wonderful well. Would you like to go up and see her? And Bessie would be glad to see you.'

In one of the two bedrooms in the attached cottage Mrs Appleyard's daughter lay in bed with her third child, new born. The coarse red-faced cowman's wife, now pale and languid, smiled faintly at Alice but let the smile expand into a broad chuckling grimace for the child to whom she turned immediately, excusing herself by saying, 'She's a beauty. We are calling her Catherine Elizabeth.'

'You're glad to have her, Bessie,' said Alice, smiling and taking up the child.

'I should think so, miss. You don't know. Don't you take any notice another time of what a woman says seven or eight months before her baby's born, when she doesn't want another. It's just nature. Still, there are mothers and mothers. Now my sister-in-law at Woodford has just had her fifth and, would you believe it, she's been asking the vicar if he knows anyone that wants a child. A pretty child, too – why, I'd like it myself, but, Lord, what would Bill say? – all that family's pretty, but this one is a white blackbird, as you might say.'

'Really,' said Alice, slowly, 'wants to give it away . . . or perhaps make a little money out of it. . . . Well, I don't wonder. Times are bad for workers. But does she really?'

'But you would wonder if you was a woman. I beg your pardon, I mean, you know what I mean. But in her it's unnatural. Only three months old, too.'

'Is it a boy or a girl?'

'A girl and the best of the bunch.'

'What is her name?'

'Rose Elizabeth, after me.'

'And it is quite healthy?'

'Yes, bless you, healthy, yes.'

'But wouldn't she want it back again, don't you think? Supposing she grew up in a good home now . . .'

'That's just what she wants. She'd make a little lady and no mistake. Some old couple, good people, gentry perhaps, would be glad of her if they only knew. They have their feelings, same as any of us.'

'And is her mother all right, except for this lack of affection?'

'Annie? Strong as a cart horse, a good-looking woman, too, in her way — she's Suffolk bred — but hard, or, well, the fact is she doesn't like Ted.'

'Your brother?'

'Yes.'

'Ah!'

Alice got up and looked out of the window at the lambs, which had been separated by hurdles from their mothers and turned into a great field of swedes, and were nibbling the tops of one and then another of the purple roots for a moment, lazily, and now and then sprawling down in the sun. She turned and asked:

'What does the vicar say, Bessie?'

'Oh, you're thinking of Annie's little Rose? He scolded her.'

'You don't think he has found anyone? I was thinking I knew, I might find, somebody who would be glad, who would consider it . . .'

'Yes, miss?'

'In fact you might mention it in case there is no one already considering it. Or I would write. My friend . . . the person I had in mind . . . I . . .'

Alice stayed a little longer, but hardly spoke, musing and pleased with the indolent pressure of the baby in her arms.

'That baby's all right, miss,' said Mrs Appleyard as Alice came out into the yard again, 'and Bessie's doing well. She'll be all the better for the rest. Healthy women like her never gets any other rest, and having me close by she'll take a full fortnight.'

'And isn't she fond of the little one!'

'Fond! And why ever shouldn't she be, miss. There's naught the matter with our Bessie.'

'Yes, but she was telling me about her little niece, Rose Elizabeth.'

'Yes.'

'She says the parents are willing to let someone adopt the child and . . .'

'So they were. I didn't want to upset Bessie, miss, but little Rose fell off a chair . . .'

'Dead! not dead?'

'No, she hurt herself though. She will live, but they will have to keep her now.'

'Oh . . .' sighed Alice in the struggle between the suddenly swollen emotion and the shock and the wish to say something of the expected kind to Mrs Appleyard who went on:

'It's a judgment on them. Why do they want to go putting off the child on somebody they don't know?'

'Yes . . . No . . . It is very sad. A crippled child . . . Most people would not think of taking it, I suppose.'

'I should think not, miss.'

'But perhaps you would give me your son's address, Mrs Appleyard. I think my friend might still . . . thank you.'

She was going away when she picked up an egg-cup full of violets from the windowsill and said:

'Violets! How sweet! I haven't found any this late season. Where did you find them?'

'Mary found them. She always finds the first. You see she is so little that she looks the flowers in their faces almost. She is so fond of them and says she likes their "pale calm blue," funny little thing!'

'Good-bye, Mrs Appleyard.'

'Good morning, miss.'

Never before had the homeward hill seemed so long and steep

as when Alice climbed back again, wearied, pulled to pieces, miserable over her new hope, her still newer despair, the scent of violets, and now . . . no! It was impossible . . . a crippled child, and a girl . . . Rose Elizabeth . . . its brain might have been affected by the fall . . . And yet was it not already in a sense hers?

'I think, Alice,' said Colonel Lacking that evening, 'you had better have a sea voyage. We will take one together, I think. Yes. This English spring is too much for us when we are no longer young. You're looking a fright.'

'It's not the spring, father, it's myself.'

'Where shall it be?' he continued, looking at a map of this world.

Sunday Afternoon

'Fear of punishment,' read Mrs Wilkins, in a clear hard percussive tone like that of two flints being struck together: 'Fear of punishment has always been the great weapon of the teacher, and will always, of course, retain some place in the conditions of the schoolroom. The subject is so familiar that nothing more need be said of it. The same is true of *Love*, and the instinctive desire to please those whom we love . . .'

Her voice burst through the ear into the brain as if with an actual physical presence, and the words themselves were apprehended dimly and fitfully like those of a man who guides us amid the whirr and hammer and throb of a factory. She held the book level with her eyes, which were for the most part fixed on the page as if it were a poor living thing whose life and death were in her power: when for a moment they were removed, it was without a change of expression, to some one of her audience of six who had seemed to betray inattention by a moving foot, a sigh, or a closing of the eyes in search of rest – vain search. Once she stopped and said to one child of the party, her granddaughter:

'Cathie, my pet, move your chair from behind your grandfather's, then you will not be so very near the fire and you will be able to see grandmother.'

Here she smiled by the mechanical act of pressing the middles of her thin lips together so as to elongate her mouth and protract the line of it upward into her grey lean cheeks. Then she continued to read with a frown at the book or at fate for having interrupted her, as in a short time happened once more. Her husband laid his huge kind hand silently upon his little grandchild's head, which it almost enclosed like the husk of a hazel nut, and there let it remain.

'Charles,' she said in the same tone, laying the book softly but firmly, and as it were cruelly, upon the black silk over her knees, 'do you really wish me to go on with this important book or not?'

'Why, yes, my dear,' he replied, instinctively smoothing the infant's hair to protect her and to encourage himself.

'Then may I ask you not to interrupt, and not to set Cathie a bad example by apparent inattention?'

'Please go on, my dear,' he said, removing the offending hand with a slight sigh of penitence and outward submission, and a twinkle of the unconquerable mind in the gay lifting of the brows over his large brown eyes that knew so well the arts of brotherhood, fatherhood, unclehood, and now for five years, of grandfatherhood.

'Then I will continue,' she said, with a rustling gesture of imperfect appeasement, 'or rather I will go back to the beginning of the chapter lest some of us should have forgotten it by this time.'

She read again: 'Fear of punishment has always been . . .' and complete silence was granted by everyone, and as far as possible by the hollow fire itself, which was now, in sympathy with the subdued audience and respect for its instructor, growing every minute more cold and black. The voice, absolutely monotonous, seemed to build an intricate structure of thin polished steel bars in the air, like a high bridge, but without obvious purpose. Most of the audience were, however, too well used to the sound to observe this effect.

Her husband was a country doctor now retired from his practice, a man, with the profile of an aged Jupiter and straight white hair and beard, who had learned in forty years of marriage to live at the same time two lives, an outer one of many duties and ceremonies for the benefit of his wife, and an inner one into which she had neither the leisure nor the curiosity to inquire, even it if had once or twice occurred to her that there was such a thing. This afternoon he was chiefly occupied in recalling to his memory Shelley's poem of 'Rosalind and Helen.'

Three of the unmarried daughters were there. They were women of thirty-three, twenty-nine and twenty-five years of age, who spent nearly the whole of their year as governess, schoolmistress and private secretary, but came home regularly at about Christmas time to worship out of long habit the mother with whom they had no contact at any other time, except by sending half of their salaries for her to invest. They admired their mother's force of character, her power of management, her indifference to the flight of time, and her clear fatigueless voice. Nervous and intelligent they suffered from the voice and the tyranny, but they, like their father, were able to quench their suffering in memories and thoughts of the separate worlds unknown to her. One of them, indeed, gave a moment or two of real attention to the words that were said, because the book was her present to her mother and she hoped to be able to say a few intelligible words in any discussion that might follow. The faces of all three were lined and thin, their black hair was going grey, and all wore spectacles. They were older than their mother. Their bony painful hands were clasped tightly on their knees; their plain dresses were ruffled over their flat chests, their heads bent. Two at least would never marry now, for their mother's knowledge of men and her exacting standard, reinforced by that voice of steel, had made it impossible for them to give way to their desires, from which this discipline was never removed. When the reader turned her eyes upon them she was reassured by three pairs of spectacles glittering attention.

In the background was another visitor but an unconsidered one, a young artist of small independent means who was supposed to be in love with one of the daughters, no one knew which. He was tall, dark, slender, mild and obviously uncomfortable, but as he never lost this expression it was unobserved, and he also was well under Mrs Wilkin's control.

The little girl was the child of a daughter who had run away to marry. The maternal discipline was escaped only for a time. Letters, visits, and that omnipotent voice had never ceased to besiege the girl after her marriage. She had consented to leave her husband and to come to live with her parents again. There, one Christmas day, in a festive house, while the north-east wind from the sea drove the sand through fast shut windows on to the hair and the sheets, into the food, into the soul, she gave birth to a child who was at once taken over by its grandmother with the words:

'Poor Alice, you see, can know nothing of children any more than she can of men. I know. All will be well.'

Mrs Wilkins took up this new interest in her crowded life of visiting the poor, making jam and marmalade, and sewing for befriended unfortunate women, as eagerly as if it were the only one.

Alice could not look after her baby, but she could cook and give her mother's advice to the neighbouring cottagers' wives. She worked hard and was feverishly content with having Cathie close at hand; she acquiesced with a faint humorous smile in her mother's judgment, 'We shall hardly make a little lady of Cathie if she has much of her father's blood.' But she crumbled slowly under the strain of her too great self-despair and self-control. One day in the next winter, as she was shutting the oven door on a half shoulder of mutton, a strong thought came into her head. She told the maidservant that she was going to drown the old cat, which she put softly into a basket with some hay and left the house. It was the first day of a thaw: the grey world dripped and reeked and gurgled and the air made the warmest clothing seem to be lined with ice. An hour later the villagers were hurrying past the house, saying that a woman had drowned herself in the river.

'What a day for her to choose, to be sure!' remarked Mrs Wilkins. 'Poor thing! I wonder who it can be. The poverty in the village is dreadful at this time of year, and there is no religion worthy of the name except in my little band. A love affair, perhaps. Why didn't she come to me? That is the pity of life – that we can't give others the full advantage of our experience. Each one wants to start afresh. The young must needs be running off to get experience for themselves, when if they only asked. . . . Look at Alice, for example. She knew nothing about men: how should she? But if she had come to me. . . .'

Then she pursed her lips with a short smile, adding thereto, as a gesture expressing modest approval of her own kindly thought, a nod of singular bird-like prettiness – for her figure and head were of exquisite regularity and proportion, well-carried and dressed with unvarying grace.

It was Alice that lay in the river, dead, with a satisfied expression. The cat came running home miserable, tiptoe on wetted paws.

Mrs Wilkins' grief at the suicide was tempered and at last quenched in a grave wondering why it should have happened, and she therefore acquiesced in the verdict of 'during temporary insanity.' 'I cannot believe it,' she said at the first news, 'she dared not.' And 'I could hardly believe my eyes,' she continued to say when describing the scene, which she would do in the same manner as when she recited 'The Assyrian came down like a wolf on the fold,' or, 'Little lamb, who made thee?'

'Now Cathie is ours to make a great success of,' said Mrs Wilkins. 'That father of hers was at any rate a strong man and she inherits his physique. As for her character, I see she has the very ways of my own sister, little Bess who died young. She would have been the best of us all, and she was as clever as she was good. She over-worked herself, Charles and died out of her mind, poor thing; and she had a love affair, too; a young man pestered her with his objectionable affections and she was too weak to reject them altogether as we could have wished, and it was too much for her. But Cathie is strong and she will be with me.'

For a few years, nevertheless, Cathie was snatched away to live in London with her father in a golden age of health and wilfulness, four years that would be a possession for ever, the richest jewel in a happy life, a crown lying at the bottom of the well of an unhappy one. But her father died and, after being passed from relative to relative, she had now arrived at her grandmother's by the sea.

At first Cathie feared the sea because there were no roads on it, and the moors round the house also, because there were no pavements on which she could get to avoid the cows. Things were too large. The earth was as large as the sky. But, on the other hand, there were black cattle and windmills on the glittering wide marsh below the house, and there was always a flock of starlings wheeling over the heather close to the door, or perched in a row on the single telegraph wire humming over the line of posts that seemed to come out of the sky — with messages from her father, perhaps, mused the child. Also there was a most ancient man who leaned against a sunny bank, as still as a tree but with a cheerful face that was chiefly eyes and whiskers like some very nice dog, clothes that were more like an animal's coat than any she had ever seen before, and a growl of a voice which somehow she knew to be kind when he said, 'Good morning, little miss, a pretty morning, little miss!' She liked walking in the little oak wood on the cliffs at the edge of the sea, where the dead leaves raced down the steep path as the rats ran after the pied piper of Hamelin, and then suddenly whirled up like butterflies and almost smothered her. On the beach there were many pebbles, and she thought that if she did a little work daily she would be able to finish a house by the time when she would wear spectacles as her aunts did, and there she could invite 'Gyp' the dog and 'Tansy' the cow and kill anybody else who tried to get in — no! not quite kill them because if they were dead they would be like her father and nobody deserved to be like that. But next day there was not a trace of her pebbles nor any footmarks of the thief, so perhaps it was her father and he was making the house in some better place.

The day after was Sunday and it was sufficiently near Christmas for sweets and nuts to be eaten in the sitting-room after dinner. She curled up in a warm chair and stared at the fire and ate continuously while the others talked and laughed more than usual, and her grandfather pitched a special sweet now and then into her lap and evidently did not want her to say, 'Thank you, dear grandpapa' before she put it into her mouth. One of her aunts played on the piano and Cathie still stared at the fire, warm and drowsy and sniffing the fruit, the wood fire, the scents of the women, and listening to the wind. She saw beautiful rockets rising straight up and spreading out like a palm tree among the stars, just as on the night before her father died. By and by the trees ceased to grow and an enormous bird stood on the earth and touched the sky: it had eyes all along its immense beak and all down its long legs, so that it could see everything as her grandmother had told her God could; so for fear lest the bird should take her last sweet she bolted it and began to cough, whereupon her grandmother said in a voice that came shooting through the music:

'Cathie, my pet, you are disturbing your aunt and spoiling our pleasure. You must not always be thinking of yourself.'

'I was thinking of God, grandmamma,' she said, but the music drowned her words. The great bird was gone, and she wished she had not swallowed the sweet because she had meant to give it to 'Tansy.' She sobbed a little and slept.

She was awakened by her grandmother telling her to sit in another chair and keep quiet while she read aloud. Again she saw the palm trees of fire, and when the golden fruit showered down there was a helter skelter of dead leaves to save themselves from being burnt, and they ran into a house made of pebbles such as she had begun to build on the beach. Now and then she heard the voice of her grandmother who was reading from a book about angels and war, which appeared to be a wicked book, but she understood little except certain familiar words – the word 'victor,' for example, reminded her of a little boy of that name and she was all ear for what followed, but in vain.

These thoughts were interrupted by her grandfather saying quietly for the second time that he could not hear, and her grandmother laying down the book and saying: 'Charles, I am reading for your pleasure, and I do think it is inconsiderate of you to interrupt . . . I think I will read a little from my own book now, Jenny's present.'

Mrs Wilkins took up the other book and read, 'Fear of punishment has always been the chief weapon of the teacher . . .' twice over, telling Cathie to sit in another chair farther from the fire.

For some time Cathie thought about nothing, and then again tried to puzzle out who had disturbed her pebbles and fancied the great bird had picked them up in his great beak, and she hoped he would swallow them and choke and be reprimanded by her grandmother. In her new seat she could see the young man, and wished she could show him her doll which was upstairs.

When the reading was over the young man rose up and looked kindly at her, and said he would go to his room and read.

Cathie looked out of the window at the moor which was now almost dark, and said to everyone:

'Why do those trees look like *that*?'

They smiled but made no reply, Jenny alone remarking, 'How sweet children are.' Mrs Wilkins was saying that they would now sing some hymns, each one choosing a favourite, when Cathie got up to follow the young man and, seeing the door shut loudly behind him, burst into tears at the thought of him and her doll both out of reach in the winter darkness. So wide opened her eyes and so far fell her mouth, so loud was her crying, that her grandmother was angry as she sat down at the piano and began to turn over the pages of the hymn book. The sound of the crying brought back the young man, and he offered to take her to his room.

'That is very kind of Mr Cardew,' said Mrs Wilkins. 'Do you hear, Cathie? But I think, Harry, she ought not to go. It is so bad for her to have her own way.'

'Then you shall sit on my knee, Cathie,' said Mr Cardew, in a vaguely protective gentle voice, not without hostility to the ruling power. He sat down and took her on his knee and encircled her as much as possible with his shoulders and both arms. She ceased to cry but not to sob and to twist the world into a tragic agony with the falling corners of her mouth, her huge eyes and lifted eyebrows of surprise.

The first hymn began:

> Shepherd Divine, our wants relieve
> In this our evil day:
> To all Thy tempted followers give
> The power to watch and pray.
> Long as our fiery trials last,
> Long as the cross we bear,
> O let our souls on Thee be cast
> In never-ceasing prayer . . .

It was the choice of one of her aunts. Cathie sobbed all through it: her sweet breath rose up to her protector and her convulsive movements shook the hymn book which he absent-mindedly watched, and shook her little head and raven curls so that she could see and think of nothing but her grandmother's icy spectacles and moving lips. At the end of each verse the aunts and grandfather glanced at her furtively. When five hymns had been sung, Cathie still sobbed and shook, and Mrs Wilkins offered to let the child choose the next instead of her.

'Now, Cathie, my pet,' she said, using the tone which she had always supposed to be soothing and endearing. 'which is your favourite? "Christ who once amongst us as a child did dwell"?'

Cathie sobbed and made no reply. She was wondering why her grandmother's spectacles looked grim as the trees outside, 'like *that*.' Mrs Wilkins continued:

'Shall it be "All things bright and beautiful," or, "Do no sinful action, speak no angry word?" . . . What was father's favourite?'

Cathie did not hear, for the spectacles were still icy and grim.

'Then I will choose for you, dear,' concluded Mrs Wilkins, removing the notes of soothing and endearment from her voice; and so they sang:

> Our God of love who reigns above
> Comes down to us below;
> 'Tis sweet to tell He loves so well,
> And 'tis enough to know . . .

At the end Mrs Wilkins said judicially:

'I think Cathie ought to be very thankful to us all for singing to her when she was a disobedient child. But she had better go early to bed now. Perhaps she is very tired. . . . Kiss everyone "Good-night," Cathie . . . Good-night, child.'

One of her aunts led her away.

'She has her mother's temper,' said Mrs Wilkins. 'Her mother was just like that. I am afraid we shall have some trouble in bringing her up as we should like, but I do not despair, Charles.'

'No, my dear,' said Mr Wilkins, not convinced that by graduating grandmother a woman became wise.

'No, she makes me feel young again,' continued his musing hopeful spouse, 'and I will bring her up as if she were one of my own.'

Cathie sobbed upstairs, and that evening it was as if the sea, and the wind on the moor and in the keyholes, were sobbing with her, until at last she slept. The wind ceased and all the house was still. About midnight she woke again to see through her window the small bright moon flying up through snowy clouds over the sea. It seemed to her that it was the very same moon she used to see at her father's house, and she smiled and slept happily.

Mothers and Sons

Years ago, continued my bald fellow-passenger, lifting his fez, I used to think that I had discovered youth. I went about repeating such phrases as: 'The respect due to age is a ceremony carried out to weariness. The respect due to youth is as great and is never paid.' I used to pretend to show that the respect paid to old men arose from the eloquence of the dying 'old John of Gaunt, time-honoured Lancaster,' and I collected the dying speeches of old men to confute my many enemies. Along with this, and by some mysterious process harmonized with it, was a great sentiment for the old things, for almost everything old in the ways of life. The new things around did not please me: I was in my own opinion born long after or before my time. For some years I conducted my attack with that cruel scorn of which ardent youth, bearing no flowers without thorns, is particularly capable. But gradually, in the wilderness I created about me, I lost sight of these sublime truths, except that I continued to consider blasphemous the world's way of not accepting the young until they show that they are as harmless as the old.

It was when I was still young, not yet thirty I should say, that I stumbled from my lofty position, in a village or small town in Wales.

I had been there many times before, but never shall I forget that one visit. In order to spend a long day there with my friend the poet I had started on foot some hours before sunrise. It was the beginning of winter. The night was cold and clear and blue, lit by a few stars and a moon so bright that it appeared to throb in the sky. My road climbed to the top of many a hill simply because some farmer who, I suppose, sometimes stooped to the valleys, chose to live there with his cows and sheep. In those days they still used to kill a cow once a year and the tallow made candles to light them to the milking in the winter mornings, the lambing at midnight, the reading of the Bible and 'The Sleeping Bard' in the evenings; and every two years the farmer had a few yards of grey fleecy cloth for a suit made at the mill below from the wool of his own sheep. Probably there had been a dwelling of some kind on those hill-tops ever since the earth rose out of the waters.

The night was still and I was going to say silent, in spite of the fact that little rivers never ceased to roar and foam below me in the ravines of the forest through which I passed. This unchanging sound comforted the ear more than silence ever can.

They had been felling much timber, and it lay about on the steep slopes under the moon, more like the crude shapes of chaos out of which trees and men might some day be made. But for the most part I saw nothing and thought of nothing. I was well and warm and pleased by the ring of my shoes upon the rocks of the wild roadways. I was living that deep, beneficent, unconscious life which is what after all we remember with most satisfaction and learn, often too late, to label happiness when the pleasures have all fallen away.

It was the dawn that recalled me to myself. I was making for the east, and in the south-east the sky, as quiet as my mind, had brought forth a scene of clouds so harmonious with my unconscious life that at first I looked upon it rather as if it had been some noble dream blessedly given to me than something which all men might see; and I was astonished as perhaps a poet is when he has wrought something lovelier than he knew out of a long silent strife.

The sky before me, almost up to the zenith and almost down to the rigid but tumultuous line of hills, dark and far off, was lightly covered with a cold marbling of bossy white clouds slightly stained by the blue behind them. Just below this and just above the hills in the south-east the clouds ceased, and there the blue had given way to a luminous silver, very soft and cold. Slowly this silver changed to a green of a saintly paleness, majestic and innocent, and the lower surfaces of the clouds above were more and more tawnily fired, while the snow of those nearest the zenith hardly flushed.

In the little white farms there were lights stirring and a clink of pans and clatter of hoofs, and many of the loops of the river beneath had begun to gleam among the still gloomy woods, but the farms and the river were infinitely small compared with the great spaces of the valleys and the dark mountains beyond and the lightening sky, and their sounds reached the ear but not the spirit, and for some time it had seemed that the brooks were hushed.

And now the green of the lower sky was crossed by long flat clouds of the colour of dark sand newly wetted by the tide, but warm, and in a little while these clouds had arranged themselves by imperceptible craft into the likeness of an immense tract of unpeopled country into which a green sea ran far, in many a bay and estuary without a sail. The clouds above had become more closely packed, so that their prominences made almost uninterrupted mountain ranges of fire.

I know not how to explain it, but I felt I was seeing this immense country and sea before me inverted by some imperfection of sight, that I was seeing only a reflection in calm water, that it was a perhaps not unalterable weakness that prevented me from seeing the thing itself. Thinking of a remedy, by a sudden impulse I threw myself down in the bracken and heather by the road the better to enter into that kingdom of the dawn. I thus shut out from my sight everything but the open sea of pale and now gleaming green, and its long inlets into the land of tawny coast and fiery hills, and the mountain ridges of the earth which were dissolved to a thin vapour under the increasing light. At first I had no doubt that I was right. That kingdom became mine in an oblivious ecstasy, just as the hills and the fallen trees and the rivers in the woods under the moon had been mine before the dawn. I was wafted upon that sea to the untrodden shore and among the hills where not even wings might travel, and there I heard the symphony which the stars and the mountains of earth and the hearts of men and the songs of rivers and birds make together in immortal ears, but make, alas! only once or twice for mortals. I closed my eyes and the scene remained.

And then, whether in an actual dream of sleep I do not know, I found myself thinking that I would take away with me the music I heard and would be happy always and show other men the way that looked so clear. But I began to struggle against falling through an abyss at some supreme command. I was aware of anger and dismay. I believed myself accused of being a spy and a contrabandist in that land which now veils of smoke were concealing from my eyes. I awoke, crying aloud that I would not have at all what I could not possess for ever, but no answer came.

When I sat up I saw that the earth was below me and the sky above, as on an ordinary day. Half of the sun was crimson above a peak which his fire appeared to burn right through, and from horizon to horizon the grey clouds were consuming themselves in crimson and in gold, except where a valley opened wide apart in the east and showed a giant company of chimneys, black and sinister, plumed with smoke as black. The earth itself was pleasant to see, especially where the moss was golden in the soft light of the old oak woods, but to my eyes it looked invalid, pathetic, and bereaved, as if that glory in the sky had been taken away from it or were indeed the reflection of something now withdrawn into the hollows of the hills. I therefore walked rapidly on towards the village dominated by those chimneys, my destination.

It stands at the meeting of three rivers, and the streets look up the crooked valleys where those rivers leap down among oaks and birches and alders, now deep enough for the otter and now only a cascade and salmon leap. Just outside the village the combined waters form an estuary, a broad and steady flood, sliding with solemnity between the level marshes at the feet of the lesser hills. At my first visit fifteen years before I swam gently down the ebbing tide and saw on one side a belt of marsh divided by a road and a thin chain of cottages from higher ground, here ploughland, there craggy pasture, or a scramble of oaks over a precipice, or the gorse-grown refuse of a deserted mine whose chimneys the ivy had bewitched: on the other side, the ancient church of the parish, standing alone, four white walls and a grey roof amidst a grave-yard encircled by white stones; then a high round barrow covered with little old oak trees; more marsh, and a mile farther on a white farm called after the name of the castle ruins at its gate; and, where the marshland narrowed, a hill of grey crags and purple bracken almost at the water's edge; more hills and coombes contributing rivulets, until the estuary wound out of sight between round brown hills to the rocks and the sea. Then I got out and ran back, as anyone could then, three miles over the close green turf, scattering the sheep and the cattle from my nakedness.

A few years earlier still the parish had consisted of three or four farms, three mills (one among the oaks of each valley), the church, a venerable chapel in a wood, and a few cottages buried away – all but their smoke and their linen shining on the gorse – in brambly chasms reached by lanes that were streams for half the year. Now only one mill was left, the cottages were empty and dislocated and long lost among the brambles.

As I entered the village I began to lose my way. In the old days the village was clustered about the streams and every road led down and across them. Their sound and glitter could not be avoided. Salmon big enough to make legends were taken from under the bridges at night, almost in the streets, and their heads, as likely as not, impaled upon the railings before the policeman's house. Nor had the huge boulders been moved from the banks. But now the streets went this way and that, according to the whim or craft of those who had land to sell, and when I came to running water it was confined between straight banks and lined with houses on both sides, in order that the inhabitants might more easily throw their filth in as well as draw out their drink. The water looked colder and blacker, the corpse of its old self, all savour of the mountains departed. The boulders were gone; so, too, the stepping-stones. The children could no longer walk half the way to school in water. One of the rivers was now increased by waste from the chemical works, and the water was of mingled yellow and red that suggested the fat and the lean of carcases in a butcher's shop when 'the time draws near the birth of Christ.' No salmon would face such a flood, but one girl, I was informed, had lately chosen the deep pool where the poison entered to drown herself. She was alone in this choice. Other suicides preferred more luxurious deaths. A young farmer had hanged himself in his barn and was not found until days later when his hair and beard had grown all over his face. Nobody had anything against him – save debts – but he was morose and discontented with everything. And so he died. It was considered an unlucky death because coal was shortly afterwards found under his land. Not long before, an innkeeper had killed himself with fox-poison because he had committed the sin against the Holy Ghost.

The streets were oily black and deeply rutted. Houses built twenty years before looked old, so dark were they and so simple compared with the new fashion which loved painted woodwork, stained glass, large balls of stone on the pillars of the gateways. Some roads led only to the railway and you crossed as you pleased. Others ended in factory yards among rusty strips of tin-like scimitars and creases, in heaps, among yellow pools, where bright, pale work-girls were going to and fro with black-faced men among engines, truckloads of the rusty tin, wreckage of machinery thrown down carelessly. Another passed alongside an ever-steaming pool where gold-fish swam among pallid reeds in water that never froze.

In the centre of the village stood its principal public house that far outshone the church, the chapels and the new school, with its cut glass and its many lights in the windows of three storeys; opposite stood two others, close together, small and homely, no longer rural though they belonged to the rural days of the village, but squalid from urban usage.

Luckily I met a youth who could show me the way and explain the changes. He told me that my friend, the poet, would not be in until midday, and I decided to look round and see the old church, the fulling mill, the otter's holt as well as the new things.

My companion knew the price of the houses that were being built. He marvelled at 'the amount of money in the place.' In half the roads trenches were being dug for the drainage, which ran at present wherever it found a slope: tired and dirty men just released from their work stood outside their gates and ate bacon and pickles while they watched the digging. The new drains, 'the pride of the village,' were to run into the estuary just past the meeting of the waters. At a corner there was an Italian ice-cream vendor, hands in pockets, by his yellow hand-cart. Over all whirled the smoke of the seven chimneys in tawny or white or black clouds. Engines panted and roared, and in black caves at the roadside half-naked men moved in front of white-hot fires and their boots squelched with sweat as they walked.

Backwards and forwards went the workers to and from their work, swift, thin men, gossiping young women, children saluting those who were lately their schoolfellows. Cattle passed through and sometimes lost their way among the planks and bricks of half-built houses or the refuse of the factories.

The streets ran in all directions, and new gardens bordered on the moss and whinberry of the bounding hills. And as there were straggling lines of houses running far out and up into the pasture and ploughland and waste, so there were still open spaces among the streets where cows or horses or pigs fed until the land was taken up, while some pieces were unfenced and trodden into mire or used for nothing or for the deposit of rubbish. One such little place was where 'the murder' took place. In the darkness, but close to the flare of a fried-fish stall, two young married men had battered the head of an older man against a stone until he was dead. When they were waiting on the platform for the train that was to take them to the gaol, they smoked cigarettes and joked with the crowd. 'When I was in the coalpit,' said the lad, 'I knew one of them. He used to make three or four of us get into an old truck with him, and he stood up while we ran at him, heads down like bulls. He liked it. We couldn't hurt him. It's lucky he's gone so soon, for he might have done more harm. But you should see his whippets, regular beauties. He was fond of them, too, yes.'

Thence a footpath led us out through the fields towards the old church, a beautiful sloping walk that followed for some way the windings of the chief river and its rustling drab reeds. 'There's nice the old church looks,' said my companion; for it was bright white amidst the green marsh turf, and the grey estuary flowed close under the church-yard walls to the bracken-coloured hills and the white clouds over the sea. Just there the sewage was to go out, and the lad laughed at the discomfiture of the cocklers down there on the coast whose trade would now be gone. In the churchyard a few new graves had been made under the sycamores, and all the occupants were over eighty, at which the lad observed: '’Twas time for them to die, yes,' and smiled because it seemed absurd in this brand-new hurrying world to live so long. The old grave-stones leaned all ways, and some were prone; few kept their legends readable. We peeped inside the church: it was white and cool as a dairy, undisturbed by the violation of the river nymphs yonder.

We ascended the gentle hill beyond the church, once a favourite walk on summer evenings, to see the sun set over the mountains. A large field had been recently enclosed as a cemetery on the brow, and already it was sprinkled with white stones and plumy sable trees. 'It will come nice in a year or two,' said my companion. We looked down at the estuary, and he showed me with delight where the new railway bridge was to be carried across it in order to save London passengers three minutes in a five hours' journey. I like to see a train going swift and low above a broad water against a background of hills, but I thought it would spoil the old view. He on the contrary was so lost in awe at the cost of the short cut that he had no thought of lesser things.

We returned by the fulling mill. There the stream was as bright
as ever and full of dash and foam. The little house was cleanly
thatched and whitewashed, the wall round it also was white, and
the apple-tree beside it was bushy with mistletoe. Brass and steel
and lustre ware shone in the firelight within. There were wall-
flowers as ever at the gate, a handful only, but perpetual. Picture
postcards of the house were to be bought in the village, I was told:
everyone bought them to send away to friends as *Souvenirs of D*.

As we walked a stuck pig began to scream, and continued to do
so while we travelled half a mile: 'It takes a long time dying,'
remarked the lad who was careless of the marriage bells that
accompanied the unwavering scream.

Before entering among the streets again I turned to see once
more in the moist sunshine the church and the sycamores and
wall, the tumulus and its oaks on one side, the river winding
bright and bowing its reeds, the estuary, the mountains beyond,
the white cloud mountains in the blue that spoke clearly of the
invisible sea below.

As I walked past the shops, neither urban nor rustic, entirely
new and as glaring as possible, but awkward, without traditions
and without originality, I was full of magnificent regrets. I ought
to have had a mantle of tragic hue to swathe myself in mysterious
and haughty woe and to flutter ineffable things in the wind, as I
trod the streets that were desolate for me.

It was now time to make for the poet's house. This was one of
the oldest houses, about thirty years old, – his age. It was a stone
building of displeasing proportions, meant to be one of a row but
standing alone, – unlike the native style, – with iron railings in
front on the precipitous road. The vegetable garden behind fell
down to the least of the three rivers, which as yet was almost
undefiled because it flowed for the greater part of its course
through a deep and narrow and very steep-sided coombe whose
rocks and spindly but dense oaks and underwood of bramble and
hazel were impassable.

Inside, the house was divided strictly into two, the poet's half
and the other half. The poet's half consisted above all of the
largest room in the house. The walls were hidden by books and
portraits of poets and bards. Its floors were almost as densely
overgrown as the coombe, with oak armchairs whose richness of
decorative carving equalled their discomfort. These were prizes

won at Eisteddfodau by the successful poem on some religious
subject or subject which could be treated religiously. The poet had
written more poems than there were chairs; for he was well-read
in English and classical literatures and had a boldness of imagery
which the judges, ministers of various sects, sometimes declared
in marginal notes to be affected. In spite of anti-macassars on the
chairs, in spite of thousands of books which generations of critics
had approved (for the most part complete sets in uniform and
unworn bindings), in spite of the poet's ever boyish face, his rough
black hair and clothes that had just scrambled up the river bed
from stone to stone and root to root of alder and oak, and the deep
melodious voice that turned prose into epic poetry as he read it, in
spite of ferns in the fireplace, the room was cold with a moral and
spiritual chill.

I was glad of the voice which summoned us into the next room,
the long flagged kitchen, a little dark, but lit as by lightning from
the great fire whose flames were repeated by lustre-ware and brass
candlesticks on the mantelpiece, a hundred brightly coloured jugs
upon the black dresser, a long polished gun hanging from the
rafters, and the glass which protected the pictures of many
celebrities and the sheets of memorial verses for dead members of
the family. There, I remember, I had read the *Mabinogion* long
before . . . Mrs Morgan, the bard's mother, greeted me as usual in
Welsh and then laughed in broken English at the fact that I seemed
to know less Welsh than ever, though I still knew the Welsh names
for King Arthur's sword, spear and shield. 'But I am glad to see
you, dear Mr Philips.'

She was a tall yellow-haired woman with a family of children
ranging from forty to ten years of age. Her decided stoop seemed
the product rather of her humility of mind than of decay, for her
activity was endless and never overtaxed. She had large bony
restless hands contrasting humorously with the decent black of
her dress. She talked caressingly in Welsh to the silent beautiful
daughter who helped her in the work of the house.

The table was set for two: such was the inevitable custom. The
poet and I sat down, and as we did so, his mother set a steaming
joint at a side table and carved it rapidly while she stood and
talked, the daughter at the same time bringing two blue dishes of
leeks and baked potatoes to the white cloth and returning,
without an interval, for two plates from the oven; these her

mother covered with meat, and they were immediately laid before us. Then mother and daughter stood, both silent now, at either side of the fire while we ate and languidly talked.

The girl was black-haired, straight, and well-proportioned, her cheeks rosy, her full-dark lips eloquently curved, her eyes large and brown like a child's, and her whole face beaming with profound brightness, simplicity, holiness. She might have been twenty-five years old, and was one of those infinitely tender, self-sacrificing girls in whom children at once salute the spiritual motherhood, who are learned in all mother's ways, can play nurse and manage, and yet, unconsciously detecting some weakness in the awful opposite sex, are destined never to be mothers in the flesh. Love and fear melt their eyes to a softness that is very wonderful and govern their silent ways; love is the stronger, but the fear though it is often forgotten is never destroyed.

When these two women saw that our plates were nearly empty they came forward, one to each of us, and helped us to more or took away our plates; and so long as I am ignorant of what it is to be waited on by angels I cannot forget this meal. They uttered no word while we talked of Virgil and Alexander Smith and the taxation of land-values, but tut! I was sick of such talk as I was of my host's apple-green tie. As I got up from the table I felt something between shame and the pride of the convalescent in his tyrant bed. We returned to the study.

Well, we talked, I know, but I have forgotten what. The poet recited some of his own verses, and we complained together in raptures of regret about the growth of the village, and as we were doing so his mother entered, but would not sit.

'I hear,' said I, anxious to speak to her, 'that they are going to open a new coal mine up by the Great Crag and the otter's holt. It used to be a favourite place of yours, Mrs Morgan, and mine too; there was not a nicer place in the country when the nuts were ripe and the harvest ending.'

''Tis beautiful, truly,' she said gravely; 'I hope the mine will give many men work; there are many needing it, Mr Phillips.'

'But they will spoil the beautiful angle of the river there. Think of it – *your* river, *your* crag – no more nuts, all the royal fern buried in coal dust.'

'Mother isn't a poet, are you, mother?' said my host.

'No, Willy,' said she, 'and if I were I couldn't tell you the things I

have seen and thought about by the Great Crag. I am sorry the
fern will have to go, but, dear me, the poor of us must have shoes
and bread and a pasty now and then, Mr Phillips, and the rich
must have their carriages and money to buy the poetry books,
Willy.'

'You've a hard spot in your heart, mother.'

'Yes, and I daresay I need it, my son. When a woman begins to
work at six years old like me and a man at five like your father,
they must get a bit hard if they are to keep on, and there's many
are all hard and small blame to them. Yes, sure, I think the world
of these soft ladies, but I can't set myself up against them; I haven't
had their privileges. Oh, I look for wonderful things from you
young ones that have had your way made easy. It will be a kind of
good world I am sure, though I'm not grumbling at what we're
living in. We old ones didn't exactly look to be happy in this world
except on New Year's Eve and the like, and yet it came about that
we were happy, too, beyond our deserts, I daresay. I have seen
changes in my time, and wages have gone up and food gone down,
and glad I was when the loaf came cheap and we could afford to
fat three pigs and sell one, but, bless you, it isn't by wages and
food that we are made happy. They were good things, and I hope
they will stay and wages be higher and food as good as it is cheap,
but there's something else, though what it is I'm not going to try to
say; that's for the poets, Willy.'

She went out to get tea ready and to leave us to our loftiness.

After tea – apple pasties, you know, home-made bread, little
flat currant cakes, all Mrs Morgan's baking – I had to choose
between staying indoors and talking about books and going to see
the Owens, Mrs Morgan's cousins. She liked to show round a
visitor from London, and she could wear her best bonnet with
violets in it and gossip freely. It was the beginning of the cooling of
my friendship with Morgan when I chose to go with his mother:
he saw that my love of poetry was only skin-deep. But what was
the good? The mother was worth twenty of him though she had
only one high-backed chair without arms were she never so tired. I
never saw a sweeter and nobler acceptance of life. She welcomed
the new without forgetting the old and gave both their due
because she felt – she would never have *said* it, for she would have
considered such high thinking arrogant – that the new and the
old, the institutions, the reforms, the shops, the drainage system,

were the froth made by the deep tides of men's inexpressible
perverse desires. On Sunday she was a Methodist, but hers was a
real Catholicism. She saw good even in the new drains, and as
we crossed the bridge over their little river she said:

'When the drain pipes are laid, I shan't have to let the slops
run into Willy's river. He, good lad, doesn't know – how should
he? he doesn't see such things – he doesn't know they run in
now. I told him he mustn't drink the water there, that is all. But
soon he will be able to. He is fond of the little river, he calls it
Castaly or something, and says it is a poet's river. It runs from
the little lake by where I was born – the pretty lake! have you
been there in your long walks? Willy never went so far and he
declares it runs from Mount Hel – Helicon. He is a true poet, I
think, Mr Phillips. But the new poets are different. There was old
Mr Jenkins, now, when he was a young preacher and poet his
sweetheart died, and when they had let the coffin down into the
grave he jumped in after it – lay down upon it and never said a
word, and when they took him out, it was thought he would not
be long for this world . . .'

The Owens' house stood opposite a waste field where the
neighbours threw broken crockery, and a donkey grazed round
the broken shell of a factory lately deserted. In ruins these mean
buildings took on some venerableness in my sight.

Mrs Owen knew less English than Mrs Morgan. She greeted
me so warmly that I was abashed to think I brought nothing but
myself.

'How are you, Mr Phillips? No more Welsh, I see, and I've
forgotten my English.'

Here the children who spoke both languages laughed with
good-humoured contempt.

'How are the children and Mrs Phillips? . . . How many
children is it now?'

'Still two,' I said.

'Two!' she replied with a smile, and wiped the dough from her
fingers in her apron: she spoke in genial irony.

'You forget that Mr Phillips is a very wise young man, Sarah,'
said Mrs Morgan, chidingly.

'He will be wiser,' snapped Mrs Owen, 'when he had had ten
children and seen five of them go away, and some not come
back. As for two, two is toys.'

I wish I could paint that tin-plater's house – not the outside which was horrible, and designed by Mr Owen himself, though I noticed that two pairs of martins had blessed its stucco with their nests in the past summer. Inside there were two large rooms, cold and stark and full of the best furniture, huge chests of drawers for Sunday clothes, family Bibles, photographs in gaudy frames, linoleum like painted ice. They were the chapels sacred to the family's respectability, and I could not understand the rites and ceremonies and sacrifices thereof. The third room had a perennial broad fire, summer and winter, for baking, cooking, and drying clothes. Everything shone with use, and aloft in Mr Owen's tobacco smoke piped the canary who seemed to wish for nothing better. The door opened into a little wash-house, where they kept the flour and the enormous sides of the last-killed pig lay white in saltpetre and brine. Bacon hung from the rafters of the kitchen itself, a whole side, a whole ham, and a long thin strip that had just supplied the frying pan which Mrs Owen was holding.

'This frying pan has fried forty pigs,' she remarked, holding back her head from the hissing rashers while she turned them.

When she was not at the fire she was opening the oven to take out an apple pasty, or getting on with the spreading of the table for the meal, or sorting the clothes that overflowed two baskets of the largest size, or buttering a slice of bread to silence the youngest girl, or telling Tommy not to play football in the room while visitors were there, or preparing the supper of bread and bacon and soup which Tommy was to take for his eldest brother to eat at his night's work, or wiping her grandchildren's noses as they flocked in to get some bread and bacon fat and stare at the stranger who knew no Welsh: or she was sighing with a smile at her weakness and lack of two pairs of hands while she rested those she had upon her hips for a moment only, and talking all the time, asking questions, giving orders, describing her visit to London which she detests ('dear me, Mr Phillips, however can you live in it? There isn't a loaf of bread fit to eat to be bought there and scarcely a woman with sense to make her own, and you daren't keep a pig, nor yet breathe for fear of swallowing what doesn't belong to you and you don't want') or singing in a wild contralto the most melancholy and most splendid of the Welsh hymns. She weighed nearly twenty stone, but she never sat down.

Her husband, a pale man whose work you might think (if you

hadn't seen him gardening, or taking his children ten miles away into the mountains with a present of seed potatoes for a cousin) had worn out everything in him but his good nature and love of a pipe of shag. The words of his conversation came from a daily paper, but he had the peace which passes understanding, and for wisdom he could depend on his wife. Neither she in her strength nor he in his sensibility had ever struck one of their children. He was whittling an oak stick, but he stopped to take me up the garden where he showed me by lantern light his tomato plants in a green-house of his own making, and then stirred out the vast pig for me to admire. He seemed to regard the pig as a kind of brother who sacrificed himself for the good of others almost willingly out of consideration for the expensive food which had fattened him; and until the day of the knife he was treated as a brother seldom is.

On the wall of the kitchen there were a few pictures, of Spurgeon, of Gladstone, of the Crucifixion, and a portrait of the eldest child, born out of wedlock and dead long ago, a pretty maid, Olwen Angharad. Six of the children were in the room, two of them married sons, pale, overworked but handsome, cheerful men who had dropped in to ask questions about London, to tell their father the weight of the pigs they were fattening and ask after his, and to exchange banter with their inexhaustible mother – their wives were not like that, but just pretty slips of women beginning to bear children and not baking their own bread, either. After their mother they admired most their eldest sister, aged eighteen. She worked at the tin-works all day and had done so for four years and was now as busy as her mother by the fire and at the table, talking little except with her eyes which flashed a variety of speeches between the look of command to her youngest brother and sister and the look of comprehension or expectancy to her mother. She had reached the perfect height of woman, which height I had never been sure of until I saw her. Her hair was of the nearest yellow to gold that is compatible with great physical energy and strength. I cannot explain how it was bound up in such a way as to boast of its luxuriance and yet leave the delicate even shape of her head unspoiled. Her face was rather long than short, her nose of good size and straight, her lips inclining to be full, kind and strong also, her grey eyes burning with splendour, her eyebrows darker than her hair and curved like two wings of a falcon, her ears – but such an inventory is absurd. Her face, whether in repose or radiant, expressed health, courage, kindliness, intelligence, with superb unconscious pride. She could bandy words with any man, and there were not wanting men to tell her – with a calculating eye for the effect of their words – that she had reached physical perfection; yet she was not wanton, nor bashful nor vain. No Roman woman could have excelled her in power and dignity, no barbarian in exuberant strength. She had grace but no graces, beauty but no beauties. She ruled – even her mother; but she did not know it. So much loved was she that her youngest sister was heard praying that her lover would die, lest he should take her away from home.

Her three younger sisters showed what she had been: the one of seventeen was still too hesitating and slender in her grace; the next, of fifteen, was too impudent, though for the moment she was quiet and sleeping away her weariness on the horse-hair sofa under the canary's cage; the youngest, aged thirteen, was still too much of a powerful animal.

Her youngest brother was fourteen, almost his eldest sister's equal in height, brawnily made, unwieldly, fierce except at home where at most he was lazily, laughingly truculent, more often grumbling amiably over some task.

They were all but pure Welsh, one grandmother being from Cornwall. The girls were fair, the boys black-haired.

Admirable as they were apart they made an indescribable harmony together. Sometimes all talked at once, the youngest boy's deep brawl almost overpowering the rest. Sometimes one told a tale and all attended. Sometimes the talk travelled mysteriously from one to another, and to and fro and crosswise, as if some outside power had descended invisibly in their midst and were making a melody out of their lips and eyes, a melody which, I think, never ceased in their hearts. Nearly always they smiled and if the gravity of the talk seemed about to extinguish this smile there was one pair of eyes or lips at least sparkling or rippling with the profound joy which no plummet of sorrow sounded. Nor was this talk mild gossip undertaken unconsciously to meet the fact that they were all of one family and in the presence of the father and the mother. For it was fearless. The father spoke his thoughts and the boy his, and there was nothing which anyone of them would have said or secretly laughed at with companions which they would not say before all.

There was noise and stir unceasing, but no haste, no care.

'What a flower bed it is, to be sure,' whispered Mrs Morgan to Mrs Owen as we concluded the skirmish of a crowded meal of new loaves, seaweed 'bread,' bacon, apple pasty, and plentiful thin tea.

'Ah, you are a poet's mother, Mrs Morgan,' she replied.

They gossiped in low tones.

'How is poor Mrs Howell's son that lost his arm in the works by you?'

'Getting on well. He has two nurses in the hospital and they are very kind. But you know these women: he wants his mother.'

'Poor boy. He was playing when it happened, wasn't he?'

'Yes. They say it was his own fault, as if that made it any better for him or the manager who will prove negligence, of course. It won't stop the boys playing, and my husband wasn't playing when he met his death. Never mind. They are going to set him up in a fried fish shop, a good idea.'

While these two gossiped the eldest boy sang 'Morfa Rhuddlan' and 'Hob y deri dando', the most mournful and the merriest of the old Welsh songs.

I was a little sad at times. I was disturbed, as Mrs Morgan could not be, at all this gaiety in the heart of the village darkness, partly because I was unable to see why it should exist, and as foolishly sure that there would never be an end to the darkness unless it eclipsed this gaiety in a revolution of some kind – impious thought and unpardonable if it had not been vain. That gaiety cannot be quenched.

I stayed that night with the poet, begging to be allowed to sit in the kitchen, where his mother left us with a parting look of reverence for those who would be talking about books while she lay awake thinking of her daughter in a London shop where she had never been, her son in the far west, her husband dead.

Next morning she took me by a long way round to the station. I remember I was wearing a coat which I had had made for me five years before with three pockets in it especially to hold copies of the poems of Shelley, of Sophocles, of Catullus; even then I bulged with the books, but carried them out of superstition, not for use.

We passed the estuary, and she pointed out the long barrow on one side and the tumulus on the other. The men in the old time had a bridge from one to the other, she had heard. We emerged from the last clustered cottages of the village on to a road high above Castaly. There were the goldfinches! – as many as ever in the rough pasture above the copse: she knew them. Didn't I think the copse the same, and the foaming river in the heart of it? One by one she named the bright farms on the side of the Great Crag opposite. White cloud rack was decamping from the red bracken and yellow larch on its flanks, and from the gaunt grey humps and cairns of its summit. The bracken was redder, the larch yellower, than ever, as if all had been the work of the spirits of the mist. The curlew's cry and chuckle were more wildly sweet. Our feet deep in the red mud of the road, we saw, fresher than ever, the gleaming wavering last hazel leaves and the stems of the oaks and hazels.

'And that is pretty too, isn't it?' asked Mrs Morgan, pointing to the seven black chimneys grouped just as I had seen them in the dawn of the day before. 'I can't walk farther than this nowadays, but I like to come here and look first at Great Crag and then at the village, then at Great Crag and then at the village again, and I don't turn any more but go straight down hill and home. You must go that way, too, to catch your train. Leave me, I will go slow and you must hurry. Good-bye, Mr Phillips. Come again and bring your books and stay a long time, and you shan't be disturbed.'

If I go again, I shall not trouble to take my books. But I shan't go. She has left the village. Her son tore himself away with infinite tears of rhyme for the river, and she silently. He got work elsewhere, and she of course must follow with her daughter, to bake the bread by which poets live.

At a Cottage Door

The cottage was built upon the rock which just there protruded from the earth; and which was the rock and which the rough stone of the walls could not easily be told, so rude was the structure and so neatly was it whitened from the low eaves down to the soil. The threshold was whitened, so also were the stones of the path, the low wall in front, and several huge fragments here and there both within and without the gate. These white stones served instead of flowers. Other ornaments outside there were not, except stone-crop on the garden wall and at the sides of the threshold flagstone, a tall solitary spire of yellow mullein growing out of the top of the garden wall, and on the thatch itself a young elder tree against the white chimney stump, and an archipelago of darkest green moss which was about to become a solid continent and to obliterate the straw. Thatch and moss beetled over the walls which were pierced by two small windows of diamond panes. The chief light, when the door between these windows was shut, came from the fireplace which, with its iron and brasswork and the door of the brick oven adjacent, nearly filled one side of the living room. But the door was nearly always open, revealing most of the dark cave within, its red flameless fire, its bright knobs and bars of iron and brass, and the polished odds and ends of copper and brass on the mantelpiece or hanging on the wall – candlesticks, snuffers, horse-trappings, a gill measure, part of an old pair of scales, a small shell from a Boer battlefield.

The cottage must have been built before the road was made, or the roadmakers had omitted to notice it; for it lay back a hundred yards from the high hedge on top of a wall, through which a stile led over a rough meadow, between almost solid hillocks of brambles and clusters of royal fern under alder trees, to the white wall, the white stones, the cabbage plot and the white house itself. To a passing child it appeared that the cottage had originally been built in the heart of a stony wood; gradually the larger number of the trees had been cut down, thus exposing the cottage to someone on the road who had then been inspired to cut through the hedge and its wall, to cross the field, to drive out the savage or fairy inhabitants, and to take possession of it. In the field there were still great butts of oak visible, and on the further side of the house, showing above the chimney, were three dead trees close together raising a few shortened, stripped, and rigid pale arms to the sky and to deities who had long ago deserted them, the house and the surrounding land of small fields as rough as a windy sea, stone walls, hedges of aspen, oak and ash, rocky rises clothed lightly in oaks of snaky and slender growth, and beyond and above, on all sides but one, hills so covered with loose silvern crags among their bracken and birch that they resembled enormous cairns – where perhaps those deities had been buried under loads sufficient to keep them dungeoned away from any chance of meddling with a changed world.

In the cottage lived a mother and son. She was very little and very old. Her hair was still dark brown, her eyes almost as dark, her skin not quite so dark as her eyes, a nut-brown woman, lean, sweet, and wholesome-looking as a nut. She might often be seen sitting and looking to the south-west when a gap in the hills framed a vision of mountain peaks twenty miles beyond; and always she smiled a little. A passer-by might have thought that she never did anything but sit inside or outside the open door unless he had noticed the whiteness of the stones and the polish on the metal in the room where she had for fifty years collected things that could be polished. Few ever saw Catherine Anne at work save her son, and he not often, for he was away early and home late. He left her entirely alone, visited of none unless on days when the smart tradesman strode up the path, deposited her weekly packages on the table while he commented on the weather, and then replacing his pencil behind his ear bade her 'Good Afternoon' in English. It was one of the few English remarks to which she could reply in English. Her only other English words were 'beautiful' and 'excursion train.' For though some of the brown in her face was a gift of tropic suns in the days when she sailed with her husband on his ship, she had learned nothing but Welsh. The old man, so she called him though dead these forty years, had been against her learning English. A God-knowing and God-fearing Methodist, he had seen in that tongue the avenue through which his beautiful young wife might receive the knowledge of good and evil. After his death at sea she had of her own accord refused all contact with the thing, and now when it was all around her she never moved from the house. Her son knew it, but at home he spoke the native idiom, and when she heard him she seemed to be once more in her father's house, or in the orchard where little red apples overhung the rocky brook at the mountain foot. There it was that she gained, no one knows how, the nourishment from mother earth that gave her the deep contentment expressed in her health and her smile, in the shining metal, and in her patience – which was not endurance or torpor – patience of an order that seemed to be all but extinct in the world. Memory and hope were at balance in the brain that looked out of her brown eyes, and the present moment, often dull-seeming or even unkind, did not exist for her. Those eyes never closed while she sat by her door, and it might be conjectured that as she gazed east and north and west she saw more than the white stones and yellow stonecrop, the alders and royal fern, the hedge following the road, the lean oak trees among the rocks, the farther hills and their curlews and cairns, the sky, and now and then the uttermost mountains, which were all that an observer could see. If the casual observer waited more than a few moments in summer he might see that she was never quite alone. The air between her and the hills was the playground of several pairs of black swifts, wheeling and leaping round and up and down and straight forward, so that the bluest sky was never blank or the brightest grass without a shadow. Out of these birds two often screamed down precipitously to the white cottage and disappeared in their nests under the thatch above her head. Catherine Anne smiled a little more at these sudden stormy visits, and there were times when it seemed certain that she received others, though neither visible nor audible.

Some thought that she believed the swifts to be some kind of spirits, and one who was very wise said that if Catherine Anne Jones had been cleverer she might have been a wicked woman.

All the other swifts lived in the church. These had singled out her roof. They always returned to her; they had been there, ever since she came, every summer, singling that little place out of the whole earth and sky. She saw them high and swift and wild in the blue, and then she felt the flutter of their wings as they arrived at the eaves, and heard their soft talk together in the darkness. On summer evenings she saw them ascend into the heavens and not return, as blessed spirits might do; only on the morrow they were back again. They were always young, always equally dashing and joyous. It was whispered that she believed them to be the souls of her two children that died as babes, and they had come to her soon after the loss. 'They were too young to know what to do in Heaven,' she was reported to have said, 'and so they were allowed to play about in Wales all the summer. But at night they have to return to see if they are wanted. Blessed birds. I daresay all birds are good if we only knew. I suppose I am too old to be one, but if it were lawful I should like nothing better than to live like them, passing the time until Judgment Day. What a lot of people there will be there to be sure – there were over three hundred in my native place when I was a girl, and I don't think there is one alive but me. I think some ought to be birds. Birds take up so little room, and they could not do any mischief if they wanted to. Now, if only the town people were all to be turned into birds. Lord, such a fright I had two years ago last February. I was sitting here, it being fine, to see the sun rise, and up from the town came a swarm of wings as many as there are leaves in yonder wood, small dark birds all close together and making a whistling noise, and I thought to myself, it has happened after all; they have changed all the people into blessed birds. No, I was not afraid about my son, for, thought I, now he will not be able to drink anything but cold water, and perhaps he will come to live in the church. I was glad. I thought of taking a walk down there just to see how the place looked, when along came the Insurance man – He isn't a bird, I thought to myself – and says: "Are you looking at the starlings, mam?" "No," says I, and I was vexed. Dear me, all those birds was a beautiful sight, and such a nice noise they made between them as if they were glad to be going away from that place. It is a funny thing about birds, how different they are. Mrs Williams said to me once when she was courting, "Why, Mrs Jones there are several kinds of birds." Several! There are as many different kinds as there are men, and that is saying a lot, and remember I have sailed over the ocean five years and went ashore in all the ports of this mortal world. They are like people, only they don't seem to do any harm. Nice things! I used to think they must be very good not to be jealous of us having all the houses and food and things, but if people only knew they would be jealous of the birds. They are all different, or else how could He know when any one of the sparrows falls to the ground. They don't know what it is to be idle or too busy, nor the difference between work and play. There are not any rich and poor, and they respect one another. They are not all tangled up and darkened with a number of things. Then look how few of them die – did you ever see a dead bird? – except men shoot them. The reason is, they are good enough for Heaven as they are, so up they go like the dew when we are not looking.'

It was not entirely due to the position of her front door that she always looked north or east or west, and chiefly west. From the back door her son's feet had worn a path which could be seen winding south over several fields until it was lost, by the next cottage, in another road, also going south, towards 'that place.'

She considered herself on the edge of the town, but still distinctly out of it. The next cottage, where the footpath joined the road, was in the town, so she thought; yet there was no outward sign of it unless that its low walls were not as clean, nor its brass so plentiful and so bright, and that its door, facing south, was often shut, and always when the wind was from that quarter.

From Catherine Anne's back door could be seen the roof and part of the wall of this cottage, another exactly like it a little beyond, then a cluster, including one not of whitened native stone, but of red brick and black mortar. All these were on the road. On either side of it, southward, there was a farm or two, white, but with sheds of corrugated iron that rattled under the mist drops from the ash trees embracing the group. From these farmyards the geese strutted across wet meadows in a line as if setting out on a long voyage. Beyond, the rough land sank, hiding all but the smoke of yet more houses in a hollow, and rose again to an unbroken line of slate roofs and dirty white walls, cutting into the bases of snowy cloud mountains whose look told that underneath them was the sea. Similar houses in irregular lines and groups were dotted on the treeless fields to the east and west of this main line. These were the first houses of the town and they were not a mile from the cottage. Beyond them the land fell away but rose again after several lesser rises and falls into great hills whose tops commanded the sea to the south and east and, on the clearer Sundays of the year, the same mountains as Catherine Anne's front door. These concealed rises and falls, and the slopes of the great hills, were the town.

From the brink, where that unbroken line of roofs notched the white clouds with its chimneys, the whole town could be seen. Over this brink fell the southward road and with it lesser roads which soon branched and multiplied into the mass of the town which choked the valleys as if it had slid down the hills in avalanches. The hills formed almost a circle, broken only by a gap on either side letting in the river from the mountains and out to the sea. Thus the town sprawled over the sides of a rudely carven bowl with deeply scalloped edges and with a bottom flat nowhere save at the narrow strip around the stream. The summits of these hills were clear of houses, and great expanses of their sides, though obviously conquered by the town, were still virgin and green and strewn with great stones.

Two of the hills on one side, that farthest from the stream, were not marked by a single street. Of these one, the highest of all, was clothed in grass from foot to ridge except on a broad lap which it made halfway up, and on that there was a house standing at the edge of a field sometimes golden with corn, and divided from it by a clump of black firs. The house was huge, both tall and wide, grey and square, with many windows towards the sea lighted only at sunset and that by the last beams in which a score of them blazed together. No road was seen climbing the steep slope to the house or leaving it for the ridge above. Some poet or haughty extravagant prince must have built it there inaccessibly with windows for the great town, the sea, the mountains. It was sombre and menacing. It was empty. It scorned the town. In its turn the town had left it up there to perish like an eagle upon a mountain ledge, shot by the hunter, but out of his reach. The neighbour hill was not so high, but it was bare not only of houses but of grass and corn and every green thing, and its only trees stood near the summit, leafless and birdless, stark and pale as if newly disinterred from an ancient grave. They were being slowly buried by the brown and fatal refuse – scarred deeply by rains and by ever new cataracts of the same substance – which covered and largely composed this hill. Out of its summit stuck a chimney and round it the black figures of men came and went against the sky.

At the foot were other chimneys, gigantic and black, and below them black buildings whose windows glowed night and day with fire such as the old house had for a few moments at sunset. The smoke mingled with white rain, and mist wreathed wildly about the brown and the green hill.

Through the river's entry below these chimneys might be seen other hills that sent down tributaries to its waters, green hills with ravines of oaks and one or two white farms, and far beyond these, more like the dream of a dreamer than rock and peat, the abode of raven, buzzard and badger, of freedom and health – the mountains of the source of the river.

The stream itself, in the midst of the town, was a black and at times a yellow serpent in a cage of steep iron-bound banks, watched by furnace, store-house, and factory. It was allowed a mock liberty only to stray into other cages of steep-sided wharves. The blackened labourer stood on the edge and spat at it where it writhed deep below. A careless child or a desperate man was engulfed by it on some night of fire and blackness, but it remained sullen and regarded not the trivial offering. The embrace with the sea was licensed, bridled, sternly watched by tall cranes, a hundred ships, and the long bleached spine of a breakwater where sea-faring men, idlers, and fluttering girls walked up and down.

The courses of the avalanches from the opposite hills were marked by white, dirty white, grey, and all but black, belts of houses broadening out to the mass in the valley. At the broad brow of the hills, in sight of the sea and of violet hills across the sea, a few farm-houses and their outbuildings still shone, while others mouldered grey and aghast and without tenants. Some of their fields were still left between the streets, but their barbed wire and patched hedgerows and walls imprisoned only an old horse or two, a temporary flock of sheep or of lean American steers on their way to the slaughter-house and the tables of the town; and even where there were no houses straight lines of streets were waiting to be built along. Across this tainted and condemned grass, even between the houses, trotted narrow brooklets over stony beds to their sepulchres in the town sewers. The houses on the upper slopes were like Catherine Anne's, though most were slated, not thatched. Fowls stalked or scuttered round about and through the open doors. The gardens were walled with once whitened stones and contained a few twisted apple trees. Old women of a former age stood on the doorsteps or moved busily in scanty undress, bareheaded. Old men pottered about, or leaned on their spades to talk or look out to sea or at the pigs. The smell of baking bread was blown from the doors. Their furniture, their Bible and theological works, were old. The curs were descended from sheep dogs that once herded the mountain flocks on these slopes. The road was still a watercourse, and the unnecessary tradesman could hardly ascend if he wished, except on foot. There was always a robin in the roadway, a wagtail in the glittering streamlet, often a rook on the square stone chimney, looking down at the town as if his ancestors had told him that it was new and might disappear any night – but as he saw that nothing was likely to happen immediately he turned his head, hopped into the air, and flew away over the hilltop.

The streets beginning on the hill-ridge ended in the thickest of the town, in a medley of steep criss-cross streets interrupted here and there by black squares of workshops with ever-burning furnaces and ever-smoking chimneys. Here every inch of the soil was covered with bricks, stones, cement, asphalte, iron-work, granite blocks. Not a tree or blade of grass was allowed to appear anywhere but in the graveyards, and even there the earth was plated almost entirely with tombstones. They were afraid of leaving any space unguarded lest Nature should show a regret, a curse or a warning. The river was unsightly, but must be tolerated alternately with insult and respect. But even here there was not an end of the 'country.' Through many open doors could be seen furniture like Catherine Anne's, and old women of her period. Thousands passed them many times a day, but they were built in days when everyone knew everyone else, and so the doors were still left open while the baking and the washing were done. The drunkard stumbled out of the crowd into the warm and rustic seclusion of his home. The child rushed out from the cradle he was tending and was swept along by the procession to meals or work. Women stood at doorways and talked, while one went on with her knitting or suckled her babe. A half-naked child wriggled through the crowd carrying tins of dough, for if they could not bake, at least they would kneed and leaven their bread, at home. Many of the children were bare-legged and headed, dirty, hungry, and quick. Out of one or other of the houses would come a bent woman, wrinkled and foul, holding a shawl over her head, looking as if she had spent a thousand years in the cellar, crushed down in rigid, idle suffering like a toad embedded in an oak root. Such creatures, chiefly women, were not uncommon. They were small, grey-skinned, with clotted grey hair; they had scarred faces, had lost an eye and most of their teeth; they wore soiled print or black dresses, bedraggled like the plumage of a dead bird in the mud and in colour approaching the foul dust of the pavement and the garbage of the gutter. In appearance they were genuine autochthons. This earth of flagstone, asphalt, granite, brick, iron, and ashes, might have protruded such a monstrous birth on a night of frost, to prove that it was not yet barren in its age and ignominy. One such crone crawling out into the light, unclean, dull and yet surprised, had a look as if she had just been exhumed; she might have been buried alive in the foundation of the town for luck, and had now emerged to see what had been done. They were seen outside the taverns with their hands hidden under the remains of aprons, or were questing in the dustbins for food or unbroken glass; often they carried babies in whose shapeless faces was hidden the power to excel their grandmothers. When they were drunk in an alley a crowd of labourers and shopkeepers gathered to watch their waving arms and poisonous faces and hear their blazing curses screeched against some unlucky man. 'There will be murder,' said one. 'It is a shame that such things are allowed,' said another. None dared to enter the mouth of the alley. The crowd recognized that a different species, a chance-begotten, mis-delivered, and curse-nourished spawn of humanity was living side by side with them, farther removed than slaves or domestic animals. It was sometimes proposed that if the streets were kept cleaner and the sewage improved this race might vanish, as if in fact it ate filth and lived in the drains. No one dared to interfere. Presently a woman rushed after the man into a house, and the door was slammed with a sound not of wood but of flesh and bone.

Such were not numerous; the majority were genuine villagers, but the minority was representative and it alone truly belonged to the place. They were villagers with a difference. One face expressed nothing but the abstraction caused by solitude in the midst of myriads. The next smiled with the intimacy of home or inn. Few had yet quite realised that they were living not at the edge of a field but in the bowels of a town, though most days it was impossible to hang clothes out to dry in the flagged or asphalted or trodden mud yards, since the air was so foul that it was worth while buying the head of a sheep fed in the neighbourhood for the sake of the copper in its teeth. Every house beheld chimneys and furnaces from one window, from another the masts of the docks or the sea and its little sails or the brown and the green hill side by side, over the ploughed sea of slate roofs. On pleasant days the smell of the sea, modified by the docks, mingled with the acrid smell and taste of smoke from the smelting of copper or the burning of carcases for manure; but at night either smell was drowned in that of fried fish. Every other house had a large window to expose fruit, vegetables, groceries, meat, 'herbal remedies,' and above all fried fish, for sale. Every corner house was a tavern, its windows foul with breath and steam within and mud, rain, and fine ashes without. The houses were small, so that tavern and church and school were conspicuously islanded among the low roofs.

But, towards the river, away from the avalanches of buildings, the houses were high and supported on plate glass windows of immense size. The streets curved and doubled after a pattern created centuries ago by the neighbourhood of a castle whose Norman masonry was still hiding in fragments behind or within some of the shops. Inns and shops were old but with glittering new faces of glass, stone, ornamented tiles, and vast gold letters. The wires of telegraph, telephone, and electric light ran amongst and over antique stone and timber work. Every inch was obviously designed or converted to serve an immediate purpose; there was no largeness, no waste, nothing haphazard, no detail forgotten through the pursuit of some ideal; all was haste, grim and yet slatternly. Here and there an old house had been pulled down, and its place hidden by a temporary wooden fence, stuck over with advertisements in black, white, crimson, and blue, of drugs, infant foods, political meetings, auction sales, corsets, men's clothes, theatres – these last showing beauteous dishevelled adulteresses and heroic gentlemen in white shirts threatening them with revolvers – men in diving costume fighting for a bag of jewels at the bottom of the sea. Everywhere the ideal implicit was that of a London suburb. The shop walker came nearest to achieving this ideal: suave and superb in dress, manner, and speech, in all but salary, he had been metamorphosed from the son of a farmer,

who spoke no English, into an effigy that put to shame the Pall
Mall clubman, though he cost the nation incomparably less. Pity
that he had so poor a world to shine in, and that his imitators
resembled him no more than they did the figures exhibited in the
tailor's advertisements, figures created merely to hold a cigarette
between the lips and a whippy cane in the fingers. His clients
included women bent on dressing extravagantly or even with
aristocratic sumptuous modesty, at a low price; young men with
white faces, riding breeches, cigarettes, and jaunty manners;
sober farmers who had tired of wearing the same old homespun so
thick that they shiver without it; wives who have come to town to
sell butter and eggs; sailors who have just found a ship, sailors
who have just been paid off, sailors who have called first at 'The
Talbot Arms'; dark-eyed, clear-complexioned girls swaddled in
blouses of red and black chequered flannel, blue and white flannel
skirts, variegated or black and red flannel shawls, but, for all their
natural and artificial plumpness, gay and continually chattering in
musical voices as they move quickly about carrying well-scoured
buckets of white wood on head or hips – women resembling
wood-pigeons in their plumpness and quickness. All were buying
what was very cheap, or very showy, or very new, or very much
like something else, or much praised as a really good thing. Cattle
and their drovers looked in at the gorgeous windows and spread
over the streets where a dozen knots of old acquaintances were
meeting for the first time since last market day. Young working
men in black whose faces had clearly been of another colour
recently but were now very white by contrast with dark eyes and
black moustaches and hair, walked up and down the pavements
doing nothing in a determined fashion and smoking, – men who
might easily have been changed into starlings in an age of
miracles. In nearly all, in men and women – except in the squalid
hooded hags who crawled by, or the work girls beside them
carrying younger sisters or bastards in shawls – the pallor,
stiffness, and haste of the town were modified by country ways, a
rolling walk as if on solitary roads, country gestures and speech
and quiet eyes. Young and old of all classes mingled on an
equality. There was no inharmonious element, it was a village
crowd, and all were united by the fact that they had been peasant
born and that they were now slaves to the town. They were
fascinated by the charm of the town, which is, that it is there easy

to fill the whole of life with a rapidly changing round of duties and necessities, where shops and all things are so convenient that life, as Catherine Anne had surmised, is swallowed up by its conveniences.

At one end of the glassy street the opposing cliffs of the house walls framed a portion of the brown burning mountain and white clouds standing above it; at the other end, under a railway arch, was a maze of gulls swaying between the steady masts of ships.

In and out of the crowd, relentless but polite, and turning round corners, passing one another, climbing this way and that the hills of the town, went the electric trams. They were polished, compact, efficient, without limbs. Like the machinery in the factories they must be of the best material and kept bright and oiled. They were tended like idols and altars with hate and fear that resembled love in its extremity. Men and women might be maimed, deformed, decrepit, pale, starved, rotten, but the wheels, the brakes, the brass-work, the advertisements, and the glass windows must be continually inspected and without spot.

Two girls of seventeen or eighteen, fair-haired – just so tall that one who cared would have said, Even so tall ought women to be – straight, quick, and graceful as mountain sheep, walked down a bye street beside the tram. They wore newly washed gay cheap gowns. Their heads were bare and their yellow hair drew down the sunlight. Their clear, rosy, small-featured faces were fresh and full of a boyish confidence – like boys among a crowd who are all companions. Their full, parted lips wavered and disclosed perfect teeth as they smiled and talked. The exquisite balance of their heads might have been called arrogant if it had not been careless and unaffected by the admiration, curiosity, and scorn of the crowd. Sometimes they held one another's hands as if unconsciously fearful of the town. It was easy to imagine these two changed into such birds of the sea-shore as terns, bright of wing and foot, for ever flitting in the sun and spray with merriment, speed and grace, and without care. They belonged to some wandering family encamped for a fair near by. A chauffeur rubbed the metal of his lamp till it flashed. There was no one to take care of these two. Instead, the town surged high above and around them to destroy them if it could, to force them to suckle gnomes at their delicate breasts.

Beyond these restless streets rose other hills away from the docks into unpolluted sea air. The town spread up on to the sides of these – first long rows of new clean houses of one pattern and few shops;

above them long terraces of houses of many forms, with gardens, shrubberies, oak trees; and still higher isolated large houses hidden by foliage, where parties played croquet and the solitary lounged with a book among flowering bushes and looked at the sea. The windy crest was free, and the half-made road ended in a deep overgrown track, now half a wood, down which the men of the mountains used to descend to the river and the ships and the sea. The oaks here were but young, yet they were stony and twisted and gaunt with the sap of other trees, stony and twisted and gaunt, that were descended from those through which the ancient men had their first glimpse of the river mouth, the small ships and the fires of their adversaries, before they plunged downward silently. Now between those twisted stems the eyes looked one way over the town to the white walls of Catherine Anne's cottage, the woods, the lesser hills, the great mountains so far away and pure that the breast heaved an involuntary sigh; the other way, in the gathering darkness, at a pale half moon of sea bounded just below by a curve of lamps low down as far as the docks, and then by the cloudy forms of hills with lights like stars upon their sides.

But at night the town irresistibly confined the gaze. It was a pit glittering with distinct small lights and glowing with the orange and scarlet furnaces that seemed to have eaten large squares out of the streets. Beyond, based in fire, the brown hill and the green hill rose indistinguishably dark into the midst of the stars. The pit was sounding with clanking and humming noises that recorded the activity of a demon, not of men, for not a whisper was heard of footsteps, voices, blows, caresses, of the love, anger, fear, anxiety, thought, argument, confusion, of men and women. It was impossible to remember that down there slept or waked those thousands of dark men, the mixed multitude, the buxom cockle-women like wood pigeons, those two fair ones like terns. The demon was humanity, a demon not born of woman, whose right hand knows not the deed of its left hand, though every nerve in its frame is a twitching soul. It knows not and recks not what it is making, as it squats there upon the earth. It feeds upon itself day and night, loading an immeasurable craw and looking up with small eyes on the sun and stars as senselessly as they look down upon it. It is cruel in ignorance, it is pitiful, and it forgets. It is hideous and beautiful. It would be noble but it must be vile. It is winged but cannot rise, so many are the claws that grapple into the earth. It is old but it is as a babe. But at this hour of night the pity and the vileness, the power and the beauty of it were under a veil. It crouched motionless, its bright eyes looked up, and the stars looked back, neither understanding, nor any longer questioning. It sang and knew not what it sang. Down there in the glimmering darkness, the demon sang, and through the obscurity of the song pierced the burden – that, with the river by which it is seated, and the mountain standing by, and the sea knocking without, and the ceiling of stars, it had a common birth; that their seeming strife is but the rude play of giant children nursed together and destined to one end; that the grass is waiting to grow upon it as upon the hills and the wreckage of fallen stars, and fire waiting to consume the grass, and the fire to burn itself out; and that in the meantime life is an inspiration of matter and must sing and must also make themes for songs. So that it resembled nothing so much as the old woman sitting at her cottage door and looking at the coming and going of the swifts from the eaves to heaven and from heaven back again, in a mystery.

The Fountain

It was a month when the sun was as a lion in the sky . . . I was walking along the beach under a vertical sandcliff that shut out all the land except a fringe of heather over the edge. A fish could have breathed as well as I in the heat. There was no escape. The cliff could not be climbed and it extended as it seemed endlessly before and behind. The sea itself simmered in the heat as it touched the burning sand. There was not a bird, or a sail, or a cloud to be seen. I could not think or give up trying to think. The solitude was unbearable. There was no rest for body or mind. Sometimes I walked quickly to make an end, sometimes slowly in the hope that it would be less wearisome. As always happens when you reach an end which you have desired only because the approach is tedious, it was no better when I came at last to the place where the cliffs gave way to a level marsh. I meant to fling myself down among the gorse between the cliff and the marsh when I saw a girl. It was as if a fountain had leaped out of the sand.

She was standing not ten yards away with her face towards me but looking at the sea. She was dark, not tall, and slender, her eyes blue and cold and still. Her brow was like a half moon under her brown hair and was of a most pellucid purity and utterly serene. The blue of her dress was very cool against the yellow of the gorse. She might have been eighteen, not more. Her hair was wet and fell down over her breast and beyond her waist in two long plaits. She had seaweed in both her hands and it hung down to the ground motionless, like dripping bronze.

I thought at once of a fountain in a desert. The purple heather and yellow gorse were mistily and drowsily coloured and fragrant, and their fragrance and colour mingled and made one effect with the murmur of bees. My path lay within a yard of her, and I walked slowly up to her and past her, bathed in the freshness of her spirit. She moved a step or two forward that the interruption might be over more quickly.

My heart was beating fast, but not with hope. She was in another world from mine. I felt that there was no possible means of contact with that form and the life which it expressed.

Then I thought that if I were a sculptor I should be able to imprison something of that life in a bronze figure lying at full length but raised on its elbows so that the outline of the young breasts should not be lost, its chin upon the linked palms of both hands, presiding over the birth of a river at a spring of sombre diamond among the mountains. If a brook might attain in a human form the embodiment of its purity, coldness, light, power, and desire to be ever moving, of its mysterious transformations in clouds of heaven and in caves under the rocks, it would be in such a form as hers. The gravity, the dark simplicity, above all the exquisite combination of wildness and meekness in the girl would be worthy of the most sacred fountain, whether emerging among moss and crags and the shadows of crags or among sunlit grass. Surely, I thought, a lymph of crystal ran in her veins. It was the darkness of a hidden spring that chilled her pellucid brow. The radiance of her eyes, her face, her whole form, was of the dawn, which I dreamed that she was one of the few left to worship – Yes! She had listened to the nightingales when the dew and the hawthorn flower and the young grass were yet dark; and the thrill of their songs had entered her eyes and lips without one passionate or confusing thought.

I fancied that I could see the way of her life. She was meek at home and in the company of others, as a large-eyed animal is meek but without surrender, or as a fairy bride was meek who consented in the old days to live with a mortal husband until he should have struck her three times, when she would forsake him and return with all the flocks and herds of her dowry to her father's palace below the lake in the hills. Only, this maid would not, like the fairy bride, laugh at a funeral, cry at a wedding; she would do all things in order, obeying in matters of the house and social life the father and mother and brothers and sisters who understood how such things should be, because it was for these that they lived. She would bound away in answer to a summons, especially if it sent her out into the air at night or in the very early morning, when she could see the stars sailing over broad blue fiords among the white clouds, or the moon like a silver fish now and then showing its side in the turbulence. And once away from these friends for whom she would easily wear away her life she was as if they were not. She plunged deep into the oblivion of other loves, as now when she looked out to sea.

I thought of her discovering one by one with serious joy the strange responses made to her heart by the earth and to the earth by her heart: how, for example, she would listen to the nightjar churring on the bough above a house where all were asleep; or watch the owl gliding over the graves softly, beneficently; or, at first fearfully, then wild with delight, follow the fox that yelled his love and hate over the winter hills at night when all that remained of the world of day was the faint light here and there in the valley which one leaf could extinguish. She tasted unfamiliar leaves and fruit, buried her face in bracken or flowers or foliage for their scent, ran and leaped and lay in far places where the sun, the clouds, the stars, the rivers, the sea, the endless wind, were her company. Her whiteness, though it was not the same and was contrasted with her dark hair and flushing cheek, called to my mind the beauty of white on an October morning, the white of mushrooms in the short turf, of the horse-chestnuts' newly cloven husks, of the fresh walnuts opened and eaten where they fell, of the nearly full moon alone in the huge blue sky an hour after dawn. As a boy it was of such a being that I used to think – though my imagination was not energetic enough to body it forth quite clearly – when I felt, in loneliest places among the woods or clouds, that my foot-falls had scared something shy, beautiful, and divine. And more than so, she was akin to the spirit abroad on many days that had awed or harassed me with loveliness – to the spirit on the dewy clovers, in the last star that hung like a bird of light scattering gold and silver from her wings in the cold blue and gloomy rose of the dawn; to the spirit in mountain or forest waters, in many unstained rivers, in all places where Nature had stung me with a sense of her own pure force, pure and without pity . . .

These were the fancies of the moment. She was in sight for less than a minute as I went up from the sea over the moor, and when I turned in one of its hollows she had disappeared and I saw nothing but sea and sky, which were as one.

The Maiden's Wood

At the upper end of a long beechen coombe that narrowed and wound and rose as it penetrated the hills, was a high ledge that looked southward down the coombe to a broad plain, an opposite range of bare and smooth hills, to other isolated hills seen above the lowest parts of the range, and, on a clear day, when the brain was tranquil and the eye at its full power, the sea beyond. This ledge was a few acres in extent, full of hollows and mounds and given up to beech, oak, and wild cherry, and it was protected from the north by a steep bank rising behind to the highest point on the hills. It was untouched by roads. The great highway that rose from the plain to the high land by a gradual ascent along the winding edge of the valley turned abruptly away from it. Once upon a time, indeed, a track had been worn from this highway to a gravel pit under the steep bank; but the pit was overgrown with bushes and fern, and, as the way led nowhere beyond, it had long been disused. The land all round was poor and mostly wild. The few inhabitants went where they liked; and the footpaths were trodden so rarely that they were slender as hare-paths and hardly distinguishable from them, and none seemed to lead to the ledge, which I discovered by following the uneven track – where the branches did not turn me aside among the trees – in search of orchises. Once there I saw that it was traversed by many faint unreasonable paths leading into one another, which from a little distance could not be seen, for the foliage of dog's mercury, everywhere of equal height, gloomy and cool and tinged with a lemon hue, almost closed over the narrow grassless ribbons of brown earth and dead leaves, though once the feet rather than the eye had revealed them they were easily followed. If they had any centre of radiation it was an impenetrable thicket of brier and hazel all overlaced by the cordage of honeysuckle and traveller's joy, in the midst of which there were a few moss-covered rotten posts, all but one lying prone; and these, hardly different from the many dead and mossy stems of trees already decayed, did not arouse my curiosity. One only of the paths was broad enough not to be mistakable. It ran along the brink of the ledge and appeared to have been artificially banked up. It was from here that the view was most perfect to the sea, or, on days less clear, to the long range and to the low plain, or merely to the wooded coombe where all the mists of the world seemed to be born and to return time after time like the sea. Once the ledge was left behind by only a few yards the view was gone, and nothing seen but the surface of the woods on the slopes below and the clouds on the blue over the topmost trees.

But the little wood was as a mountain kingdom apart, not merely on account of what could be seen from it and from it alone. It was divided from the woods of the coombe sides by earth walls, still high and once hedge-grown, like ancient fortifications; from the high lands behind by the precipitous bank; from the treeless trough of the coombe by the all but impassable steepness at the beginning of its descent. It was the home of the sun. East, south, and west, the sun never forgot it, and the twisted lean trees, many of them dead, did nothing to keep it out. So used was it to the sun just here, the great bee was careless of the heavy spring rain as he went feeling from white bloom to bloom of the dead-nettle.

The path at the brink was cut off short by the earth walls at either end. I thought that the whole ledge had been forgotten: the estates on these miles of half-precipitous wooded declivities were very large, and entirely neglected, the fallen trees lying where they fell because they were inaccessible; and there were no gamekeepers – what then could these two or three acres matter, even supposing that they were duly distinguished from the surrounding country on the maps locked up half a century ago by a lawyer? There were long days of every season when I believed it my own, or what was better even than possession, I felt entirely free there and alone and without responsibility. I used to wander idly and without asking who the owner was, for I concluded that it had an owner in the sense that my occupation could be disputed if it were avowed. Day and night I used to go. In all those enormous woods there were only two sounds by day – the sudden laughs of the green woodpecker and the oceanic music of the wind which, even when it slept, seemed to dream there aloud. There was one other sound, but it was not often heard simply because it was always there, the noise of a streamlet running down among the woods; seldom did I notice it except in still cold nights when the huge forest hills were black and the sky starless and grey, and then the harsh sound was unceasing and ghostly, as of a river running in the sky. Once when the trees were all white under silent snow one heron came up the long empty coombe, grey and lean and slow and like a solitary ship entering the keelless foam between the untrodden shores of some mighty estuary long ago; and he also was silent. But on that ledge between the forest and the high open land no bird was afraid to come, and whether that long kingdom of green leaves was roaring or silent I could always hear a bird singing among these trees or stirring the dead leaf. The stillest days of Spring, when the leaves could yet be numbered, were best savoured here where the enormous silence of the world was threaded by rivulets of song. By night there was the hoot and the shriek and the soft chuckling of the owls. Many a windy, cold night, dripping and black, I climbed up there and heard the owl crying his loudest and clearest into the echoing coombe, a strong happy voice when all other life but that in my own breast seemed to have passed away into the wind and rain.

Now and then I tried to picture the man or woman who had been there last. Whose were those footpaths? Or were these ribbons of earth, always bare among the green, not footpaths at all, but to be explained some other way?

I had been there a score of times without making anything like a full survey and inventory of my kingdom. It was becoming part of me, a kingdom rather of the spirit than of the earth, and I was content to see what I had seen on my first visit. In the neighbouring woods I had sought for orchises but after finding half a dozen kinds here at that time I had not looked for more. The other flowers were the usual flowers of the woods, the minute green moschatel, the stars of stitchwort and later woodruff, the bluebell and a few more, such as I was glad to greet for the twentieth time with more familiarity than ceremony. But one day I not only learnt that the wood was not my own, but that there was a further mystery. At the first moment the other visitor seemed to be its possessor, so much at home was she and so strange did I suddenly feel. It was a woman, how much past middle age I could not guess. Her hair was flaxen, her face as much weathered as it was possible to be without ceasing to be pink and fresh, her thin mouth at once childlike and shrewd, her eyes of a sparkling grey so that in each of them seemed always to be a drop of quick-silver sliding. She was short and plump and had a kind of briskness that I imagined to mean a nature of the utmost independence and unworldliness. She came towards me gathering flowers which she put into a basket on one arm. She looked at me with those intensely brilliant eyes that certainly saw me as I had never been seen before and saw in me something of which I was unaware; she curtsied and went on picking flowers. I was just about to step off the narrow path so as not to disturb her, when, still bending and without looking at me, she hopped aside and I passed by. Indeed I should not have spoken to this extraordinary human being, in spite of her rarity and fascination, if it had not been for the flowers which I caught sight of under her face. Though I am not a botanist I see most of the flowers in my path and I know the names of most; but I recognized none of these. They were bells and cups and stars clustered or single, in spires and bunches, that I had never seen growing wild before.

'There are many here in this wood,' she said in answer to my questions. 'Yes, only here.'

'Can you tell me their names?' I asked.

'No. They have never been christened that I know of,' she replied.

Seeing some orchises among them I said:

'But you know these?'

'Yes, they are fly-hawkins and butterflies' nests,' she said, perverting the names of the fly-orchis and bird's nest and butterfly orchises. She smiled, I did not know why; but it was a smile as fitting to her as her childlike mouth and complexion, her quick-silver eye, her briskness, and her hop to one side. I asked her the name of the wood. 'The Maiden's Wood,' – she said, 'It has always been called the Maiden's Wood . . . I do not know the meaning of the name.' And she went on picking flowers. I now saw that these unfamiliar kinds were to be found everywhere in the little wood.

Twice again I saw her in the wood, and I liked to see her alone and undisturbed, at ease and at home there like a bird questing among the dead leaves when it has no fears of being observed.

Now that I saw the wood was not unknown I did not hesitate to ask questions at the nearest inn, several miles away, in the hope of learning more. I asked a young labourer. Yes, it had always been the Maiden's Wood. Old Mrs Malkin knew all about it, he said, for she went everywhere for flowers, and she got the curious ones in the Maiden's Wood, so they say – for he had never been there himself. I next asked an old man. He gave it the same name. There was a story, he said, but he did not belong to these parts, and he did not rightly remember it – something about a great lady, he believed, who had a garden there, hundreds of years ago it must have been. I asked him had there been a house there. No, no house; she did not live there; in fact he thought she was a ghost, though he had not seen it, or a fairy, or something.

Another old man said it was a queen had owned the place, he did not rightly know which queen, but she had stayed at the big manor house, now a farm, with the ancient wall round its orchard, which was the nearest building to the Maiden's Wood.

The farmer was a young man with a fine chestnut horse and a polished trap that was always rushing here and there on its bright yellow wheels. I hardly expected him to be able to tell me more. But I caught him out of his trap one day, having come to look at the wool in a barn where there was a boastful shearer who cut the flesh every minute in his effort to show himself the swiftest of his craft in the county, when he was being watched. The farmer was a practical man of few words, but he said that his father would be glad to have a talk, so he took me upstairs, backward and forward, as it seemed to me, the whole length and breadth and height of the big house that looked as if it had grown by some natural process of conglomeration, room by room; and at the top, in a corner no one could have suspected from the outside, he showed me in to the old man. He was sitting in a high-backed chair, as stiff and as rugged as a tree, a huge grey-bearded man, as still as a tree too, for he could not rise to show his pleasure, which he did, however, by very soon setting out to talk very slowly in a voice that seemed to echo in his head before it left his lips, but without noticing any of my interruptions.

'I cannot tell you,' he said, 'when it was first called the Maiden's Wood, but I knew the Maiden. This was her room when she came to stay at the farm when I was a boy. The estate belonged to her and two brothers, this long bit from here up to the brow and that little bit you were speaking of as well, the Maiden's Wood. She was the Maiden. Some call it the Maiden's Garden. But her real garden was out there' — and looking out I saw a long wide border, under a fruit wall, full of flowers such as I had noticed in the wood — 'and it was her fancy to take the seeds out there into the wood and sow them there. She did it all herself. Many's the time, when they were ploughing up to the edge of the steep bank there, that they could see her down below in the wood as they were turning the horses round to begin another furrow. She used to walk up and down, up and down, and round and back again, rain or shine, no matter. She never had anyone with her there, and never would let anyone else go in except when we built the arbour for her in the middle of the wood: you have seen the posts of it, I dare say, but the thatch has gone long ago. Are the roses there now? I suppose not — oh, dear me, no, what am I thinking of? They would not last, pretty lady's roses they were with long Jerusalem names. She was pretty herself, too — not what everyone would like, you know, and some of them saw nothing in her, but like one of these ladies in pictures. She always wore the same kind of dress; like a maybush she looked in it, and one of the men seeing her and not knowing who it was took her for a blessed ghost. I was about eighteen then, and she was not any older. No. I liked to see her down there. But she wasn't our sort. Queer, something wrong or funny about her, and a well-born lady, too. The young have not any business to be like that. I never saw her speak to anyone. She always came here alone to stay. She used to talk to herself a lot, and it sounded as if she was saying poetry and lots of outlandish words out of books. She would have a book with her and hold it in her hand hanging down, as she walked back and forth. I laughed to myself about her many a time, I did. I and my brother helped to put up the arbour. It was her idea. What did a young thing want to be playing about by herself in the wood like that, I should like to know? It was the time of the Crimean war. She didn't care. I remember one day I was just turning the plough at the top by that bank above the Maiden's Wood when Jacob Stout went by galloping on the hard road a good mile away. He saw me and the team and he stopped his mare, and shouted "Victory," so that the horses pricked up their ears, wondering what was up, and off he went again. Now it so happened that Miss West was walking down below at the time, and having nobody to talk to after I had told the horses all about it and promised them an extra sieve of oats to eat Her Majesty's health with, I shouted "Victory" myself, pretty loud. She stops dead, looks up at me, and says: "John!" So I scrambles down, and there was she standing like a queen, and she gives me a crown. "That's for the good news, John;" but I would sooner not have had it if only she had spared me the look she gave when she said, "But I don't like to be disturbed, John." I was feeling proud, too, and my view halloo used to be a good one, I promise you. You might have thought she was at her prayers, or courting. She might have been in love with somebody that had not the sense to love her back again – she was a beauty, dear me! such waste of time it was for her to be walking there all alone and looking for the sea, if you please. "A clear morning, John," she used to say some days, "I ought to be able to see the sea this morning." Funny thing. There was she with health and strength, riches and good looks, everything mortal wants, and not unhappy either, walking up and down among those trees just as if she was on a ship. She made those paths, every one of them, in her idleness. The only thing she ever *did* was to sow seeds there. She used to go out into the garden there after a warm day at harvest time and fill her pockets with seeds from her fancy plants, and then she would scatter them in the wood. It looked pretty for a time, but there are only a few left for Jenny Malkin by this time, I doubt. It was not one year only – you might have understood that. These young ladies with nothing to do must have their whimsies. But one two, three, four, five – the year I was married – yes! five years she was there, and all the spring and summer, half the autumn too, and Christmas time. What can you make of it? And then she did not come any more. The estate had to be sold. The brother went abroad. We missed her, too. She was kind and sensible in her talk; and then her looks did you good, ay! a bonny face. I never set eyes on her again. It was just after this we opened the gravel pit, and many a joke the men had about the arbour. The children found it out when they got a bit venturesome, and they pulled it about sadly. But after they began to work about the farm they never went more, not till my eldest went courting there, and then it was a rare sort of a lovers' nest for them all in a smother of weeds and climbers and roses, and the flowers there still; and when Mary came in wearing the pretty things I used to fall awondering what might have happened to Miss West that planted them. That must have been how it came to be called the Maiden's Wood, I should say. Albert and his sweetheart used to call it that, I recollect, and that is what we always call it.'

Light and Twilight

(1911)

A Group of Statuary

I had walked several miles through streets whose high, flat-fronted buildings made me feel as if I were at the bottom of a well, or in a deep, weedy river-bed with cliffy banks, from which it was impossible to climb out, though I could turn aside into many tributaries even more narrow and as deep. The sky was stagnant and dull; the fever and heat of the air came not so much from the sun as from underground, and from the walls on either side – a volcanic fire out of the earth's depths and the hearts of men. The plaited streams of men and women were restless. Their bodies were glad of the heat, but the gladness was repressed, and could show itself only in a darkly burning eye, a caged smile, a beautiful contrast of colours, a restlessness that knew not its own cause, far less a means of satisfying itself. They thought of the country, of the sea, of leisure, of resting on the grass, of sleep, of dreaming, of love; of everything which the prison made impossible, or of nothing at all, merely undulating with the waves of vague desire and discontent. Thousands of faces and figures passing me by were full of capacities, of strength and love. They were like weapons, swords, spears, axes and daggers, slender scimitars and curious twisted edges, hanging on the walls of a museum. They had the same look of being unnatural and out of place as objects in a museum. If only they were to begin taking them down, trying their edges, brandishing them!

One such street led me at last out into a wide pool. A score of streets opened into it, yet it was broad and almost empty. It was dotted with islands where people could take refuge from the stream; only there was no stream; and the islands also were empty. It was a grey flat space, surrounded by many-windowed buildings of a grey that was almost black, a chapel, a factory, a school, public-houses, at the several corners, and all of this same hue. It was shapeless, like a natural pool. It was far larger than the largest cathedral in the world, and it allowed a view of the sky, both overhead, and on every side above the roofs and between the walls of the streets running into it. The islands were girt by low, thick posts. On some there were pillars surmounted by lamps. They were wonderfully silent and still, as if detached in some way from the conditions of the surrounding world.

The largest of the islands, lying at one corner of the pool, was shaded by three plane trees; or rather, being trees, and retaining a few colourless, dusty leaves, they suggested the thought of shade. At first sight, the trees, the emptiness, the space, the quiet, gave the place a rustic or cloistral air as of a cathedral or market town; bullocks in rows, sheep and pigs, crates of geese, farmers going slowly to and fro would have been in keeping with it – or a priest walking at ease with a fine lady. But under the trees there were seats without backs, and the flagged pavement was irregularly worn into many hollows, and plastered with dust and moisture in blotches. On the seats were figures which few could have had difficulty in recognizing at a short distance as those of human beings no longer young. It was they who spread round about them the silence which possessed the islands.

Even more fitting than a market or ecclesiastical group was this assembly under the planes. For like a market group, in a market square, it had a look of entire fitness, as if it could not have been changed, as if it had been there from the beginning. The dull, grey figures might have risen up out of the city soil, with some of it still clinging to them, rude and shaggy after the effort of birth, to sun themselves and look about. Their greyness was wintry, the rasping greyness of north-east wind that turns dry roads, asphalt, flagstone, plough-land, and meadow in the country, within the mind, to one grey, the colour of ashes. Nothing in them responded to the heat out of the sky. They were of the dark earth.

Before the discovery that they had faces with eyes and lips and hair, it might have been seen that they were men and women, and that for two reasons: first, they wore clothes which subtly suggested those of the people in the crowd, without in the least resembling them; second, they were miserable. I think that the clothes alone, the misfits and cast-offs of scarecrows, would have betrayed them, but I am not sure; I cannot separate the clothes from them, and not them or their clothes from misery. By a swift intuition the spirit penetrated those recumbent or propped-up frameworks of old black clothing, and divined their humanity — penetrated the clothing straight to the spirit, without thinking of the flesh. For in these abjects, as in the sumptuously apparelled, there is something terrible about the mere naked flesh, and it needs the inhuman ironist to think of it with serenity. Of all those who, full of meat and hope, or one of its equivalents, passed by that island, and turned an eye for a vacant second upon those under the planes, not one failed to recognize that these were of one species with themselves. Not one got so far beyond that profound truism as to think of them and to see them naked, merely human, in their approximation to the appearance of a child bathing, a beloved woman a-dream on a summer morning, or a quoit-thrower poised. Had anyone so beheld them he would have stood thinking half the day over it, or he would have run away and stopped his eyes against the siren-sphinx: I saw neither the thinker nor the fugitive.

For all of us it was the clothing that had a meaning, the clothing of other men and other women. The clothes were the human things. The clothes held them together and made them the men and women they were, and these upon the benches had a look as if they would have crumbled away had they been divested of their rags. The body beneath was unconsciously known and feared as something diabolical or divine. The Master Sculptor had wrought them daily throughout a lifetime, and somebody had always come to their rescue on the day when the drapery had seemed no longer to perform its part sufficiently. One man, it is true, lay half along a seat with his head and shoulders in the lap of a woman whose head had fallen forward so as to hide his face with her hair, and his trouser leg had rolled up and disclosed a yellow bone. But the chances of ordinary life do frequently bring to sight a man's bare arm, breast, or foot, though usually it is whitish and something more than bone. This was a yellow bone. Still, it might pass. There was nothing here to outrage those who were not only full-fed but rightly and confidently expecting to remain so. Had it been a woman. . . . Apparently there are always enough black stockings left in the poor world to cover the yellow bones of the distressed mothers, sisters, wives, casual mistresses, and daughters of Englishmen; if not a loaf, yet a black stocking. There were men and women lying – men and women doubled up as the cavemen used to sleep and die – men and women with folded arms, and faces looking down or straight over the grey pool at nothing – on the warm seats under the planes. There was not an attitude that could not be equalled among birds on a frosty branch, and, for all that it was not designed for them, their clothing was like a natural covering of plumage or fur, but mangy and soiled.

One of the women was doing up her dusty hair. She had laid her black bonnet on her knees, and her locks fell to the pavement as she drooped her head to one side and combed them with her fingers, her eyelids closed, for there was no mirror. It was a touch of nature. The gesture is always pensively beautiful, and could never fail to remind one of his mother when he was yet a child, and another of his young wife – but there was nobody near, neither were there any windows or private houses looking that way. No one of them spoke, or wept, or sighed. The woman who was doing up her hair coughed now and then. The man with his head in a woman's lap turned over once to spit – he was wide awake. As he once more made his head comfortable the woman revealed her eyes. There was nothing else of her save rags, and the eyes seemed hardly to belong to her. They expressed no private grief or hope or fear, any more than do the eyes in the portraits of Christ. It was a jest of gamesome providence to light those lamps in her face unknown to her, a jest like that of a small boy who chalks another's back. She bore about with her those beautiful brown eyes, and, save that no doubt men would kiss her for them, they served no purpose which is not served by the eyes of a weasel or crow. In a musician, now, in a lovely woman living among mountain lakes – such eyes would have done many missions for the soul. They were like wild-voiced nightingales in their silence. But in this cage . . . Had they really belonged to her, it was inconceivable that she should have been content to sit in that dusty retreat under the planes. A musician or a poet with such eyes would have told us subtle, remote, lustrous things, and, if we had not listened in his lifetime, yet, when he was dead and known to all, his eyes would still be remembered. A passer-by, seeing these eyes, would have been startled, but would have controlled himself by reflecting that they could be matched in a cow's or Irish terrier's, and he would have gone on to remember even with amusement what very foolish people have glorious eyes; it is the inner eye and the soul that count; indeed, what better proof of this could be given than this vision on the bench in the dusty heart of the city, in a corner where refuse had been swept up and left to lie, as by a careless housemaid, because nobody would notice it in such an out-of-the-way place. A girl passing dropped a paper bag opposite to the woman with the eyes, and they saw it. She raised the man's head in her hands, and looking to learn if any of the others had seen, let his head down on the bench. She rose and walked to the bag. First she put her foot gently upon it to make sure that she was right in thinking that it was not paper alone. She was right. She picked it up, thrust in her hand, filled her mouth with something, and putting the bag in her pocket, returned to her seat. Since she saw nothing more that was unfamiliar, or in any way new or worth attention, nothing which she could not see as well without them, she closed her eyes.

All were now still. They absorbed the dry, dull heat.

The pool and its islands appeared to be empty. For no one notices the statuary of London unless it is made for display or to divide the traffic, not to form a decoration appropriate to a particular site, as in the case of these figures under the planes. In all the city there was no group so perfectly in keeping with its greatness and aridity. I had seen equestrian figures, symbolic groups, nudes, semi-nudes, figures in frock coats, in stone or bronze; thousands of living creatures, joyous or beautiful or tragic in their capacity for joy, in harmony with the burning sun, yet having nothing to do with this city which was the work of the giants, the heaven-besieging giants, not the gods. But these thirteen or fourteen recumbent, leaning, seated, and bowed figures, in their dignified dismay, forming neither a circle nor a square, but a group as of a herd or flock, were in their place, thoroughly native, children of the city clay – fit lords of the scene, if they had but known – perfect citizens of no mean city. Why should it trouble to house Grecian marbles when it had these eternal ones wrought with its own hands? Could they have been petrified at that moment, and duly proclaimed as the costly work of the most famous living sculptor, none would have denied their pre-eminence. One by one the alien transitory crowd in the surrounding streets, after venturing up to glance at the wondrous art, would have slunk away and have left the city in their possession as theirs by right and theirs only.

It was very still. The sun in the sky was the one thing that moved. I dreamed that this exodus had taken place. I was a traveller in a desert city whose sons had all been dead thousands of years, but were known still to the stranger by these mighty marbles among which the planes had taken root. The tradition of the dead race was so powerful that not a bird or beast or any wild thing cared to visit this memorial of it, except curious men. And I was a man. I consulted the learned authorities and found them divided between two theories. One was that it was a group of that ancient people preserved in their natural attitudes, 'while the flesh was yet between their teeth, ere it was chewed' by a petrifying plague. The other was that these were their gods, whose uncouth names I was not skilled to interpret. It seemed to me that the second theory was the better of the two, and, except Stonehenge, I had seen nothing approaching its sublimity in my wanderings.

Home

A little square sitting room, not very high, and hardly wider than it was high, yellow-lit by a brass lamp in the centre, and shutting out the visible world by three walls of a pleasant dull gold and indistinguishable pattern, and by three narrow curtains of a ruddiness that was dreamily heavy and sombre. On the walls, five pictures at the same height above the tops of the dark chairs, the mantelpiece and the sideboard; and on one, three shelves of books. A very still, silent room; and in it, motionless as in amber, a man standing before the books, and a woman with raised eyebrows and stiff but unquiet hands, dove-tailed together, staring into the black-crusted fire. The man, chin on one hand, elbow on the other, tall and upright and dark like a pinnacle of black rock, looking sternly out of kind eyes at the books as at children. The woman, trying to drowse herself through her eyes by the fire and through every pore of her body by the silentness, yet aware all the time of the husband between her and the windows, as though his shadow blackened her instead of half the books. These two, separate and careful not to look at one another. Had they been utterly alone they would hardly have looked thus. They were not alone. In the stillness and silence, despite the walls and curtains, there was another presence, and a greater than they. It was London, a presence as mighty as winter, though as invisible. Its face was pressed up against the window; its spirit was within. And there was yet another, almost invisible, and as frail as the other was mighty – the spirit of the one who saw the room and felt the enchantment of London upon it. Neither the man nor the woman knew what was this second spirit in their room, yet the room was its home. It was the spirit of a young soldier dying in a far land. He was calm and easy now, without pain and without motion. Only his dark eyes told that he lived. As still was he, with bright fixed eyes, as a bird sitting on its nest. One had just left him who had spoken a few words intended to comfort him; but all the words had faded as soon as spoken, just as wavelets on a burning sand which they do not even stain, all except 'for your country.' He had heard these before without considering them, though he would have struck the man who mocked at them. This time they remained because they instantly recalled the first time he had heard them used, eighteen years before. His father had said to him one morning, 'Johnny, I am going to take you to see your country, to-morrow.' His pale mother had smiled her patient, weary smile — with some gentle ridicule added — at these words. Then she looked admiringly at her husband, the big, gaunt wry-faced man, whose eyes laughed so under his black brows. She had no country. She was born in the great city where they lived, where Johnny was born, and she had never left it. Nearly everything outside her home inspired her with wonder, awe, or fear, and she held her husband in awe because he had a country of which he frequently talked, where they spoke a different language, had queer names, different food, different ways and, as she dimly conjectured, a kind of common life as of one big family. Her husband had told her often that he had only to take a train to his country and get out at any station over the border, and somebody, most likely a cousin, would step up as if he had been waiting, and say, with his face all cut up by a smile, 'And how are you, David John, this long time?' But somehow he never went until this April. He had had to be content with talking, with taking the boy on his lap and singing the songs of his country, grand wailing songs that would often make him happy for the rest of the evening, merry, quick songs that made him tap the ground with his toes and yet brought tears into his eyes, so that he set the child down and went out into the street and came home, bitterly, hours afterwards to the dark house and the meek waiting wife.

But now he was really going to his country. 'To-morrow,' he said, 'we will take the train at midnight, and before noon we will be finding a curlew's nest on the moor just by where the old battle was.'

'What battle, father?' said the boy.

'Why, one of the old battles when we beat the English, I suppose,' said he.

'But what was the name of it, and when was it fought?'

'Ah, I cannot tell you that now: it is not in the history books. But the river there is called the River with the Red Voice, and there is a battle mound. The air is so clean there that a collar lasts you a fortnight.'

'Dear me,' said his mother, waking with a start from her musing.

Then the boy fell a-dreaming about his father picking up mottled eggs among dead men's bones by a river that ran red with blood.

Those bright eyes in the hospital tent saw now the railway station like a huge palace, sprinkled with lights and paved with multitudes of men and women, and good silent trains stretched out among them which the people had caught by a hundred handles and were mounting, to persuade them to carry them far off into the black night beyond, the unmapped black night with its timorous lines of small lights. He and his father entered the multitude and crept in and out alongside the train; and it was very wonderful, but many of the groups who talked were talking in the tongue in which his father used to sing, and he looked up at their pallid faces and black hair and agitated smiles and boldly moving lips, and was inclined to be afraid, but remembering that they were his father's people he was not afraid, but filled with wonder and admiration. Even some very little children, smaller than himself, were chattering in that same tongue quite easily; it seemed to Johnny that they were very clever little children. How kind everybody looked now! He had never seen so many people smiling and talking friendly before.

'Where is our country now?' said Johnny, and as soon as he had sat down with his face towards the land of his desire, the train was gliding out past a hedge of white faces and white lifted hands into the darkness.

The carriage was full, and the boy liked pressing up against his countrymen on both sides and touching their boots with his toes, and watching the thoughts on their faces and the books and papers they were reading, and how they would sometimes let their books and their papers fall on their laps, and look out at the wild-starred night seriously as if, perhaps, 'it had come . . . their country.' In a corner opposite sat a young woman, and next her a young man. He was reading. She was doing nothing but thinking, with her eyes turned towards Johnny. Soon the man closed his eyes; his head sank upon the woman's shoulder, but she did not move, only took away the book lest it should fall, and she offered Johnny a sweet, but he was too busy looking at her, and would not take it. The young woman's brown eyes fixed on him softly, and, his father's arm round him, he began to dream; and he awoke, surprised that he had been asleep, at a cold glittering station with a few faces staring in from the platform, looking for seats. 'Is this –?' He was going to ask his father if they had arrived, but he saw the name of a well-known town on the seats and lamps and again closed his eyes; the others also had looked and immediately closed their eyes. Then nothing – tiny lamps in the darkness – nothing again – then over a hill a large moon began to light a watery sky, black cloud and blacker earth, and looked afraid of the huge world over which she reigned. Another stop, a well-known name on the lamps, and then sleep to the sound of the train expressing steadiness, determination, and content in its rhythm and hope in its speed. If he opened his sleepy lids he saw the young woman's soft eyes, and the earth now grey and not black, and the moon high, without a cloud around or below, with groups of houses lost – as it seemed – in the night and cowering under the trees, here and there a light burning where someone, perhaps, was enviously watching the train on its march of discovery and conquest; or, still later, a pale sky lit from below and behind, as well as from the now invisible moon above, a river gleaming, a horse knee-deep in white mist looking up at the train, a church upon a hill that seemed awake but alone, small contemptible stations where they did not stop.

The fixed bright eyes in the bed saw these stations again in their dreariness, and saddened with the dream that he now was upon such a station, and the lighted train was rushing by and forgetting him, with its proud freight of living men looking ahead towards their country.

Nodding awake again, he saw the girl eating an orange, a wide water like a sea and the pale moon shrivelled beyond it, a farm and its cattle streaming out under a hill covered with crooked oaks, and the cattle were bowed under the weight of their long horns. 'It is near,' whispered his father: he slept.

When he awoke he was upon his father's knee, and both with cheeks together were looking, over frosty meadows and blown trees, at sand hills and sea beyond, and on the other side at hills crimsoned with bracken, their summits invisible, so steep were they. 'This is it,' said the father. 'Yes,' whispered the son, and both looked through and beyond the mountains and the sea to their country, the country of their souls, so that the child's first thought – that this was not what he had expected – never appeared again, until now in the tent. When a gap in the near hill showed them greater giants beyond that appeared to have descended out of the sky, and only half descended as yet, for their crests were in the clouds, the two were not more moved; they could see, far beyond these distances, greater hills, a land even more free.

They stopped, and there were wizard faces waiting, and the strange tongue that was the boy's own was spoken, and they seemed to welcome him. He began to step down from his father's knee to get out – but no, not yet.

They stopped again where there was only a black-bearded, tall man and a sheep-dog waiting. They could hear the thrushes sing, under the clear blue and the lightless moon, from out of dark thickets in a hollow rushy, land, backed by the sea and the orange sails of vessels that caught the dawn. 'Over there,' said his father, pointing beyond the ships, 'is the land we have come from.' It was as faint and grey and incredible in the distance as his own land was clear and true; and he sighed with happiness and security, and also with anticipation of the further deeps that were to be revealed, the battlefield, the curlew's eggs, the castles, the harps, the harpers harping all the songs of his father. He had got so used to the faces of the men, which were like his father's, that when his father asked him whether they were not different from the English, he said 'No,' and was scolded for it.

The sun and the bright world dazzled his eyes. He slept. Then, a black barren land, a host of tall black chimneys between hills and sea, fountains of black smoke, sheaves of scarlet flame, red-hot caves. . . . Young men crowded into the carriage and burst out into a song. It was in the language that Johnny spoke, but the beauty of their voices in harmony made it different from anything he had heard before that day.

A marsh and a thousand sheep, gaunt hills on one side, sea on the other, and the young men singing a war march in their own tongue at his father's request. It made him afraid at first. Then he fancied that the battlefield was not far off, and they were going to it, and the song was sung to hearten a host of which he was one.

He felt grim, but glad and bold as he looked at the dark young men and thought of 'his country.'

'My country,' muttered the dreamer lying still, and blinked his eyes as the tent flapped and he saw outside the sun of another country blazing and terrible as a lion above the tawny hills. The country that he had been fighting for was not this solitude of the marsh, the mountains beyond, the farms nestling in the beards of the mountains, the brooks and the great water, the land of his father and of his father's fathers, of those who sang the same songs, the young men and the old, and the women who had looked kindly on him. Where were those young men scattered? Where had their war march on that April morning led them?

A grim, black-bearded face was bending over him, with smiles deeply entrenched all over it. He was lifted straight into a cart behind a chestnut pony with his father and the man.

The sun was hot. They climbed up high among the hedgeless and pathless mountain, always up. The larks sang. The mountain lambs skipped before the cart.

They alighted by a solitary cottage under the road, whence a maid brought ale for the men and milk for the boy. They sat down among gorse bushes and ate apple tart and cheese, wafers of oat and currant cakes. The men talked. Johnny wandered up from the road with a girl of the cottage. And there with the rough strange mountain boys they set fire to the gorse and dead bracken. The flames leapt up like the genii out of the imprisoning jar in the Arabian tales, and he drew back. The earth was crowded with little flickering plants of fire spreading this way and that. Huge whirls and rounds of the yellow-white smoke soared up against the milky sky. The smell of the smoke heated by fire and sun was delicious. When the earth was black they moved on, while some sent the grey boulders galloping downward till they bounded over the road with a hero leap, and struck sparks out of other boulders or plunged into the gorse. The boys roared, the girls shrieked. All disappeared. But all day they could see the smoke of one conflagration pouring upwards before the wind in a great river, lost awhile in the hollows, seen again continually surging towards the high crests mile after mile, like a gigantic engine smoking wildly over the wilds.

Outside one cottage there stood a little old man, naked to the waist, washing himself and talking to three foxes chained up to a shed. The foxes seemed to understand his tongue and he theirs, and neither heeded the cart as it drove on. And now, careless of waterfalls thundering among low woods beneath the road, of flames and smoke clouds hunting upwards over the moor, and of mountains such as he had dreamed lying across their course a day ahead, Johnny fell asleep, content, not even rousing himself to make sure whether that was the cuckoo he heard upon the hillside.

The dream of the fixed open eyes wreathed and wavered. Was it the same day – it was morning and about noon – when he stood by the door of a long white inn fronting the sun? The wide courtyard, bounded on one side by the road and on the other by a green hedge, was dotted with fowls pecking idly or lying down. In the midst rose a brown oak, very thick and stiff and well stricken in years, and at its side a very tall gentleman with a fishing-rod was mounting a trap; and the boy watching him and thinking of his wealth and happiness was happier than he. On the hot white pavement by the door all the dogs were lazy in the sun. Each one, except the big, smooth pointer, had a bone, and each snarled as the pointer strolled past. There was a greyhound, a spaniel, a sheep-dog with one eye almost white, a mongrel, resembling both the spaniel and the pointer, and a fox-hound. From time to time the spaniel's puppies – pure spaniels – broke in among the fowls, and the mother raised her head and left the bone under her paws until the pointer re-appeared. It seemed to Johnny that the sun was always full upon that white inn, that the dogs were always lying down there in the sun, and that it had been so and would be so for all time. He longed to have an inn with a white wall facing the sun, and many dogs to take the sun upon the pavement in front. The fisherman drove away.

The father and son walked in a solitary wood upon the side of a steep hill, and at the foot of it was a green vale that wound with the windings of a broad stream running fast, and at the top of the hill, where it was a precipice, hung a castle with trees growing in its crevices, and its windows looked out through ivy thicker than its vast walls down at several miles of the green vale on either hand, at the sun-bathed gloom of the oakwoods of the opposite slope, at the other castles, bleached crags which could be recognized as the work of men only because they were even bolder and more gaunt than the natural crags round about. Sometimes it rained, sometimes the sun shone, and the father and son were glad of both as they gathered blue violets and white sorrel in the dripping and glistening woods. Under the castle wall they sat down, and the father brought out a book and read: 'King Arthur was at Caerlleon upon Usk . . .' and Johnny began to think of bowmen shooting through the ivy about the windows, of king and queen walking in the grassy courts within the walls, whose roof was the sky. His father told him that the book was written by his countrymen about the heroes of his country, and the child made over to those heroes the glories that had once been Aladdin's, and the Marsh King's, and King Solomon's . . .

The dark eyes gleamed like a thrush's upon her nest when she is watched.

They saw more mountains, and the cart creeping over them and among them, small as a stone upon the road. And by and by they got down by a brook and began to travel upward towards the source. There were clear and dark pools in the brook where the trout darted and the man with them said: 'The fish runs away, who knows that man has sinned.' They were among steep woods of oak trees as dense almost as grass, all twisted and grey as if made of stone and very old, but based in greenest leaves and flowers of white, of gold, of golden green. The blackbird sang, and the brook gushed, but they did not speak, except that as they left, the strange man said: 'This is the Castle of Leaves.' Now, there was no longer a path, and the way was over whistling dead grass and grey stones, like ruins of a palace that must have been lofty as the heavens, and when they had gone further still the man said it was 'The Castle of the Wind.' And now the mist washed over all and hid everything but silvered stones and dead grass blades underfoot, and the rain that was like bent grass blades of crystal, through which for a moment a sheep crept up and crept away again, or a hare, grey as the grass, but blackened as if by fire, leaped up and dived into the wind, the mist, and the rain. Stumbling still among the ruins of the wind's castle, they continued to climb, until the rocks, now tall as a man and so dense that some had to be scaled, came to an end at the shore of a lake which they surrounded – 'The Shepherd's Lake.' The cry of a raven repeated at intervals from the same spot high up above told them that the mountains rose higher yet and in a precipice. The boy sat upon a rock while the two men went out of sight to the other side; his father to bathe, as he had done twenty years before when a young man. The wind hissed as through closed lips and jagged teeth. The mist wavered over the polished ripples of the lake that resembled a broad and level courtyard of glass among the rough hills. The men were silent, and the sounds of their footsteps were caught up and carried away in the wind. The boy was thoughtless and motionless, with a pleasure that was astonished at itself. He could not have told how long he had been staring at nothing over the lake when, at his feet, his father's head was thrust up laughing out of the water, turned with a swirl, and disappeared again into the mist. He had not ceased to try to disentangle that head from the mist when once more he heard that wailing song that used to make his father so glad, and he himself sang back such words as, without knowing their meaning, he remembered; his brain full of the mists, the mountains, the rivers, the fire in the fern, the castles, the knights, the kings and queens, the mountain boys at cricket, the old man with the foxes, the inn dogs lying in the sun . . . the sun . . . the mist . . . his country . . . not the country he had fought for . . . the country he was going to, up and up and over the mountains, now that he was dying . . . now that he was dead.

The Stile

Three roads met in the midst of a little green without a house or the sign of one, and at one edge there is an oak copse with untrimmed hedges. One road goes east, another west, and the other north; southward goes a path known chiefly to lovers, and the stile which transfers them to it from the rushy turf is at a corner of the copse.

The country is low, rich in grass and small streams, mazily subdivided by crooked hedgerows, with here and there tall oaks in broken lines or, round the farm houses, in musing protective clusters. It is walled in by hills on every side, the higher ones bare, the lower furred with trees, and so nearly level is it that, from any part of it, all these walls of hills, and their attendant clouds can be seen.

I have known the copse well for years. It holds an acre of oaks two or three generations old, the roots of ancient ones, and an undergrowth of hazel and brier which is nearly hidden by the high thorn hedge.

One day I stopped by the stile at the corner to say good-bye to a friend who had walked thus far with me. It was about half an hour after the sunset of a dry, hot day among the many wet ones in that July. We had been talking easily and warmly together, in such a way that there was no knowing whose was any one thought, because we were in electrical contact and each leapt to complete the other's words, just as if some poet had chosen to use the form of an eclogue and had made us the two shepherds who were to utter his mind through our dialogue. When he spoke I had already the same thing in the same words to express. When either of us spoke we were saying what we could not have said to any other man at any other time.

But as we reached the stile our tongues and our steps ceased together, and I was instantly aware of the silence through which our walking and talking had drawn a thin line up to this point. We had been going on without looking at one another in the twilight. Now we were face to face. We wished to go on speaking but could not. My eyes wandered to the rippled outline of the dark heavy hills against the sky, which was now pale and barred with the grey ribs of a delicate sunset. High up I saw Gemma; I even began trying to make out the bent star bow of which it is the centre. I saw the plain, now a vague dark sea of trees and hedges, where lay my homeward path. Again I looked at the face near me, and one of us said:

'The weather looks a little more settled.'

The other replied: 'I think it does.'

I bent my head and tapped the toe of my shoe with my stick, wishing to speak, wishing to go, but aware of a strong unknown power which made speech impossible and yet was not violent enough to detach me altogether and at once from the man standing there. Again my gaze wandered dallying to the hills – to the sky and the increase of stars – the darkness of the next hedge – the rushy green, the pale roads and the faint thicket mist that was starred with glow-worms. The scent of the honeysuckles and all those hedges was in the moist air. Now and then a few unexpected, startled and startling words were spoken, and the silence drank them up as the sea drinks a few tears. But always my roving eyes returned from the sky, the hills, the plain to those other greenish eyes in the dusk, and then with a growing sense of rest and love to the copse waiting there, its indefinite cloud of leaves and branches and, above that, the outline of oak tops against the sky. It was very near. It was still, sombre, silent. It was vague and unfamiliar. I had forgotten that it was a copse and one that I had often seen before. White roses like mouths penetrated the mass of the hedge.

I found myself saying 'good-bye.' I heard the word 'good-bye' spoken. It was a signal not of a parting but of a uniting. In spite of the unwillingness to be silent with my friend a moment before, a deep ease and confidence was mine underneath that unrest. I took one or two steps to the stile and, instead of crossing it I leaned upon the gate at one side. The confidence and ease deepened and darkened as if I also were like that still, sombre cloud that had been a copse, under the pale sky that was light without shedding light. I did not disturb the dark rest and beauty of the earth which had ceased to be ponderous, hard matter and had become itself cloudy or, as it is when the mind thinks of it, spiritual stuff, so that the glow-worms shone through it as stars through clouds. I found myself running without weariness or heaviness of the limbs through the soaked overhanging grass. I knew that I was more than the something which had been looking out all that day upon the visible earth and thinking and speaking and tasting friendship. Somewhere – close at hand in that rosy thicket or far off beyond the ribs of sunset – I was gathered up with an immortal company, where I and poet and lover and flower and cloud and star were equals, as all the little leaves were equal ruffling before the gusts, or sleeping and carved out of the silentness. And in that company I had learned that I am something which no fortune can touch, whether I be soon to die or long years away. Things will happen which will trample and pierce, but I shall go on, something that is here and there like the wind, something unconquerable, something not to be separated from the dark earth and the light sky, a strong citizen of infinity and eternity. The confidence and ease had become a deep joy; I knew that I could not do without the Infinite, nor the Infinite without me.

The End of a Day

Towards evening of that tempestuous day the west began to clear
and brighten under a swaying heavy curtain of cloud, and the
primroses to shine with a cold light out of the black earth, as I left
the road to cross a corner of the moor. Before me and moving
athwart my path in the slant rain was a young girl. Though the
rain was in her eyes and hair, and the wind enveloped her with its
cold kisses, she was young and proud. Her head was lifted up and
her lips parted with pleasure at the rain upon them. She had come
out at the sight of the brightening west and was walking towards
it. She was lightly dressed as knowing that the rain was spent, or
not caring, and she had not gone many steps before me when it
ceased. The dark woods behind her still roared with the dying
wind and the dripping rain, yet upon the moor there was a
walled-in silence through which she walked, and upon her and the
dead grass fell a watery cold light out of the white pane that
widened every moment more radiantly in the western sky. And to
me, losing all memory of the storm and the peace-making, it was
as if the day had led up to this, as if a long resounding avenue had
led to a still glimmering lawn as broad as the earth and mingling
with the bright heavens. I had emerged out of the darkness and
mist into an immeasurable and wondrously open world, and
across it moved the figure of the girl. My steps became slower and
slower. I no longer drove my heels into the ground. My lips ceased
to murmer all manner of songs, poems, fragments of tunes,
hunting cries, fantastic exclamations remembered or invented. In
a minute or two I sat down on a boulder in the grass, and leaned
forward wearily with hands and chin upon the handle of my stick.

The girl was beautiful. Breasting the rain at first, and now
facing the restful and splendid west, any springy maid might have

painted herself upon my brain for an hour or so. But she so raised my thought that suddenly at this noble end of a great day I felt myself weary, at once weary and very glad. Had she leaped out of the earth or out of the sky to express in human shape the loveliness of the hour, she could not have been made otherwise by a sculptor god – solemn and joyous and proud with the pride of things that are perfect and know it not, yet have as it seems attendant spirits offering them praise and courtliness wherever they go. No princess barbarically and multitudinously escorted could have walked with greater magnificence than this girl thinking her thoughtless thoughts. She now was the triumphant one, as I had been when I looked over plain and hill and saw them faint and quiet as in a tale. Not for one moment, but all the time of watching her, I felt as though I were looking out of a grave where I lay stiff and still but with wide eyes and untired spirit, and with those eyes and that spirit saluted and loved the beautiful living creature passing by regardless.

I watched her plant her feet firmly and rise up lightly as one might do to whom these things were impossible and marvellous. She had a slightly swaying motion which, graceful in itself, was fascinating, partly because it suggested how much more so it would have been had she been utterly unencumbered by dress. This swaying from hip to heel was the most obvious expression of the indolence which went side by side with her force, and was one with it, since it showed how much of that force was subdued in the effortless exercise of walking. She could have run, she could have leapt and climbed, almost it seemed that she could have flown, yet she but walked steadily across the moor. She was perfectly at peace, untried by pain and strife and sorrow, or passion.

The unaccomplished hours hovered about here as she went. She might some day be a Helen, a Guinevere, a Persephone, an Electra, an Isoud, an Eurydice, an Antigone, an Nimue, an Alcestis, a Dido, a Lais, a Francesca, a Harriet. She was a violet-eyed maid walking alone. Yet these were the spirits that attended her. Helen whispered to her of Theseus, Menelaus, Paris, Ulysses, of calm Lacedæmon, and burning Troy; Persephone of the lone Sicilian meadows, and the dark chariot and Dis; Dido of Carthage and Æneas and the sweet knife of despair; Eurydice of Orpheus and Hades and the harp and silence; Isoud of Tristram and the ship and joyous Gard; Lais of many lovers, and not one love;

Electra of her brother; Alcestis of her spouse and death; Harriet of the poet, and the water that quenched love. And there were many more upon the grass under the western light. They were tempting, guarding, counselling, warning, wailing, rejoicing, vaguely whispering. They waited on her, some wistful, some imperious, but all drawn after her whithersoever she went, all praising her for her sweet lips, her long brown hair and its gloom and hidden smouldering fires, her eyes and her eyelids that were as the violet opened flower and the white closed bud, her breath sweet as the earth's, her height, her whiteness, her swift limbs, and her rippling arms and wrists and hands, made for love and for all fair service; her straightness, that was as the straightness of a tulip on the best day of spring; and for her life, because it was all before her, pale and mysteriously lit, without stars yet with the promise of stars like the sky which had now dismissed all clouds but one dark bar, and was expanding around and above without a bound. Into that sky, into the gorse of the moor and a wild multitude of birds, she slipped out of my sight; and I rose up, and knew that I was tired, and continued my journey.

Hawthornden

Hawthornden was always home to tea, except once, and it was a significant exception.

When he was about thirty-five Hawthornden moved out into the country, partly because rents were less and he could have a governess for his three children, and so put off for some years the difficulty of choosing a school; and partly, but this was unconsciously, because he had few friends left. As a young man, clever above the common, reckless (within certain limits) and open-handed, he had attracted men of very different types, both at the university and in his bachelor lodgings. But after he married, at twenty-eight, his friends never came to see him, except when they were definitely asked to dinner, though his wife was charming and clever and anxious to meet them, and though he was not too fond of her to attend to them. He seemed to have stiffened and chilled. His smile began to have an awkward catch in it. It was so awkward that it ought to have been dignified, but was not quite. And at the same time as his friends were neglecting him he was not making any progress in domesticity. He had decided against entering a profession, and as he could live on his private means, he was at home very much. But there he gave himself up chiefly to solitary reading, and saw his wife chiefly at meals, and, on evenings when he wished to go early to bed, after dinner. He had thought of writing, but he was squeamish and touchy, and had destroyed his early verses and prose with great care, burning them in his room one summer evening, with a tense, red face, and then, by an after-thought, preserving the ashes in a small cherrywood box. He read many books of almost every kind, except criticism. Criticism he had taught himself to hate, because it seemed to him absurd that the writing class should not only produce books, but circulate its opinion of them among people occupied – like himself – with the business of living at first hand, not at second hand. In the days before criticism life and literature had both been finer things. It was the men with no standards of taste at all who made the arts of the great periods. When there was no one to tell men what to put on their walls, how to build their houses, what to wear and what to read, the glorious things were being created which men instructed at every turn in these matters were content to imitate. Hawthornden sought to recover this freedom by allowing no middleman between art and himself as a human being. As it was, however, physically impossible to keep pace with modern literature without a guide, he neglected it without noticing that this was a concession; and as the old literature had been well sifted by the efforts of the very criticism he despised, he had little left but to enjoy, and he discovered, with some annoyance, that he read and thought – so far as he could express himself – very much like everybody else. Nevertheless, he continued to read abundantly, and for the sake of books put off year by year the problems which his own life offered him. He got out of touch with his wife, ignored her friends, and only by an insincere though, determined effort, from time to time, succeeded in quieting her hysteria and relieving her melancholy. As to his children, he made spasmodic and more and more conscious efforts at pleasing and understanding them, and, observing that they could do without him, he plumed himself upon their ingratitude, and left them to the natural methods of his wife, of which he expressed his disapproval from time to time. Yet he was fond of the poetry of passion. He would look up from a poem sometimes and see his wife reading or embroidering, and then take his eyes away with a sigh and only the faintest dissatisfied recognition that he was becoming more and more incapable of being passionate himself and of meeting the passion of another. He also continued to sigh for the simple antique attitudes of the emotions in their liberty, and cursed a time when they could only be seen travestied on the stage. It was literature, nevertheless, and the stage, that had given him the standard which he unconsciously applied to scenes in life which he thought should have been heroical, for example, and were not. Nor was he shaken from his dim-pinnacled citadel of unreality by his one experience of something near tragedy at home. His wife rushed at him one day, with stiff, drawn, red-spotted face and staring eyes, and a shrill voice he had never heard before, to tell him that one of the children was injured. He drew her head to his breast and kissed her hair, and felt at first a kind of shame, then an instinctive disgust at the stains and rude prints of her grief. The same with beauty. He could not have defined it, but he had a standard which he applied to loveliness like a yard-wand, and never suspected that it was the standard that was wanting. It was expression that he feared in living beauty. He wanted the calm of antiquity – of death – of the photographs of celebrated women. A dark face, burning and wrenched with eagerness or delight, disturbed him, and – was not beautiful, because he had been at the trouble of putting aside the expression, and observing that the nose was too small, the eyes unequal, the lips too full, and so on.

He was fond of reading fairy tales and books for and about children, and had acquired strong opinions as to what they needed and liked. He was a great lover of liberty, of liberalism, of freedom for thought and action. He could be heard late at night reading aloud in a deep voice poems on liberty, and even at breakfast would relieve himself by muttering impressively –

> And in thy smile and by thy side
> Saintly Camillus lived and stern Atilius died.

The children looked up and said, 'What did you say, father?' or 'Do say some more like that'; but he stirred his tea, and made haste to leave the table for the study. He admired books of curious character and adventure, such as Borrow's and adored the strange persons who frequented once upon a time, and perhaps even now, the inns and roads of England. He was indignant with civilization which threatened to extinguish such men, and used to cut from newspapers passages describing the efforts to chain up gypsies and tramps.

When he moved into the country he was prepared for adventures. Gypsies should be allowed to camp near his house and he would be familiar with them. He would invite the tramps into his study for a talk and a smoke. He used to sit by the roadside, or in the taproom of an inn, waiting for what would turn up. But something always stood in the way – himself. He grew tired of paying for a tramp's quart, and was disconcerted, now by too great familiarity and now by too great respect. When a tramp came to the back door, his maids or his wife reported it to him, and they sometimes had interesting fragments of a story to relate; for the women had human sympathies along with unquestioning commonplace views of social distinctions. Sometimes he saw the man coming or going, and formed romantic conjectures which made him impatient of what he actually heard. He thought at one time that perhaps his mistake was in keeping too near home; he would walk far over the hills, and stay away for a night or two. But it was always the same. He dressed negligently and carried a crooked stick, and when he complained of his failure to get at the heart of the wayfaring man, his wife flattered him by saying that any one could see what he really was, whatever his disguise; he liked the flattery, and remained discontented.

Perhaps his whole plan was wrong. He had bought many maps, special walking clothes and boots, compact outfits, several kinds of knapsacks, rucsacs, haversacks, satchels, uncounted walking sticks, just as in other departments of his life he found himself buying pipes suitable for this purpose or that, half a dozen different species of lamps, pens, razors, hats and so on. He tried simplicity for a while, but this also meant a new outlay, and he was soon unfaithful.

Among the people of the neighbourhood he received a reputation for unconventionality. He was said to know the country and the people better than anyone. He was mistaken for a genius, a poet, an artist, a Bohemian, an eccentric millionaire, especially as he had a genuine dislike to parties and picnics and to the sound of men and women trying to put emotion into the words, 'Isn't the weather perfectly glorious?' by drawling them or emphasizing one word or each word in turn. He liked the mistake.

But one thing, above all others, gradually disturbed him. He was always home to tea.

He liked a certain kind of tea – the milk or cream of a precise quantity poured out first into his cup and then the tea on top of it, to scald it and produce a colour and flavour otherwise impossible. Then the sweet home-made cakes . . . Once or twice he went into cottages for tea, to chat with the poor and see them *au naturel*. But he saw nothing, and was therefore keenly alive to the fact that the tea was bad, and the cakes all but uneatable – so that he had a second tea when he arrived home. Mrs Hawthornden was glad of this; she liked him to enjoy himself, and to praise her cakes. She made cakes regularly, and saw that they were of the kinds he preferred. When he started early for a long walk, she used to ask him when he would be back. 'Oh, I cannot possibly say!' he retorted at once; but added, on reconsideration, 'But perhaps by four or five.' He was rarely later than four, and she smiled. He made special efforts not to be back by five – dreading the habit – and yet at last walked so hard as to tire himself in the effort to reach home at that time. So at last, when his wife asked the question, 'When shall I expect you back?' he used to say, sometimes smilingly, sometimes with a submissive despair, sometimes with irritation, 'Oh, I am always home to tea!' When he was not punctual, he was proud – but regretted the cakes – and read Borrow with greater relish. But the next day he would find himself home again to tea, and eating too many cakes with equanimity. He knew they were too many, and the thought at length prevented him from enjoying them, but not quite from eating them; there was a relic of virtue in this inability to enjoy them, though he knew that it might have been greater. At times, in an ancient cathedral or in the midst of a tragic tale, he started with the thought that he was almost forgetting his tea, and then his pleasure was at an end. Lying awake at night, he reproached himself, 'You are always home to tea.' He was haunted by it, as men of noble families of old time were haunted by their fate, and in his moments of complacency it crept suddenly upon him.

One day he went out to a distant part of the county to explore a ruin. It was a fine August day, and he spent most of it in the castle. He left it late in the afternoon, and then began to run. There were several trains that he might have caught; nevertheless, he ran. That day he did not return to tea. His wife looked out a train, and expected him first by one and then by another. It grew dark, and he was not back. The afternoon had been hot, and he had run too fast for a man of his build. He was found lying beside the path. He had achieved his ambition. He had not only not come home to tea, but had ceased to think about tea, so far as can be known. He was dead.

Olwen

Olwen was eighteen, a Welsh girl, with light brown hair so loosely coiled and so abundant that no fancy was needed to see it down to her knees; an oval face, not plump enough to conceal the bones of cheeks and bold chin; a clear, wild-rose complexion, lit up from within as by moonlight; dark eyebrows that had wild, clear curves like the wings of some bird of free waste lands, and curved lips that never hid the perfect teeth when at rest. She wore the clothes of a slattern. She walked and stood still and sat down with the pride of an animal in the first year when it has a mate. The curlew, the hare, the sheep upon the mountain, were not wilder, or swifter, or more gentle than she. Her face and stature were those of a queen in the old time, whose father was a shepherd on the solitary mountains. Being as strong as a man, she had finished her work early in the factory and come straight home, and, tucking up her skirts, had scrubbed and polished her mother's house. There was no pleasant way of being idle in the daytime, for, except with her lover, she did not care to walk to the mountain or to the black village streets. She laid tea, served it, and washed up. She was the only one who was not going out for the evening, for she had to bake the week's bread. Before the lamp had to be lit, her brother's wife came in with her baby. The first batch of cakes was already out of the oven. Their perfume streamed out through the open door, which let in the song of the blackbird, the wind from the mountains, and the majesty of evening. Olwen could rest now; she took the baby, and they sat down and began to gossip.

The married girl was a little older, slender and dark-haired, with small, sharp features and full lips, pleasure-loving, gay, and sharp-tempered, rapid in her speech. This was her first child, and she kept, as yet, all her maiden attractiveness and irresponsibility, and added to it the different power of one who is captive but unconquered. She sighed lightly now and then, as if she relished and remembered over-much the youth she retained. She seemed to feel the advantages she had over the unmarried Olwen, without being able to overcome a phantom of admiration for her that might at any moment turn to envy.

Olwen, being the eldest of ten, held the baby like a mother. Her face bent down to it, her shoulders and arms walled it, in an experienced way. She knew all that she would ever know about the care of infants – even their death. The young mother, watching her, would now and then cull the baby from her lap and press it to herself, and cover it with kisses. If there were cries, it was Olwen who silenced them in her deep breast; but the mother had the craftiness to let the maid seem to be their cause, and when the child was with the other she would tease it, in the hope of being the comforter. It would have been hard for a stranger to say whose was the child, since Olwen's attention to this one baby out of many was as perfect as the mother's to the only one. The mother was lively and effusive, yet careless; the maid was calm and tender, and never forgetful. The mother could have been a model for Aphrodite, the maid for Demeter. The mother was a lover first; the maid was born maternal, and her heart could be stormed by a sweetheart, but ruled only by a child. The mother was destined for a man or for several men; there was somewhere a man destined for the maid, to open for her a kingdom which she would enter alone. The mother pressed the child to her with a luxurious smile, as if the lover were there, too; the maid resembled some noble animal, calm, but with a half-hid ferocity that would have talons if need were, even for the father of its brood. The mother was an elf, a not purely human creature, a haunting, disquieting form of life, a marshlight out of the wilds of time, and to be blown away with time again; the maid was the beginning and the end of human life, necessity itself made beauty, mere humanity raised to a divine height, the very topmost plume on the crest of life's pride. And yet behind the physical glory of Olwen, her bold, easy gait, her deep voice, full of nobility and sweetness, behind all her courage and robustness and independence, there was a something like the timidity of the stag who stands on the rock in the moment of his greatest power and joy, without fear, and yet with an ear and a nostril for every breath of the summer gale.

The baby was with its mother when Olwen's lover entered the

room. It was still half-lit by the great fire and the pale sky after sunset. Seeing the two girls and the child, he sat in the darkest of the chairs and kept his cap in his fingers. The mother gave the child to Olwen, and the young man became silent. The maid hardly looked at him, while the young mother, glad to see a man, bantered her visitor in vain even when she said laughing:

'Olwen has a baby now, John, and you see she can do without its father.'

The young man fingered his cap, but looked musingly at Olwen out of the shadow. She had no eyes or ears but for the little thing that was now fully awake and standing on her lap and putting its hands into her mouth and eyes. Now she caught it quickly under the armpits and, throwing back her head, lifted it at arm's length and let it plant its feet upon her throat, then between her breasts, and so on down to her lap; it crowed and waved its limbs. The mother looked into the fire. Again Olwen stood the baby upon her head where its curled feet were entangled in her hair; her eyes were towards the young man but not looking at him, though her thoughts might have been of him. Still turned towards him, she lowered the child to her knees and jutted her bright face forward, pouting her mouth for kisses while the child tried to take away one of her glistening teeth; then she let it down flat on her knees and buried her head in the laughing and quaking form. The young man's dark eyes fixed upon her grew more and more dark and sullen, with admiration of her, jealousy of the child, and indignation that she was so careless. She had not given him a glance. She sang, she talked, she laughed, she feigned to cry, she cooed, for the child. She allowed it to do as it liked and as nobody else had done except in thought. Her cheeks glowed with pleasure and exercise and thoughts unexpressed; the white skin of her brows and throat gleamed moist and whiter than ever; her grey eyes flamed softly. Never had she been happier, and the happiness was at one with her beauty, so that a stranger watching might have thought that her happiness made her beautiful, or even that it was the consciousness of her beauty. She looked taller and her shoulders more massive than before, her back more powerful in the gentleness of its maternal stoop, her breast more deep, her dark voice more than ever the music of her noble body and blissful nature. Fit to be the bride of a hero and the mother of beautiful women and heroes and poets, she gave herself to the child.

Presently the child grew more silent, playing with a lock of her hair which now fell half over one shoulder down to her lap. She smiled musingly and caught the eye of her lover and began to tell him what she had been doing that day — how the manager had told her not to work so fast, and then asked her when she was to be married — but he remained silent. The child reared itself up by her hair and pulled at her chin and ears. She took no notice save to smile good-humouredly and shake her head, and continued to talk. Her two arms imprisoned the child; her head was raised in a pretence of keeping her chin from the enemy. Cheated of the smooth chin and soft ears the child was still a little while, and remained so still and so silent that it had been forgotten, when suddenly the mother broke into a laugh and cried:

'Well, I never, Olwen, the impudence of the child, you will be suckling her next!'

Olwen rose up undisturbed, smiling to herself, and then glancing over at John as she fastened two buttons below her neck.

'Now, Caroline,' she said, 'you take a turn with baby and let me talk to John.'

John stood up and came forward very slowly and very stiffly, and took the child from her arms. It began at once to cry and the mother, rising in a temper, carried it swiftly away, leaving the lovers silent:

John was the first to speak, saying:

'And what did you say to the manager, Olwen? Shall we get married this summer?'

'Yes,' she said; 'waiting is not much fun for you, John.' And she gave him a kiss that he was too slow to return, so that she broke away, saying:

'And now I must take out these cakes. You light the lamp, John. Yes, come along, no nonsense. Bless me,' she added, opening the oven door and letting out a smell as sweet as the first heat of May. 'It's lucky I wasn't a minute later. There! Take one while it's hot and don't burn yourself. Hot cakes and maids' lips, John.'

And John split the cake in two and buttered it, and they ate the halves together.

The Attempt

Several seasons had passed since Morgan Traheron had so much as looked at his fishing tackle, and now he turned over, almost indifferently, the reels and lines and hooks and flies which had been carefully put away in an old tool box of his great-grandfather's. He looked at the name 'Morgan Traheron' cut neatly inside the lid, and shivered slightly during the thought that one of his own name had bought it in 1776 at the ironmonger's and brazier's under the sign of the 'Anchor and Key' near Charing Cross, and that the owner had been dead nearly a hundred years. Cold, cold, must he be! Even as cold would be the younger bearer of that name, and he anticipated, in a kind of swoon, the hundred years that would one day submerge himself from all known friendliness of sun, earth, and man.

He was seeking, not any of the fishing tackle, but a revolver that lay amongst it, and a small green box containing only one ball cartridge. He had often thought of throwing the revolver away. His wife always looked wonderingly at him when he cleaned it once every year or so, but if she had urged him to throw it away he would have scoffed at the fear which he detected, all the more heartily because the sign of her concern inflated his vanity. She, lest she should provoke his mood in some way which even her consideration could not foresee, remained silent or asked him to tell again how he shot the woodpigeon fifty yards off, actually within sight of the gamekeeper's cottage. It was a thrilling and well-told tale, albeit untrue.

It was not a mere accident that one ball cartridge was left.

Morgan took out the revolver and the cartridge and shut the box. The lock was stiff and the chambers would not revolve without the use of both hands. To fire it off, it would therefore be necessary to twist the loaded chamber laboriously round to its place and then force back the hammer to full cock. The barrel was brown from rust, but probably the ball would force its way through as it had done before. It was a cheap, ugly, repulsive weapon; it impressed him with unsuitableness. He did not stay to oil it, but putting it in a pocket and the cartridge in another, he prepared to leave the house.

'Won't you take Mary with you, Morgan?' said his wife.

'Yes,' said Mary, his little daughter, laughing not so much because there was anything to laugh at as because she must either laugh or cry, and certainly the chance of a walk was nothing to cry for: 'Take me with you, father.'

'Oh no, you don't really want to come, you only say it to please me,' said Traheron, mild but hard.

'Yes, I am sure she . . . Good-bye, then,' said his wife.

'Good-bye,' said he.

The thought of kissing his daughter turned him back for a moment. But he did not; the act occurred to him more as a part of the ceremony of this fatal day than as a farewell, and he feared to betray his thought. She was the immediate cause of his decision. He had spoken resentfully to her for some fault which he noticed chiefly because it disturbed his melancholy repose; she had then burst out crying with long, clear wails that pierced him with self-hate, remorse, regret, and bitter memory.

Why should he live who had the power to draw such a cry from that sweet mouth? So he used to ask in the luxurious self-contempt which he practised. He would delay no more. He had thought before of cutting himself off from the power to injure his child and the mother of his child. But they would suffer; also, what a rough edge would be left to his life, inevitable in any case, perhaps, but not lightly to be chosen. On the other hand, he could not believe that they would ever be more unhappy than they often were now; at least, the greater poverty which his death would probably cause could not well increase their unhappiness; and settled misery or a lower plane of happiness was surely preferable to a state of faltering hope at the edge of abysses such as he often opened for them. To leave them and not die, since the child might forget him and he would miss many a passing joy with her, was never a tolerable thought; such a plan had none of the gloss of heroism and the kind of superficial ceremoniousness which was unconsciously much to his taste. But on this day the arguments for and against a fatal act did not weigh with him. He was called to death.

He was called to death, but hardly to an act which could procure it. Death he had never feared or understood; he feared very much the pain and the fear that would awake with it. He had never in his life seen a dead human body or come in any way near death. Death was an idea tinged with poetry in his mind – a kingly thing which was once only at any man's call. After it came annihilation. To escape from the difficulty of life, from the need of deliberating on it, from the hopeless search for something that would make it possible for him to go on living like anybody else without questioning, he was eager to hide himself away in annihilation, just as, when a child, he hid himself in the folds of his mother's dress or her warm bosom, where he could shut out everything save the bright patterns floating on the gloom under his closed eyelids. There was also an element of vanity in his project; he was going to punish himself and in a manner so extreme that he was inclined to be exalted by the feeling that he was now about to convince the world he had suffered exceedingly. He had thus taken up the revolver, and blurred the moment of the report by thinking intently of the pure annihilation which he desired. The revolver was the only accessible weapon that entered his mind, and he had armed himself with it without once having performed in thought what he had committed himself to do in fact before long.

As he mounted the hill by a white path over the turf, he felt the revolver strike against his hip at each stride. He was in full view of anyone who happened to be looking out from his home, and he pressed on lest the wavering of his mind should be seen. Recalling the repulsiveness of the weapon, the idea of a rope crossed his mind, not because it was preferable, but because it was something else, something apart from his plans which now had a painful air of simplicity.

When he was among some bushes that concealed him and yet still gave him a view of his house, he paused for breath. He half-longed for an invasion of sentiment at the sight of his home; but he was looking at it like a casual stranger, and without even the pang that comes when the stranger sees a quiet house embowered in green against which its smoke rises like a prayer, and he imagines that he could be happy there as he has not until now been happy anywhere. The house was mere stones, nothing, dead. He half wished that Mary would run out into the garden and compel him to a passionate state. His will and power of action were ebbing yet lower in his lifeless mood. He moved his eyes from the house to the elder hedgerow round it, to the little woods on the undulations beyond, to the Downs, and, above them, the cloudy sun perched upon a tripod of pale beams. Nothing answered his heartless call for help. He needed some tenderness to be born, a transfigured last look to keep as a memory; perhaps he still hoped that this answer that was not given to him could save him from the enemy at his side and in his brain; even so late did he continue to desire the conversion, the climacteric ecstasy by which life might solve its difficulty, and either sway placidly in harbour or set out with joy for the open sea.

He mounted the upper slopes and passed in among the beeches. He turned again, but again in vain. There was little in him left to kill when he reached the top and began to think where exactly he should go. He wished that he could hide away for ever in one of the many utterly secret mossy places known to him among beech and yew in the forsaken woods; the foxhounds might find him, but no one else. But he must go farther. The sound of the discharge must not be heard in that house below. Almost with tenderness he dreamed of the very moment when his wife would hear the news and perhaps see his body at the same time; if only that could be put off – the announcement must not come to-day, not under this sun in which the world was looking as he had always seen it, though more dull and grey, but on some day he had not known, a black, blind day yet unborn, to be still-born because of this event so important to him. Who would find him? He did not like the thought that some stranger who knew him by sight, who had never spoken to him, should come across the body, what was left of him, his remains, and should suddenly become curious and interested, perhaps slightly vain of the remarkable discovery. If only he could fade away rapidly. Several strangers with whose faces he was familiar passed him in a lane, and he assumed a proud, hard look of confidence, as he hoped.

He quickened his steps and turned into a neglected footpath where he had never met anybody. He took out the revolver and again looked at it. It was just here that he had come in the hottest of the late summer to show his daughter cinnabar caterpillars, tigerish yellow and black, among the flaming blossoms of ragwort. The ragwort was dead now, blossom and leaf. He recalled the day without comment.

He was now hidden, on one side by a dense wood, on the other by the steep slope of a hill, and before and behind by windings of the path which skirted the wood. He inserted the cartridge and with difficulty forced it into position; the brass was much tarnished. Now he revolved the chambers in order that the cartridge should be under the hammer, but by mistake he turned them too far; he had to try again, and, losing count of the chambers, was again defeated. Where the cartridge was he could not be sure, and he looked to see; its tarnished disc was hostile and grim to his eye, and he hid the weapon.

Moving on, he now looked down upon a steep wood that sloped from his feet, and then rose as steeply up an opposite hill. They were beech woods with innumerable straight stems of bare branchwork that was purple in the mass. Yews stood as black islands in the woods, and they and the briers with scarlet hips close to his eye were laced with airy traveller's joy, plumy and grey.

Traheron now turned the muzzle to his temple, first letting the hammer down for fear of an accident. He had only one shot to fire, and he could not feel sure that this would enter his brain. His ear, his mouth – the thought was horrible, impossible. His skin ached with the touch of the steel which was very cold. Next he turned the weapon to his breast, and saw that he had better pull the trigger with his thumb. The hammer was now at full cock, the cartridge in place. The hideous engine looked absurdly powerful for his purpose. The noise, the wound, would be out of proportion to the little spark of life that was so willing, so eager, to be extinguished. He lowered the weapon and took a last sight of the woods, praying no prayer, thinking no thought, perfectly at ease, though a little cold from inaction.

Suddenly his eye was aware of someone moving above the opposite wood, half a mile away, and at the same moment this stranger raised a loud halloo as if he had sighted a fox, and repeated it again and again for his own delight, feeling glad, and knowing himself alone. Traheron had been watching the wood with soul more and more enchanted by the soft colour, the

coldness, the repose. The cry rescued him; with shame at the
thought that he might have been watched, he raised the revolver
and turned it to his breast, shut his eyes and touched the trigger,
but too lightly, and breathless, in the same moment, he averted the
barrel and hurled it into the wood, where it struck a bough
without exploding. For a moment he dreamed that he had
succeeded. He saw the man who found him pick up the revolver
and examine it. Finding but one cartridge in the chambers he
concluded that the dead man was a person of unusual coolness
and confidence, with an accurate knowledge of the position of the
heart. Then, for he was cold, Traheron moved rapidly away, his
mind empty of all thought except that he would go to a certain
wood and then strike over the fields, following a route that would
bring him home in the gentleness of evening.

He opened the door. The table was spread for tea. His wife,
divining all, said:

'Shall I make tea?'

'Please,' he replied, thinking himself impenetrably masked.

Cloud Castle
and Other Papers

(1922)

Morgan

The storm is over; Morgan is dead. Once more we can hear the brook's noise, which was obliterated all night by the storm and by our thoughts. The air is clear and gentle in the forest and all but still, after the night of wind and of death. High up in the drifting rose of dawn the multitudes of tall, slender trees are swaying their tips, as if stirred rather by memory of the tempest. They make no sound with the trembling of their slender length: some will never sound any more, for they lie motionless and prone in the underwood, or hang slanting among neighbour branches where they fell in last night's storm, and the mice may nibble at crests that once wavered among the stars. The path is strewn with broken branches and innumerable twigs.

The silence is so great that we can hear, by enchantment of the ears, the storm that passed away with night. The tragic repose of ruin is unbroken. One robin sings, and calls up the roars and tumults that had had to cease utterly before his small voice could gain this power of peculiar sweetness and awe, and make itself heard.

The mountains and sky, beautiful as they are, are more beautiful because a cloak of terror has been lifted from them and left them free to the dark and silver, and now rosy, dawn. The masses of the battlemented mountains are still heavy and sombre, but their ridges bite sharply into the sky, and the uttermost peaks are born again. They are dark with shadows of clouds of a most lustrous whiteness that hang, round above round, like a white forest, very far off, in the country of the sun, and the edges of the rounds are gilded; seen out of the clear gloom of the wood, this country is as a place to which a man might wholly and vainly desire to go, knowing that he would be at rest only there. In the valley between this forest and the mountains the frost is rosy with the roses of the zenith.

As we listen, walking the ledge between precipice and precipice in the forest, the silence seems to murmur of the departed tempest like a sea-shell, and we also remember again the sound of the dark hills convulsed with a hollow roaring as of an endless explosion.

Trees were caught up and shaken in the furious air like grasses; branches were stricken and struck back, were ground and beaten together and broken. The sound of one twig was drowned by that of myriads; the sound of one tree by that of leagues; and all were mingled with the sound of the struggle in the high spaces of the air. Between earth and sky there was nothing but sound and darkness plunging confused. Outside the window branches were brandished wildly, and their anger was the more terrible because the voice of it could not be heard or distinguished amidst the universal voice. The sky itself seemed to aid the roar. It was dark with the darkness of black water, and the planets raced over it among floes of white cloud; dark, menacing clouds flitted on messages of darkness across the white. We looked out from the death-room, having turned away from the helpless, tranquil bed and the still wife, and saw the forest surging under the wild moon, but it was strange and no longer to be recognized while the earth was heaving and be-nightmared by the storm. Yes, the forest is still under the awe of that hour. That is why its clearness is so solemn, its silence so pregnant, its gentleness so sublime. But not for that only. It is fresh after the sick room, calm after the storm and after the vain conflict with death, sad because every thought in it leads to death, and made majestic by the character of the life that has ended and never saw this dawn. It is as if his soul had bereaved the forest also. The robin's song is poured into the silence and shivers and is chilled by falling into the dark cave of death, as a brooklet falls over a cliff into a sunless sea.

The blue smoke rises straight up as if nothing had happened from the house of death, over there among the white fields. As if nothing had happened! But we have been walking here an hour, and have come to see even in that smoke a significant tranquillity as of a beacon or sacrifice. It comes from the room where the wife sits and looks at the white face peering through its black hair like seaweed, and still speaking of the old ecstasy, solitude, and irony that it had in life. A strange life – of which the woman who shared without breaking his solitude can tell nothing, and would tell nothing if she could: for she wishes only to persuade us that, in spite of his extraordinary life, he was a good man and very good to her. She has become as silent as he is and as he was. Nevertheless, they say that twenty years ago, when she began to live with him on the mountain, she was a happy, gay woman, the best singer and dancer in the village, and had the most lovers, while now her wholly black, small Silurian eyes have turned inwards and have taught her lips their mystery and Morgan's, have taught also that animal softness to her steps and all her motions. It would not be surprising were she to strive to be buried along with him, if only she had not lost so much of herself in losing him. She guards him like a hound and like a spirit. She shadowed and clung to the doctor and the minister, so that their offices were a mockery, yet they dared not attempt to keep her away. Perhaps she will go back to his Tower and live there alone.

If this winding path between two of the forest precipices be followed to that bank where the eastern sun now falls upon the dazzle of a myriad celandines, the top of Morgan's Tower, or Folly, can be seen against a wedge of sky among the hills; there are no trees at that height, and it is distinct and unmistakable. It is a slender, square tower containing three rooms one above the other, and above these an uncovered look-out. If she returns there she will be able to visit the upper room and the look-out for the first time.

Morgan built the Tower before he was thirty, and he dwelt there nearly thirty years; whether out of cruel constancy to his first resolution, no one knows; but once he had gone there he never left it, except to die in the great house where he was born, and where he chiefly lived, until the building of the Tower. For a time he tried to live entirely in London, devoting himself and his riches to social reform, which seemed the only way to gain some tranquillity and save himself from too often remembering that he was in hell. He drew back because he could not understand the town life, and it was absurd to reform what he could not understand. At first, and for several years, the sight of the men and women and children living a pure and simple town life allowed him no rest. It was easy to provide them with things which seemed to him to be good for them. But it was not easy, it was in the end not possible, to put away the thought that his motive was a false one, and yet one for which he could see no practical alternative. He was trying to alter the conditions of other men's lives because he could not have endured them himself, because it would have been unpleasant to him to be like them in their hideous pleasure, hideous suffering, hideous indifference. He saw in this attitude a modern Pharisaism, whose followers desired not merely to be unlike others, but to make others like themselves. It was due to lack of imagination, he thought, of imagination which would enable the looker-on to see their lives as compared with their conscious or unconscious ideals. Did they, for example, fall farther short from their ideals than he from his? He had not the imagination to see, but he thought perhaps not; and he did see that, lacking as their life might be in antique beauty and power, it yet had in it a profound unconsciousness and dark strength which might some day bring forth beauty – might even now be beautiful to simple and true eyes – and had already given them a fitness to their place, such as he himself was far from having reached. He never hesitated when it was food and warmth that were lacking, but beyond supplying those needs he could never feel sure that he was not fancifully interfering with a force which he did not understand and could not overestimate. So leaving all save a little of his money to be used for giving food and warmth to the hungry and the cold, he escaped from the sublime un-intelligible scene. He went up into the Tower, that he had built upon a rock in his own mountains, to think about life before he began to live. Up there he hoped to learn why it was that sometimes, in the London streets, beneath the new and the multitudinous there was a simple and pure beauty, beneath the turmoil a placidity, beneath the noise a silence which he longed to reach and to drink deeply and to perpetuate, but in vain. He desired to learn to see in human life, as we see in the life of bees, the unity which perhaps some higher order of living beings can easily see through the complexity that confuses us. He had set out to seek at first by means of science, but he found that science was only the modern method of looking at the world, possibly a transitory method, and that too often it was an end and not a means. For a hundred years men had been reading science and experimenting, as they had been reading history, with the result that they knew – some science and some history. So he went up into his bright Tower.

From there he looked out at the huge, desolate heaves of the grey beacons. Their magnitude and pure form gave him hours of great calm. Here there was nothing human, gentle, disturbing, as in the vales. There was nothing but the hills and the silence that was God. The greater heights, set free from night and mist, looked as if straight from the hands of God, as if here He also delighted in pure form and magnitude that was worthy of His love; and the huge shadows moving slowly over the grey spaces of winter, the olive spaces of summer, were as His hand. While Morgan watched, the dream came, more and more often, of a paradise to be established upon the mountains when at last the sweet winds should blow across a clean world that knew not the taint of life any more than of death, and then his thought swept rejoicing through the high Gate of the Winds that cleft the hills far off, where a shadow ten miles long slept across the peaks, but left the lower wild as yellow in the sunlight as corn. Following his thought he walked upward to that Gate of the Winds, to range the high spaces, sometimes to sleep there. Or he lay among the gorse – he could have lain on his back a thousand years hearing the cuckoo among the gorse and looking up at the blue sky above the mountains. Or in the rain and wind he sat against one of the rocks among the autumn bracken until the sheep surrounded him, half visible and shaggy in the mist, peering at him fearlessly as if they had not seen a man since the cairns were heaped on the summit; he sat on and on in the mystery, part of it but divining it not, and in the end went discontented away. The crags stared at him on the hill-top, where the dark spirits of the earth had crept out of their abysses into the day, and still clad in darkness looked grimly at him, at the sky, and the light. More and more he stayed in his Tower, since even in his own mountains, as in the cities of men, he was dismayed by numbers, by variety, by the grotesque, by the thousand gods demanding idolatry instead of the One whom he desired, Whose hand's shadow he had seen far off. Looking on a May midnight at Algol rising out of the mountain, the awe and the glory of that first step into the broad heaven exalted him; a sound arose as of the whole of time making a music behind him, a music of something passing away to leave him alone in the silence, as if he also were stepping up into the blue air – always to stumble back. Or it was the moon rising. Then the sombre ranges to eastward seemed to be the edge of the earth, and as the globe ascended the world was emptied and grieved, having given birth to this mighty child; he was left alone, and the great white clouds sat round about upon the horizon and judged him. For days he would lie desolate and awake and dream and stir not. Once again he returned to London and saw the city pillared, above the shadowy abyss of the river, on columns of light; and it was less than one of his dreams. It was winter and he was resolved to work, and was crossing one of the bridges, full of purpose and thought, going against the tide of the crowd. But the beauty of the bridge and the water took hold of him. It was a morning with a low, yellow sky of fog. About the heads of the crowd swayed a few gulls, interlacing so that they could not be counted, and they swayed like falling snow and screamed. They brought light on their long wings, as down below a great ship setting out slowly with misty masts brought light to the green and leaden river upon the foam at her bows. And ever about the determined careless faces of the men swayed the pale wings like wraiths of evil and good calling, and calling to ears which do not know that they hear. And they tempted his brain with the temptation of their beauty; he went to and fro to hear and see them until they slept and the crowd had flowed away. He thought that they had made ready his brain, and that on the mountains he would find fulness of beauty at last, and simplicity, so he went away and never returned. There, too, among the mountains was weariness, because he also was there.

But not always weariness. For was not the company of planet and star in the heavens the same as had bent over prophet and poet and philosopher? By day a scene unfolded, as when the first man spread forth his eyes and saw more than his soul knew. These things lifted up his heart, so that the voices of fear and doubt were not so much in that infinite silence as little rivers in an unbounded plain. There were days when it seemed to him the sheer mountains were the creation of his lean, terrible thoughts, and he was glad, and the soft, wooded hills below and behind were the creation of the pampered luxurious thoughts he had left behind in the world of many men. It was thus, in the style of the mountains, he would have thought and spoken – but language, except to genius and simple men, was but a paraphrase, dissipating and dissolving the forms of passion and thought. Then, again, time lured him back out of eternity, and he believed that he longed to die, as he lay and watched the sky at sunset, inlaid with swart forest, and watched it with a dull eye and a cold heart.

So much was known or could be guessed from his talk. For in those early days of his retreat he was not silent to those who met him upon the mountains, nor did he turn aside so as not to encounter them. And much more was told in the legend that flourished about the strange truth, and at last entangled and stifled it, so that the legend was all, and no one cared about the man. He was said to have buried money somewhere in the caves of the hills. He was said to worship a God who had never entered chapel or church. He was said to speak with raven and kite and curlew and fox. He was said to pray for the end of man and the world. He was called atheist, blasphemer, outlaw, madman, brute. But the last that was known of him was that one summer he used to come down night after night courting Angharad who became his wife. One of the most persistently reported of his solitary obsessions was the belief in a race who had kept themselves apart from the rest of men though found in many nations, perhaps in all. Some said the belief was from the Bible and that this was the race that grew up alongside the family of Cain, the guiltless 'daughters of men' from whom the fratricide's children took their wives. These knew not the sin or the knowledge or the shame of Adam, Eve, and Cain – so he was said to believe – and neither had they any souls. They were a careless and godless race, knowing neither evil nor good. They had never been cast out of Eden. Some of the branches of this race had perished already by men's hands, such as the fairies, the nymphs, the fauns. Others had adopted for safety many of men's ways, and had become moorland and mountain men, living at peace with their neighbours and yet not recognized as equals. They were even to be found in the towns. There the uncommon beauty of the women sometimes led to unions of violent happiness and of calamity, and now and then to the birth of a poet or musician or a woman who could abide neither with the strange race nor with the children of Adam. They were allowed to live and compelled to suffer for their power and beauty. Their happiness – it was considered by men to be something other than happiness, lighter, not earned or deserved, mere gaiety – was the cause of envy and hate, and it met with lust or with torture. They were feared, but more often despised, because they retained what was charming in the animal with the form of men, and because they lived as if time was not, and yet could not be persuaded to a belief in a future life. Up in his Tower, Morgan came to regard his father as one of these, the man who had forsaken his wife before the child was born, and left only a portrait behind. If only he could capture one of this race, thought Morgan, and make her his wife, he would be content. And Angharad, the shy and bold and fierce and dark Angharad, whose black eyes radiated light and blackness together, was one of them. So he took her up to his Tower.

After that these things only were certainly known: that she was unhappy; that when she came down to the village for food she was silent, would never betray him or fail to return; and that he never came down, that he also was silent, that he looked like a wild man with unshorn hair. He was seen at all hours, always far off, on the high paths of the mountains. His hair was as black as when he was a boy. He was never known to have ailed, until one day, the wild wife knocked at the door of his birth-place, and asked for help to bring him where he might be tended as was necessary, since he would have no one but her in the Tower. And so he came and last night he died, having thanked the Earth for its strength and its beauty, for what it had given him and for what it might have given had he been wise, having prayed that his body might be dutiful to Earth in the grave and bound up more purely than it had been during his living days 'in the bundle of life with the Lord my God.' She has not always been silent, but has cried aloud with a voice far wilder than the curlew's because she is left alone with the children of men. And that is why this gentle morning is so grave and so forlorn, and why Morgan's Folly stands up so greatly and notably in its blackness against this dawn.

(1913)

Helen

Twenty-five years ago the chief inhabitants of Crowbit lands were squirrels, the chief crops hazel nuts and flints. To-day it is a forlorn declining old-new settlement, with the look of a wrecked suburb, and resembling a village only in that it has one idiot and one great house, every pane of every window in it broken by the stones of happy children. In another twenty-five years the old condition will probably be restored. It is the highest land on a high plateau and the plough has never been over it. The greater part is treeless, but the slopes bear copses of poor oaks and in the bottoms are families of ancient beeches and enough grass for many rabbits. One straight main road crosses it now as it has long done, but for some reason it is avoided, and in spite of an old man always bent over it the weeds and grass grow apace. The other roads are, and were, broad green lanes deeply fringed with untended hazel and bracken and the purple and gold flowers that love to be among bracken. Even twenty-five years ago no tract of southern England was richer in green lanes almost without rut or footprint. Perhaps a gipsy came one day, but next day was not there. One farmhouse there was, and the only reason for that seemed to be to avoid the scandal of so large a district in this prosperous country being without one. Every year or two it was partly painted and the garden half weeded, lest the predestinate tenant should see it and pass by: once or twice there were tenants – not farmers, but a poor middle-class family with an indigent mother or sister, or children too young for school – for not more than six months. The great house was at the very edge of Crowbit, turning its back on the misty plateau, its face towards a better land of dairy and corn in comfortable proportions. It was a square grey house among oaks, dull and substantial, a perfect breeding-place for men about town, like the Salanders. They could not live there because the consumption of cigarettes and spirits which it enforced gave it a reputation for unhealthiness and costliness; but they had been happy there as children and they liked to come down in the autumn for pheasants, in the summer for trout – not in their own land, which had not one flash of running water. The Salanders had some reason for expecting trouble: in fact, the only reason against it was that it had long been delayed. The only way out was work – and that was impossible – until one day a low, but amusing friend of George Salander offered another. The lord of the manor had just landed a game trout and held it in his hand with a sunny hard smile, saying in compliment 'Jolly plucky little beggar,' before putting his thumbnail deep into the spine of a creature which, he knew, had done its best to give him pleasure. At Johnson's proposal he smiled in the same way.

Within a year the plan was a success. The healthy situation and lovely scenery of Crowbit, the fitness for poultry and small fruit farms, and the convenience of a five-mile-distant railway station upon a branch line, were enthusiastically advertised by Johnson, the railway company, the Press, and in a quiet way, by Salander himself. The newcomers were old and middle-aged men who had saved a little money in shops, young men at their first venture and men no longer young at their last. They enclosed parallelograms of an acre or half-an-acre with wire-netting; they planted trees which died; they dug up plots of innocent grass where forthwith exulted the hardiest and most offensive weeds; they erected low buildings of corrugated iron, white framed windows and doors and many lace curtains. The old farmhouse received a corrugated iron roof from ridge to eaves over its thatch and the name of 'The Laurels'; and inside or outside of it could be heard a cheerful baritone voice singing 'The Boys of the Old Brigade.' Many lengths of the green lanes were furrowed hither and thither by heavy wheels, and the mud well mixed with broken glass, crockery and coloured paper. Gaps were torn in the hedges for gateways and to allow a view when the mist cleared. Everywhere, the sound of hammers on deal and corrugated iron. Chickens made paths in all directions. Faces of extreme cheerfulness or extreme anxiety went up and down riding bicycles or eagerly pushing them.

Salander had ready-money. He came down to see the place and told Johnson, 'It is like a damned circus, only it won't go away.' He was genuinely enraged with Johnson.

Some of the people did, nevertheless, go away before long. Some who had hoped they would be isolated were wedged in a dense row: others found it lonely in a lane with no sound but their own chickens: some longed for the town, some for the country. But enough had been sold to overcome Salander's distaste; he was able to send his idle eldest son, Aylwin Salander, to a mining school, and later on to Canada.

Some of the invaders stayed. The Browns, for example, kept to their little red house, and in ten years' time they alone remained of the original settlers. The slope up to their front door and its white wooden steps were carefully mown and broken into beds of lilac and laburnum, roses, sunflowers and nasturtiums in their seasons. Of the half-dozen spruce trees only one had lived through the first summer, and this was the nearest to the house. It was absurdly near, as Mrs Brown pointed out; it grew apace and its branches brushed the wall of the house. On the night when her first child was born, and on other nights she could then remember, she was tormented by this tree rasping the corrugated iron in the rainy wind. 'You devil,' she said to it when first she stepped out with little Helen in her arms; but she let it remain, and it continued to flourish while its companions rotted very slowly in the ground. Helen flourished like the tree, which she watered all through the summers; and Salander, passing by a shed one day where she was playing, threw away his cigar to have a good look at her. Outside, it was a day of glory in the sky and of harvest peace and abundance on the earth: inside, the child was in deep shadow and looked down at him with eyes bright, glowing cheeks, rosy lips, and teeth glistening, all the more lovely for the shadow which her face overcame and seemed to illuminate like a lantern. He tried to talk to her, and she said 'Yes' or 'No' or sometimes nothing. He remembered as he looked at her an old countrywoman's remark to him when he was a boy: 'Birds have great wisdom; not one of them except the cuckoo has said a thing men can understand, not since the Creation.' Before he left she reminded him still more of a bird, for she suddenly put on a face like an owl which was evidently a favourite accomplishment. This she maintained for about half a minute and then broke into laughter, under cover of which Salander departed. He did not profess to know anything about women until they were seventeen or so, and none that he had ever troubled with was like a bird; yet his complacency was hurt by the bird-like Helen. She grew more and more beautiful, to the confusion of old and afterwards of younger Salander. She had a peering face, narrowing down to the chin and sharpened forwards – a face that asked many questions no man could answer. She had olive eyes, long dark lashes, and dark eyebrows, a rather more than usually projecting mouth which seemed to make the whole world wreathe in a smile with it; her skin was nothing rarer than damask; her pale yellow hair was open to the imputation of tow, inclined to stick together in tails, and only just rippled out of the straight, yet radiant and original whether it swished about her in running or was held across her mouth for her to bite while she spoke; perhaps only her ears could be called perfect, being of a unique simple curve up, round and down, and within of a subtlety suggesting with even a shade of painfulness in its subtlety, the hidden brain which it furnished with the sounds of the world. Many other women had some of these elements in more perfection, not a few had them all: there was never one who combined them in these proportions to this result, which was so much more than the sum of them all that one like old Salander could pretend to see it as such only when there was a Crowbit mist moaning and shaking the spruce against Helen's home and the rain drummed on corrugated iron, and he felt in his teeth that he was old. He was, in fact, deeply impressed by her beauty. It was the most surprising fact within his knowledge that this brand-new, rasping new, never-to-be-old, settlement and two plain parents could produce one like Helen, could nourish and preserve her year after year, while she ran up and down the deep-rutted lanes and over the scratched flinty fields among the chickens, climbed his great beeches in the bottoms still mainly belonging to the squirrels, and later on raced about on a rattling bicycle with a milk can or a parcel from the station. She wore bad clothes, always torn, often dirty – but so much the better! they gave her laughing loveliness another triumph. It was always laughing, though not perhaps for what Salander or most others would have called happiness. Her mother was angry with her for laughing at nothing: she did not know, she believed the child did not know, why this laughter; and she accused her of pretence, the more certainly because the gravity of her eyes was never disturbed by it. At school she learned only to fear school-teachers and lofty rooms with shiny pictures. All her wisdom was in the quickness of her feet and the light of her eyes. Some thought her daft.

When Helen was seventeen, old Salander died suddenly. Aylwin had returned from Canada, something worn by indolence, but still handsome. He was a perfect Salander externally – had a neat head, close-cropped mouse-coloured hair, regular features and excellent teeth, but also a melancholy and rash futility that grinned at the masterly military exterior. He wooed Helen outright. She was now a woman of a great new beauty, neither of the town nor of the country. She was the offspring of the union or conflict between country and town, the solitude of Crowbit and the corrugated iron. The union showed itself in the astonishing blend of the wild and the delicate in her beauty, the conflict, in her uselessness – she could do nothing with her hands or her head, she could not even sing, though her voice was worthy of her – in what the neighbours called her stupidity or imbecility. She was like a deer enchanted into a woman's form, nothing like a deer except sometimes in her gesture of suspicion, and yet a deer underneath. Salander used to come down to the 'King's Head' at Newton Salander for several days at a time and make opportunities to see the wandering Helen instead of fishing. At some visits he sat down and drank peaceably for hours, to fend off the sad looks of Crowbit; at others, he would not touch alcohol, for the same reason; in both moods he would talk of fitting out two rooms at the manor-house, of keeping fowls and Arcadianizing. It was pretty well known why he came, and Mr and Mrs Brown, though not yet consulted, saw no reason to be sorry, since it might do them good and would, at least, take the solitary and useless girl off their hands. The neighbours blamed sometimes them and sometimes Helen, when they knew her entire liberty with Salander. They accused the Browns of thrusting her upon him. His friends, on the other hand, thought it would be quite unnecessary for him to marry her.

Helen herself seemed to take no notice of him, to be the only person who could not see what was happening. Then suddenly it was known that she and Salander were to be married. It was said that he had lain in wait for her in one of her secret haunts, and that there for some reason she had struck him so that he fell and was stunned. It was said that his helpless body had raised her pity; she had tended and kissed him back to consciousness. After this he could apparently do anything with her, except persuade her to leave 'Fair View' where she was born. She used to compare herself to the solitary spruce-tree. She had never lived anywhere else, and she never could. But as soon as possible Salander meant to take her right away from it.

After the wedding Helen was gay and gentle with all, until she came to the gates of the manor-house. She trembled and leaned heavily on her husband's arm, and he was all but carrying her as they approached the door. At the threshold she was powerless; he lifted her in, helpless and drooping as a sheaf of barley.

She is now what all would call mad. She fell into silence, untranslatable sounds, and her old laughter. She refused to sleep anywhere except in her birthplace, and as she was not admitted there she stayed out of doors. She thought that she was a spruce fir, and spreading out her arms with a grave look she shivered and made a sound like the wind in fir needles without opening her lips, and having gradually become silent she burst out into laughter and turned away. Salander was much condoled with by her parents, and in his watchfulness he was often out all night, following her until he was tired and she disappeared. His fowls arrived, but he made a present of them to his father-in-law. In a few weeks he departed, leaving the key in the door with a hope that she might return. He comes down now and then to see if she is changed, but when he appears she runs fast away. They have relented at 'Fair View,' and she sleeps there once more. She works hard in the garden and among the fowls, and goes on errands. If the little boys of Crowbit stop her and say, 'Helen, what is that noise?' she stands still, slowly extends her arms and moans like a fir-tree, and the boys grin at one another until out comes her wild laughter, and they grin no more. The people at Crowbit are not proud of her, though she is still as beautiful as the dawn; but at the next village an old woman says it is good to have one idiot in a place, and very lucky – 'It keeps things quiet,' she says.

(1911)

Seven Tramps: A Study in Brown

We were a close-knit and easily divisible covey of seven tramps – a woman, two boys and a girl, and three men; there was, too, an ass, but he was a gentleman and had belonged to a great house that lay near our path one summer night. We were the most dirty of mankind. No tramp ever joined us, except one, who was an artist. He painted us and said that we might have belonged to the middle ages. 'Yes,' said one, demanding ale, 'we have known better times.' We thought ourselves honest tramps; for we never robbed a poor man, not even the artist, who had art in his head instead of brains. He could not paint dirt, he confessed, and he unscrupulously invented and painted a sash on the girl of eight, so that she cried when she felt in vain for the pleasant crimson thing.

This girl was our only burden; she was like a doll some child has defaced, and had a thin, coughing laugh that went into my heart like a needle at times

The two boys were in place of a dog. They could clean a copse of pheasants' eggs, or mind the camp. The arm of one of them, 'Snag,' would go through a letter box, a natural gift which he never abused. They lived more wildly than we, having come to us from a London working family, as apprentices or 'halves.' The elder, 'Hag,' was sometimes called grandfather; when he had been drinking, he looked older than anyone I have ever seen.

Of Nell, the woman, it is hard to say anything except that she was a woman and could weep. She bore children who died, and helped the ass up hill. She 'married' Tim when she was seventeen, a gay dairy beauty from Devon; but when she was twenty she was 'that ugly that to see her when she got up in the morning was a curse.' She was foolish when drunk, mad when sober, and talked continually at the top note of tragical expression. None was more cruel to her child than she. Our cruelty, which I confess was great, she rather encouraged. I hear her laugh sometimes; it *walks* in the winter evenings and is all that is left of her now that she is dead. But she alone was kind to the girl, and should any other use endearments towards the child she became a fury. She practised kindness as a secret indulgence; I have overheard her making the child shriek with her desperate caress. I have said that she was a woman, mainly because she re-arranged her rags with coquettish assiduity; her face was not that of a woman so much as of a type that had been created by an artist in love with mere despair.

Her husband, a brown, haystack man, had an almost romantic interest in female beauty. Chamber maids, barmaids, and sporting women, he worshipped, and would consequently attend at meets of hounds. The white skirts and well-polished boots of servants raised his speech to rhapsody. Yet he cared for his wife and beat her only during periods of very good or very bad fortune. He could snare a bird or rabbit exquisitely, and a certain pedantic hate of careless work sometimes left us supperless. Had he been clean I should have said there was a polish in his ways. 'Not a pigeon, your honour; 'twas a handsome cock pheasant,' was his scrupulous interjection in court. I believe he gloried in the name of tramp and could have confounded a clever man by a favourable comparison of his profession with the rest. 'A quart of six on a wet night – a strange, neat girl in a long, long lane – to knock your man down – to have a bonny child on your knee on Christmas day' – such was his ode to life.

'Partridge' could make the most superior farmer or gamekeeper impotently ridiculous by touching his cap and keeping within the letter of respect. The finesse of insult and abjection were his life-study. He was master of all the arts of eloquence that are not in Cicero. For he had been a waiter and was a linen-draper's son. But I will not attempt to put his eloquence in print lest I should prove him to have been second-rate. According to our standard he was the gentleman of us all. He stood five immaterial feet high; grasped an oak wand taller than himself; and wore his hair over his face. I value his memory for the way he had of cajoling the basest of men, all the while looking like an early Czar . . . He had the brow of a great man, a singular thing. Of old the brow made the man and the God. It was his natural gonfanon – the brow of Jupiter – of Aphrodite – of Plato – of Augustus – was for centuries an altar where human thoughts and dreams did reverence. The history of sculpture is a *te deum laudamus* to the brow. Now the soul has descended a step of the temple and dwells in the eyes. On the stock exchange, in parliament, in the army and in literature, victory is won by the eyes. 'Partridge' had that calm and ample span of curving bone, but his eyes slept, and he was a failure. Having once caught a partridge, the accident was considered apt to give him the name by which he was known.

As for 'Mud' (short for Muddle), he was a poor human creature, and a tramp by accident. He would never tell the facts of his early life, though his way and conversation made them a subject for secure surmise. He had left his own class and become a labourer. His health failing, he had taken to the road with no certain aim. After spending his money unadventurously he lay dying when we passed near, and Nell lifted him on to the ass and made him one of us. He recovered, but always seemed to be dying; his voice was a long sigh; yet was he the happiest of us all. I have heard him utter sour words, only against 'the rich,' 'the world,' and 'men,' who were the mainstay of his incurable pessimism of thought. His behaviour with men and women belied the theory of this gentle optimist in practice. Should any decisive political or social movement stir the world, he would not fail to point out its anti-human tendency, its trifling probable influence upon the sum of things. But the man – the politician or agitator at the helm – even if he happened to be well-fed, attracted his sympathy at once: he would insist on the man's character as a man, and on the way in which every man's actions when extended out of the reach of his sight will vary from their original cast. I believe he was an idealist. He spent whole days in searching for straight hazels in the copses and returned with a bundle like Jupiter's quiverful of lightning. 'I tried to get them perfectly straight,' he explained. He seemed in truth to have in his mind a long shelf of platonic ideas, dusty, rusted, moth-eaten by sorrow and the ills of the body. To these he referred all he saw in real life. His ideas were castles, Dulcineas, Micomiconas; and since he rarely met anything better than a Maritornes, his dull sight – or perhaps his charity – raised up the hands of these mortal, rotten things to his cobwebs and his gods, associating them. He would single out some poor house or inn, some unlucky girl's face, and transfer to them the glowing sentiments which he had once reserved for his inner, ideal vision of these things. He saw a miracle where there was in truth but a second-rate dawn. He felt an enchantment when everybody else felt cold. He thought that the ways of a tramp sorted better with the history of mankind than any other. Responsibilities and duties he had, but should he perish none would suffer. The responsibilities were co-terminous with the length of life which chance had planned for him. Nomadic, unencumbered by property, relatives, or social status, he was a creature in keeping with an unaccountable world. No storm, no social disaster, no philosopher or tyrant concerned him save as a spectacle. The stars in their courses were not more serene, more lonely than he. Such a friend of night was he, the stars were nearer to him than man. 'If only they would warm my hands!' he cried. When the north wind blew, it killed someone's sheep, broke windows, laid the corn; his ears tingled, he grew silent, and I believe that he rode upon the wind as happily as a witch or a brown leaf. A noble sound, the sight of the sea, or the perfume of a lane – 'I eat and drink them,' said he. Thus he seemed to me the half, as it were the female half, of the greatest poet that ever did not live. By difficult ways and strange, such a man is made a poet. He was once narrating the wonders of an evening in a wood; he paused and paused as I became expectant, and at last said with some shame that the very trees were 'like a church full of men when the organ begins; and I was no better than any one of them.' In outward appearance he was, like the other six, a brown tramp.

(1902)

Death by Misadventure

As the train slowed down between the long grey platforms all the men in the carriage dropped their newspapers to their knees and raised their eyes, without any appearance of thought or emotion, in short with a railway-carriage expression, to scan the name of the station, the small groups by the bookstall, the two or three intending passengers just coming through the doorway of the booking-office. On steeply rising ground above the station flocks of white linen flapped wildly and brightly in the back gardens of rows of new cottages. Above these, white clouds went nobly through the sky like ships ages on some long quest of love or of war.

When the train was still, there was not one shout. No one called out the name of the town or the place for which we were bound. No one cried 'Chocolate,' 'Paper' or 'Violets' though the vendors of these things were at hand a moment ago.

A stout man in black coat and black gaiters opened the door of our carriage and got in puffing, yet saying as he closed the door:

'Man killed. Carelessness. Nobody's fault except his own. Teach platelayers a lesson. Smoker and drinker, I'll be bound.'

People began to hurry past our windows towards the engine. Those in the carriage who sat nearest the windows put their newspaper on their seats and in turn put out their heads to look. 'You can't see anything,' said one.

The train backed slowly a few yards. 'He was under the engine,' said the observer. Some of us were dimly pleased to have had an experience which not everyone has every day; the stout man was disturbed by the delay; others were uncomfortable during this movement, as knowing that they were in part the cause of the accident and that their weight was now helping to crush out the blood and life of a man; one wanted to jump out, but while no one was willing to leave the carriage, all were bent on taking their turn at the window.

A policeman walked smartly by, and one of the seated passengers remarked that 'on the Continent' they arrest the engine-driver as a matter of course. Two porters followed with a stretcher.

'Now they are picking him up, but I can't see for the crowd,' said the one who now had his head out. 'Here he comes. . . . No. He must be dead . . . There is some more.' The train backed yet a little again. 'They have got all of him.'

In the little gardens the housewives and daughters were already watching. Old and young, buxom and slender, fresh and worn, in their white aprons and print dresses, leaned over the low fences, one stood upon the fence and stared. The scent of death had not taken a minute to reach those women whose sons and husbands and fathers and lovers include some — it is not known which of them — who are destined to die bloodily and unexpectedly. There was not a sound except the hissing of the steam, until the guilty train began to grunt forward again and take us past a little group of uniformed men with ashen faces surrounding the brown humpy cloth which covered the remains of the chosen one.

(1911)

Mike

For two or three years it had begun to be assumed and the probability even mentioned aloud that Mike would some day die. Not that there was any evidence that would bear sifting by one who was intimate with him. He was strong and hearty, and never had any wretchedness except when I threw a stick at him in anger. Looking back, we could say that his life's thread was spun 'round and full out of their softest and their whitest wool' by the Fates. He could still walk as far as ever. If I travelled twenty or thirty miles over the Downs he would walk and run two or three times as far. For he was nearly always hunting at full speed, visible or audible half a mile away, or he was examining every inch of the path, seeking an excuse to be off; and if that was not to be found he would look up to see whether I was thinking or otherwise inattentive to him, and then, his thievish thighs endued suddenly with all the wolf, he was off at his best speed which no shout could stop. In the rapture of the hunt his bark became a song, but as a rule it was hard and explosive.

Seven years before, when he became mine for five shillings – he was a stray – I used in my ignorance to beat him for hunting. Never having thought about it, I took it for granted that the habit was bad because dangerous and forbidden, and also a piece of wantonness and defiant self-indulgence. I did not cure him; I did not even make him dislike me; and therefore I began to laugh at the folly of lashing myself into a fury at the vice of disobedience under the pretext of improving the morals of an excellent dog. He forgave me so readily that it took some time for me to forgive myself. And so for seven years not a day passed but he hunted, and many were his whole nights spent in the woods. It was he who discovered for me that a partridge is eatable in May. He had no evil conscience by nature or from me, and so was often superficially unwise in choosing his bird; he would make his leap into the hedge where the partridge lay when the landlord was only a few seconds distant. But I learnt that there is a providence watching over such simple wants. However much the pheasant screamed as it flew a few yards and then dropped with fear to run certain other yards before the dog, no harm came except to the bird; as the glade rang with screams of alarm and yelps of delight I tried to look as if Mike was not mine; the keeper was beneficently detained or deaf.

He was a magically fortunate dog, and it was fore-ordained, that however boldly he might be leaping through a wood, he was always to alight with his four feet clear of traps. Wire nooses he often ran into, and many a hare and rabbit he must have saved by first entering a snare intended for them and then freeing himself by force or subtlety, returning sometimes with the wire and its peg still fastened on his leg as an inconvenient decoration. As he hunted in his first year so he did when the judicial minds, who knew nothing of him except what they believe to be common to all dogs, began to aver that he was getting old, with a kind of smile that one so mighty and so much vaunted should be giving way before them. They pointed out that he was silvering everywhere, that his head was almost pure white, that he lay dozing long after the house was astir; but I could see no real reason for believing that this change might not go on, as the phrase is, 'for ever,' and then when he was all silver he might have another life as a silver dog. So with his teeth. It was evident that the fangs which held on to a stick while humorists swung him giddily round and round were now very much shorter (I concede this), but still they held on; he ate as well as ever; he drew blood from the enemy as before. If a stump was as useful as the polished and pointed fang, why should not the bare gum of the hero be equal to the stump?

Gradually I got into the frame of mind which was no longer violently hostile to the proposition that one day Mike would die. But this did not affect my faith; it was an intellectual position with no influence on life.

He was no ordinary dog. That, the sceptics tell me, goes without saying: they argue that because all people regard their favourite dogs as extraordinary, therefore all, including Mike, are ordinary and will turn white, lose their teeth and die. In the main he was an Irish terrier. But his hair was longer than it 'should have been,' and paler and softer. His face was more pointed than was right; his ears, darker than the rest of him and silky (so that a child once fell asleep sucking one), usually hung down. His hindquarters approached those of a collie. Also his tail when he trotted along curled over his back and made children laugh aloud; but when he was thinking about the chase it hung in a horizontal bow; when stealing away or in full cry it was held slightly lower and no longer bent, and it flowed finely into the curves of his great speed. He was eloquent; his yawn alone, or the twitching of his eyebrows as he lay with head between extended paws, expressed a score of shades of emotion. He was very excitable, very tender-hearted, very pugnacious. He was a rough, swift dog, yellowish-brown above and almost white beneath, who was here, there and everywhere and always forgiven. He would attack any dog of equal or greater size, and test the magnanimity of the mastiff and the churlishness of curs running behind carriers' carts. But if a little dog attacked him, he lifted up his head, fixed his eyes on me, and looked neither to left nor right, but muttered: 'You are neither dog nor cat; go away.' As for a mouse, he thought it a kind of beetle, and was curious but kind. He would, however, kill wasps, baring his teeth to avoid the sting and snapping many times before the dividing blow.

I should like to be able to say that he had no tricks. The most splendid array of tricks only gives colour to the vulgar notion that a dog is, as it were, a human being manqué, a kind of pitiable amusing creature unfortunately denied the gifts of Smith and Brown. But this loud-voiced dog of violent ways, who leaped through a window unscathed, this fighter, this hunter, had been taught one trick before I had him: he would beg when commanded, but unwillingly and badly. The postman, cobbler, and parish clerk, a little wizened philosopher, would never let him beg for the lump of sugar which he carried as a daily gift: 'I would never beg myself,' he said, 'and I don't like to see a noble animal beg neither.' As for faults, I think he had them all, the faults, that is, which human beings call such in dogs – abruptness, invariable vivacity, the appetites . . .; they merged charmingly into his other qualities; isolated, they looked like faults, but good and bad together swelled the energy, courage, and affection of his character. Wondering wherein lay my

superiority to Mike, I found that it was in my power to send him
out of the room – as it lay in Alfonso's power to shackle Tasso.

Once in his life he became, for one hour, a lap dog. A child had
just been born in the house. In the evening all was very still and
silent; strangers flitted up and down stairs and along passages;
Mike's mistress was not to be seen as she lay motionless in bed, but
from her side came cries which he had never before heard –
therefore he leapt up into my lap and would not move for an hour.
Seldom did he do a thing which harmonized so well with those soft
brown eyes in a face that was all eyebrows.

So long as he was out of doors he was inexhaustible, and he
took every opportunity of trying his strength by hunting, racing
to and fro, and asking even strangers (with head on one side,
eyes expectant, forelegs stamping as he alternately retreated
slowly and leapt forward) to throw him a stick or stone. Perhaps it was in this expectant attitude that he looked his best,
every limb braced, his steps firm and delicate as he tripped
backward obliquely, his ears erect, his mouth open, and white
teeth, flame-like tongue and brown eyes gleaming together as
he repeated his commanding bark. 'What a nice piece of lean
bacon it would make,' said a child, looking at his tongue. He
fought with every inch of his body, and his movements were no
more to be followed than those of a wheel. His fury and
alacrity never ceased until intervention ended the fight, however
long. And as profound as his energy was his repose. After a
fight or a night in the wood he showed no fatigue until he was
indoors. Then he fell flat on his side and slept with quiverings
and snuffling yaps; and even then anyone's movement of pre-
paration for going out discovered a new fount of activity, and
he was up and had burst out of the door before the latch was
released.

When he was at least ten years old and looked very white slipping
through the beeches and troubling the loves of the foxes under a full
moon I confess that even I used sometimes to say that I hoped he
would die in full career with a charge of shot in his brain. He never
began to grow stout, and was never pampered; it could not be
thought of that he should come down to lying in the sun and taking
quiet walks of a mile or so, and living on pity and memory and
medicine, though memory, I think, he would have been spared.
Better far that, if he had to make an end, one of the keepers (a good

shot) should help him to it in the middle of his hunting. That would have been a fortunate death, as deaths go.

But he did not die. He forced himself through a dense hedge of blackthorn, came out combed and fine, stood hesitating among the first celandines, and was off after a hare. He never came back. If he could not bolt out of this world into a better, where there is hunting for ever, yet with his head on one side, ears cocked, eyes bright, he would not be refused entrance by any quadruped janitor of Paradise. But then we do not know what stage the belief in a future life has reached among dogs, and whatever the dogmas, heresies, scientific doctrines (that the fleshy dog manifestly does not survive, etc.), they doubtless have no power to influence the law and lawgiver, which are unknown to those it most nearly concerns. I only hope Mike is – or, rather, I wish he were – somehow, still hunting. There seemed no reason why he should not go on for ever.

I tried to believe that each one of the Cleeve houses had a canary, or a book, or piece of furniture, or an Irish terrier, to slip a kind of a soul in among its walls – that is in the case of houses not occupied by persons whom Christianity or Maeterlinck has gifted with souls.

(1911)

Saved Time

I dreamed that I walked far along a solitary and unknown road. Nobody met or passed me, and though I looked through many gateways on either hand I saw nobody at work in the vast plains. Nor had I passed or seen anywhere in the land one house, one coil of hearth smoke, or even one ruin, when suddenly at the roadside between two trunks of oak, and under their foliage two small windows gleamed faintly in the shadow. The glass was dark with cobwebs, dead spiders, and dead flies caught in the webs of the dead spiders; nothing could be seen through it but vague forms, yet darker than the darkness within, such as are to be seen under water in a momentary half calm. But there was a door between the two windows, and I entered as if I had been expected, though never had I seen or heard before of a house in the heart of an empty and boundless wilderness, but resembling a low second-hand furniture or marine store in a decayed part of London.

The door would not open wider than just to admit me sideways, so full was the room of its shadowy wares. These were all objects for holding things – cupboards, chests, and nests of drawers of all kinds, delicate cabinets, heavy oak chests, boxes massive or flimsy and of every material and workmanship, some no bigger than children's money-boxes, iron safes, small decorated caskets of ivory, metals, and precious woods, bags and baskets, and resting in numbers or solitary on the larger articles were trinkets with lids, snuff-boxes, and the like. They were clear and dark in a light of underground, the rows and piles that I could see mysteriously suggested one invisible infinity of others. As I trod a haze of dust rained and whispered unceasingly down upon them and from off them. Through this haze, or out of it in some way, like an animal out of its lair, appeared a small old grey man with cobweb hair, whiskers, and eyebrows, and blue eyes that flashed out of the cobwebs and dust whenever they moved. His large long grey hands wriggled and twitched like two rats cleaning themselves. He was all head and hands, and shadowy grey clothing connected him with the carpetless floor of rotten planks on which he made no sound. The dust fell upon him unnoticed and from time to time dribbled from his hair and beard to the ground.

'This,' said I suddenly, 'is a useful kind of box. I should like to open it, if I may, to see whether it would suit me. It is for papers that I shall never look at again, but may serve to light a fire or make a footnote for an historian in my grandchildren's time. If you would brush the dust off . . .'

'Have you the key?' he asked in a voice that made my throat itch into a cough. Did he think me a locksmith, or what? I was annoyed, but said questioningly, 'No.'

'Then I am afraid it cannot be yours.'

'But of course not. I wish to buy it.'

'It is not for sale.'

'It is reserved then for one of the multitude upon this highway?'

'Well, yes. But I hardly expect the owner to come for it now. It has been here some fifty years.'

'You can't sell it?'

'Oh, no! I assure you it would be of no use except to its owner. It is full.'

I rapped it, thickening the haze of dust and glancing at him to see the effect of the hollow sound on his expression. It had not the effect I expected, but he raised his eyes for a moment and said:

'You hear? It is quite full.'

I smiled with a feeling in which amused expectation swamped my contempt for his deceit.

'You have made a mistake. Try one of the others,' he said patiently.

I cast about for something as suitable, and having found an old oak tool-box of not too heavy make, I pointed to it and asked if he would open it. Again he replied simply:

'Have you the key?'

'Naturally not.'

'Most unnaturally not. But if you have not, then the box cannot be opened. I am afraid, sir, you have come under a pretence or a mistake. This box, like all the other receptacles here is owned by

someone who alone has the power to open it, if he wishes. They
are stored here because it is found that they are seldom wanted.
All are full. They contain nothing but time.'

'Time?'

'Yes, time. It is abundant, you perceive. All those boxes, bags,
etc., contain time. Down below' – here he pointed to the decayed
floor – 'we have more, some of them as much as fifty thousand
years old.'

'Then probably you have time to explain,' I said, hardly
covering my amazement, and in a moment awed by the reverbera-
tion of my words in a cavern which the echoes proclaimed as
without end. The planks rippled under me. My eyes wandered
over the shop until they stopped at a very small copper box
enamelled on the sides with a green pattern as delicate as the
grass-blade armour of a grasshopper; the top had the usual grey
fur of dust.

'What is here?' I asked.

'That is the time saved by Lucy Goldfinch and Robert
Ploughman twenty years ago. They were lovers, and used to walk
every Saturday afternoon along the main road for a mile, and then
by green lanes three miles more, until they came to a farm where
her uncle kept twenty-five cows, and there the old man and his
wife gave them tea. After they had been doing this for two years
Robert learnt a path going straight from the main road to the
farm, thus saving a mile or nearly an hour, for they kissed at the
gates. By and by they gave up kissing at the stiles and found that
they could walk the whole way in three-quarters of an hour. Soon
afterwards they were married. She died long ago, but he probably
has her key. Neither of them has ever called here. This,' he
continued, touching a plain deal box with iron edges, 'This is
another box of his. After they had been married a little while he
thought there was no good reason for walking three miles into the
town to his work, so they moved into the town. The time thus
saved was deposited in this box and it also has not been called for.'

Against Robert Ploughman's box was a solemn chest of oak
with panelled sides, and I asked what it was.

'This may have to go back at any time,' said the manager.
'Many times Mr Beam has been expected to send for it, though it
is only three or four years old. He was a squire, whose day was full
from morning till night with country works and pleasures, mostly

the same thing. There was no doubt that he did very much, what with planting, building, and so on, and that he liked doing it. Sometimes he used to turn his horse Fencer up an old road and let him do as he liked, while he himself sat on a gate and read Virgil, at least such parts as he had succeeded in thoroughly understanding at school. But at last the horse died and before he had begun to remember at the thought of the old road that Fencer really was dead, a kind friend gave him a motor car. He could not read Virgil in a motor car nor could he go up the old road, so that it was clear that he saved many hours a week. Those saved in this way are sent down here, but as he has not yet learned what to do with them or had any need of them, here they remain.'

He spoke with the same grey voice, scattering dust from his beard as his lips moved. I glanced here and there. The boxes were without end and I could no longer see the windows and door. The room was vast, and neither walls nor ceiling could be seen through the rows and piles. Most were of similar pattern. They were square, made of yellowish brown tin, or deal, or wicker, of about the size which holds the property of a young general servant. In the midst of some of these monotonous groups were chests or cabinets of more massive or more delicate make. I pointed to one of the groups and asked what they contained. He thrust his finger through the dust on top of the master box which was an iron safe.

'This,' he said, 'holds the savings of a man who invented machines for saving time. In a few years he grew rich and bought the chief house of his native parish. He employed four gardeners. He did not live there, but occasionally paid visits with business friends. The boxes you see round about belong to his less fortunate neighbours in the parish. They also have saved time. For when he went out into the world the women used to bake their own bread, make most of the family clothes, and work in the fields half the year. Now they do none of these things, but they have saved time.'

No ordinary shopman could have refrained from pride in the neat regiment of boxes over which he waved his hands at these words. But he turned with me to a solitary cabinet at the side of another group. It might have been supposed to hold letters or a few hundred cigars, and was scarcely large enough for my purpose.

'It contains,' he said, 'the savings of a young journalist. He was an industrious youth, earning a living without quite knowing why or how. He bit off the ends of many penholders, and often blackened his mouth with ink. He had an old pewter inkstand, once the property of a great-great-grandfather who was a pirate. He used to say that out of this inkstand he got more than ink, but his friends proved that this was not so by emptying it and showing that it was free from sediment. They advised him to buy a fountain pen because it wasted no time and it was impossible to bite the end of it. This he did. He no longer bit his pen or paused with the nib in his inkstand which was now put on his mantelpiece and polished faithfully once a week. He saved a quantity of time as his friends told him; but he did not notice it, for he continued to be industrious and to earn a living just as before. His friends, however, were right, and that box is full of the hours saved by him in ten years. It is not likely that he will come in search of them. He is busy saving more time. There are thousands of similar cabinets, saved by fountain pens, typewriters, cash registers, and the like. We have also some millions ready for holding the hours to be saved by the navigation of the air.'

He became verbose, enumerating tools, processes and machines for time saving. In one parish alone enough time was saved to extend back to William the Conqueror; in some cities it went beyond the landing of Cæsar to the Stone Age and even, according to some calculators, to the Eolithic Age – if such an age there ever was. But most of this time was now in the underground chambers that gave so solemn a resonance to my footsteps. To this too mathematical monologue I was indifferent and I strayed here and there until I seemed to recognize a home-made chest of deal. I had made several myself of the same pattern in former years. The proportions and peculiar workmanship marked this one surely as mine. I felt in my pocket for my keys and with some agitation chose one from the bunch. Yes! . . . No, not quite. Or . . . I could not open it. Yet I could have sworn . . . Meantime the manager had come up.

'This is my chest,' said I excitedly.

'Have you the key?' he asked.

'This almost fits.'

'Then you must wait until you have found the right one. People sometimes lose their keys. This chest contains . . .'

But what he said was so absurdly true that I raised my hand to strike him. He fled. I followed, thundering after him through the haze of dust and the myriad chests and caskets. I slid, I waded, I leapt, with incredible feats of speed and agility after the silent grey man until he went perpendicularly down. I plunged after him into space, to end, I suppose, among the boxes containing hours saved in the time of Lear; but I awoke before I had touched ground in that tremendous apartment. Forcing myself asleep again I recovered the dream and heard much more from the shopman which it would be tedious or ridiculous to mention.

(1911)

The Last Sheaf

(1928)

A Third-Class Carriage

When the five silent travellers saw the colonel coming into their compartment, all but the little girl looked about in alarm to make sure that it was a mere third-class carriage. His expression, which actually meant a doubt, whether it was not perhaps a fourth-class carriage, had deceived them; and one by one – some with hypocritical, delaying mock-unconsciousness, others with faint meaning looks – they began to look straight before them again, except while they cast casual eyes on the groups waving or turning away from the departing train. Even then every one looked round suddenly because the colonel knocked the ashes out of his pipe with four sharp strokes on the seat. He himself was looking neither to the right nor to the left. But he was not, therefore, looking up or down or in front of him; he was restraining his eyes from exercise, well knowing that nothing worthy of them was within range. The country outside was ordinary downland, the people beside him were but human beings.

Having knocked out the ashes, he used his eyes. He was admiring the pipe – without animation, even sternly – but undoubtedly admiring what he and the nature of things had made of the briar in 1910 and 1911. It had been choice from the beginning, not too big, not too small, neither too long nor too short, neither heavy nor slim; absolutely straight, in no way fanciful, not pretentious; the grain of the wood uniform – a freckled or 'bird's-eye' grain – all over. In his eyes it was faultless, yet not austerely perfect; for it won his affection as well as his admiration by its 'cobby' quality, inclining to be shorter and thicker than the perfect one which he had never yet possessed save in dreams. A woman who by un-prompted intelligence saw the merit of this favourite could have done anything with the colonel; but no woman ever did, though when instructed by him they all assented in undiscriminating warmth produced by indifference to the pipe and veneration for its master. As for the men, he had chosen his friends too well for there to be one among them who could not appreciate the beauty of the pipe, the exquisitely trained understanding of the colonel.

He was not merely its purchaser; in fact, it was not yet paid for. The two years of expectant respect, developing into esteem, cordial admiration, complacent satisfaction, had not been a period of indolent possession. Never once had he failed in alert regard for the little briar, never over-heated it, never omitted to let it rest when smoked out, never dropped it or left it about among the profane, never put into it any but the tobacco which now, after many years, he thought the best, the only, mixture. Its dark chestnut with an amber overgleam was reward enough.

As he filled the pipe he allowed his eyes to alight on it with a kindliness well on this side of discretion, yet unmistakable once the narrow but subtle range of his emotional displays had been gauged. He showed no haste as he kept his pale, short second finger working by a fine blend of instinct and of culture; his whole body and spirit had for the time being committed themselves to that second finger-tip. After having folded the old but well-cared-for pouch, removed the last speck of tobacco from his hands, and restored the pipe to his teeth, he lit a wooden match slowly and unerringly, and sucked with decreasing force until the weed was deeply, evenly afire. The hand holding the match, the muscles of the face working, the eyes blinking slightly, the neck bending – all seemed made by divine providence for the pipe.

When the match was thrown out of the window, and the first perfect smoke-cloud floated about the compartment, only the eye that sees not and the nose that smells not could deny that it was worth while. The dry, bittersweet aroma – the perfumed soul of brindled tawniness – was entirely worthy of the pipe. No wonder that the man had consecrated himself to this service. To preserve and advance that gleam on the briar, to keep burning that Arabian sweetness, was hardly less than a vestal ministry.

There was not a sound in the carriage except the colonel's husky, mellow breathing. His grey face wrinkled by its office, his stiff white moustache of hairs like quills, his quiet eyes, his black billycock hat, his unoccupied recumbent hands, the white waterproof on which they lay, his spotless brown shoes matching the pipe, were parts of the delicate engine fashioning this aroma. Certainly they performed no other labour. His limbs moved not; his eyes did not see the men and women or the child, or the basketful of wild roses in her lap, which she looked at when she was not staring out at the long, straight-backed green hill in full sunlight, the junipers dappling the steep slope, and whatever was visible to her amongst them. His brain subdued itself lest by its working it should modify the joys of palate and nostrils.

At the next station a pink youth in a white waterproof, brown shoes, and hollycock hat, carrying golf-clubs and a suit-case, entered the carriage. The colonel noted the fact, and continued smoking. Not long afterwards the train stopped at the edge of a wood where a thrush was singing, calling out very loud, clear things in his language over and over again. In this pause the other passengers were temporarily not content to look at the colonel and speculate on the cost of his tobacco, his white waterproof, and his teeth and gold plate, on how his wife was dressed, whether any of his daughters had run away from him, why he travelled third-class; they looked out of the window and even spoke shyly about the thrush, the reason of the stop, their destination. Suddenly, when all was silent, the little girl held up her roses towards the colonel saying:

'Smell.'

The colonel, who was beginning to realize that he was more than half-way through his pipe, made an indescribable joyless gesture designed to persuade the child that he was really delighted with the suggestion, although he said nothing, and did nothing else to prove it. No relative or friend was with her, so again she said:

'Smell. I mean it, really.'

Fortunately, at this moment the colonel's eyes fell on the pink youth, and he said:

'Is Borely much of a place, sir?'

Every one was listening.

'No, sir; I don't think so. The railway works are there, but nothing else, I believe.'

'I thought so,' said the colonel, replacing his pipe in his mouth and his mind in its repose. Every one was satisfied. The train whistled, frightening the thrush, and moved on again. Until it came to the end of the journey the only sound in the carriage was the Colonel knocking out the ashes of his pipe with a sigh.

The Pilgrim

The 'Dark Lane' is the final half-mile of a Pilgrim's Way to St. David's. It may be seen turning out of the Cardiganshire coast road a little north of the city. Presently it crosses the 'Roman road' to Whitesand Bay, and then goes doen into the little quiet valley that holds the cathedral and a farm and a mill or two. Travel has hollowed out this descent; bramble and furze bushes on the banks help to darken it. Yet the name of 'Dark Lane' is due rather to the sense of its ancientness than to an extremity of shade. Perhaps on account of the shadow it may cast on the spirits of men it is now little used, unless by the winter rains; and some days of storm had made it more a river than a road when I walked up it, away from St. David's. I looked back once or twice at the valley, its brook — the Alan — its cathedral, and the geese on its rushy and stony pasture. I had no conscious thought of antiquity, or of anything older than the wet green money-wort leaves on the stone of the banks beside me, or the points of gorse blossom, or a jackdaw's laughter in the keen air. If the pilgrims never entered my mind, neither did living people. The lane itself, just for what it was, absorbed and quieted me.

I was therefore disturbed when suddenly, among the gorse bushes, I saw a young man kneeling on the ground, his back turned towards me. If he had not heard me approaching he knew, as soon as I stopped, that some one was there. He was more surprised and far more disturbed than I. For in a flash I had seen what he was kneeling for; and he knew it. He was cutting a cross on a piece of rock which had been left uncovered by money-wort. Obviously he felt that I must think it odd employment for him on that December day.

He was not a workman carving a sign or a boundary stone, or

anything of that sort. He was nothing like a workman, but was clearly a young man on a walk. A knapsack and a thick stick lay at his side. He was dressed in clothes of a rough homespun, dark sandy in colour, good, and the better for wear, and with nothing remarkable about them except that the coat was not divided and buttoned down the front, but made to put on over his head. As he wore breeches he showed a sufficient pair of rather long legs. His head was bare, and his brown hair was untidy, and longer than is considered necessary for whatever purposes hair may be supposed to serve. He might have been twenty-five, and I put him down as perhaps a poet of a kind, who made a living out of prose.

He looked at me with his proud, helpless, blue eyes; his lips moving with unspoken words. He shut the knife he had been using as a chisel, and opened it again. I knew that he would have given anything for me to go on after saying 'Good morning,' but I did not go. I asked him how far it was to Llanrhian, and if the main road beyond here was the original continuation of the 'Dark Lane,' or if part of it was missing, and so on. He answered, probably, by no means as best he could, for he was thinking hard about himself. In a few minutes he could no longer keep himself to himself, but began to talk.

'I suppose you wonder what I was doing, cutting that cross?' he said in a defensive tone.

'Was there an old pilgrim's cross there?' I asked innocently. 'I have heard they carved crosses on some of the stones along the road.'

'I have heard so too,' said he, 'but I have been looking out for them all the way from Cardigan and have not found any.'

'Then you have carved this yourself?'

'Yes; and I suppose you wonder why. Well, I don't know; I can't tell you; I don't suppose you would understand; I am not sure if I do myself; and at any rate it is no good now.'

'I hope my interrupting you . . .'

'Oh, no, I don't think so. But when I began I thought it would be a good thing. I got as far as this at daybreak, and I was feeling . . . what is it to you? Seeing this old stone, which is perhaps the last before I reach the cathedral, and no cross on it any more than on the others, an idea came to me. I had been thinking about those pilgrims, some of them with torn feet, some hungry, or old, or friendless, or with an incurable disease. And yet they came here to

St. David's shrine. They must have thought there was some good in doing so; they would be better, even though their feet might still be torn, or they might still be old, or hungry, or friendless, or have their incurable disease. But the shrine is now empty. I did think that perhaps the place where the relics used to be, when they were not carried out to battle, would have some power. All that faith would have given it some quality above common stone. But I doubted. Then I thought. "But faith is the thing. If those pilgrims had faith there was no special good in St. David's bones, except, again, that they believed there was." I tried to think in what spirit one of them would have carved a cross. Perhaps just as a boy cuts his name or whatever it may be on a bridge, thinking about anything or nothing all the time, or sucking at a pebble to quench his thirst. At the sight of this stone — I may have been a fool — I thought — I had a feeling that while I was doing as the pilgrims did I might become like one of them. So I threw off my knapsack and chiselled away. . . . Please don't apologize. In any case it would have been no good. The knife was already too blunt, and I was cold and aching and also thinking of a wretched poem. Do you think a pilgrim ever had such thoughts? If there was such a one he would never have got far on his road.'

I tried hard to lure him into a Socratic dialogue to disclose what had brought him so far. He went on:

'The quickest city in the world is St. Pierre, which was overwhelmed by the volcano on Mont Pelée. But one cannot easily become a citizen of St. Pierre. Well, well, what is it to you that I want in some way to be better than I am? I must be born again: that is certain. So far as it is in my power, I have tried hard. For example, there is no ordinary food or drink or article of clothing I have not given up at some time, and no extraordinary one that I have not adopted. There remains only to wear a silk hat and to drink beer for breakfast.

'I have been to physicians, surgeons, and enchanters, but they all want to know what is the matter with me. I answer that I came to them to find out. Then they listen gravely while I tell them about a hundredth part of the outline of my life. They write out prescriptions; they order me to eat more or eat less, or to be very careful in every way, or not to worry about anything. They shake hands, saying: "I was just like you when I was your age. You will be all right before long. Good-bye."

'My family paid a specialist to come to see me at the house once. He and I had the usual conversation. Then he was given lunch, which he ate in complete silence, except for a complaint about the steak. After receiving his cheque my mother asked him rather tragically what to do. "Don't hurry him on, Mrs Jones," he said, "and don't keep him back, Mrs Jones."

'For forty days I visited an enchanter continually. He did not promise to cure me, though he also said that at my age he was just like me – which was untrue, for he had a Yorkshire accent. Day after day in his room I sat with closed eyes, repeating "Lycidas," silently with the object of not thinking about anything, especially the incantation. This consisted of a whispered, slightly hesitating assertion that I should get well, that I should be happy, that I should have faith, that I should have no more doubt, but confidence, concentration, self-control, and good sleep. After several minutes I always heard the enchanter take out his watch to see if he had given me enough. From that time until the end I was doing little but listening to the crackle of his shirt-front and cuffs. It was so funny that I was even more serious about it than he; but after forty days I had had enough. My rebirth did not take place in the house of the enchanter.'

'When I was your age . . .' I began; but luckily I was inaudible.

'I have tried many medicines,' he continued. 'I have been to a physician who offers to cure men who are suffering from many medicines. All in vain. I tried a medicine which all great writers take, and which presumably makes them greater or keeps them great; but it had no effect on me – my literary ambition died.'

Here he took out his watch.

'Zeus!' he said. 'I have been two hours at this thing,' and he rose up. 'I must photograph that cross and put it in my book. That will pay for the wasted time.'

He photographed the stone and cross, and departed with long strides down the 'Dark Lane' before I could ask about his book, but I see no reason to doubt that he was writing a book.

Tipperary

To the tune of 'It's a long, long way to Tipperary' I have just travelled through England, from Swindon to Newcastle-on-Tyne, listening to people, in railway carriages, trams, taverns, and public places, talking about the war and the effects of it. They were people, for the most part, who worked with their hands, and had as little to do with the pen as with the sword. The period was from August 29th to September 10th,[1] when everybody in town and village, excepting as a rule, the station-master, was discussing the transport of Russian troops down the country – 'if they were not Russians, then they were Canadians or else Indians,' as a man said in Birmingham. I shall write down, as nearly as possible, what I saw and heard, hoping not to offend too much those who had ready-made notions as to how an Imperial people should or would behave in time of war, of such a war, and while the uncertainty was very dark. For their sakes I regret that men should everywhere be joking when our soldiers were fighting and our poets writing hard. Though not magnificent, it is war. At Coventry a fat man stepped stately off a weighing machine. Seventeen stone, accumulated in peace. A lean man with a duck's-bill nose at once attacked him. 'You're the sort of man that stays behind, while a lot of fine young fellows go to fight for their country. I suppose you stay to take care of the ladies. When the Kaiser reaches Coventry he'll see a lot like you, You ought to be ashamed of yourself. You will be.'

Every one had his joke. The porter who dropped something and caused another to jump, covered up his fault by exclaiming, 'Here come the Germans.' Precisely the same remark was made when

[1] 1914.

small boys let off crackers after dark. The hostess with the false
hair, being asked if her husband had gone to the war, and how she
liked the idea of his being in Paris, replied with a titter that she did
not fear — 'the gay girls have all left Paris.' More serious, but not
more satisfactory, were the thousands of young men streaming
away from the football ground at Sheffield on a Saturday
afternoon. Yet even at a football match recruiting can be done and
the hat sent round. Some professionals were paying five per cent
of their wages to the Relief Fund, as men in a number of factories
were contributing 2*d*. or 3*d*. a week. And a man in blue overalls
said to me in Birmingham, 'If a man doesn't fight, he will do better
to go to a football match than to drink in a pub or stay indoors
moping.' On the other hand, everyone seemed to acknowledge
that the war was the great thing; at the free library a hundred
shuffling coughers were studying war to one that concentrated on
Aston Villa.

The most cheerful man I met was reading *The British Weekly*,
and continually saying rotund and benignant things. 'The Irish,'
he would pronounce, 'have responded manfully. In fact, this
unfortunate business has bound people together more than
anything else could have done.' A young Northumbrian recruit
was the most wretched. He had walked twenty-six miles to enlist.
'I wish to God I was back again in the village,' he said, 'though it is
a cock-eyed little place. Since I came here I haven't had a wash or a
brush or changed my clothes. If I were you I would sit farther off. I
have had a cement floor for a bed, and some of them singing till
three in the morning. We have to be out at six. The food's all right,
but it's worse than a dog's life. I wish I could get back, and I will
too.' Here a recruit of slightly longer standing, and already
wearing a uniform, cut in with, 'I wish I had your chance, I'd be
off. We have been moved fifteen times since July.' 'You'll be all
right in a day or two,' said a decent, wooden-legged man, flicking
away this fly from the jam of patriotism.

Most men fell short of the recruit in wretchedness and the
reader of *The British Weekly* in benignity. Unless the Kaiser was
mentioned they used, as a rule, the moderate language of sober
hope or philosophic doubt. The one act of violence I witnessed
was an oldish man, with a head like a German Christ, knocking
down a sot who persisted in saying, 'You look like a – German.'
More typical was the man I overheard at Ardwick, talking of the

black and white pig he was fattening for Christmas, regardless of
the fact that the Kaiser had God 'magnificently supporting him.'

Wherever I went I was told that employers – 'the best firms' –
were dismissing men, the younger unmarried men, in order to drive
them to enlist. 'Not exactly to drive them,' said one, 'but to
encourage.' Nobody complained. They suggested that the 'Gov-
ernment' had put the employers up to it, or that 'It don't seem
hardly fair,' or 'It comes near conscription, and only those that
don't care will give up good wages and leave their wives to charity.'
One old man at Sheffield remarked that it used to be, 'Oh, you're
too old' for a job; now it's 'You're too young.' It was added that the
men's places were to be kept open for them; they were to receive
part of their wages; if rejected by the doctor, they would be taken
back. 'They *have* to like it,' said one man. These were not the
only men who had lost their work. The jewellery-makers of
Birmingham, for example, young or old, could not expect to be
employed in war-time. Collieries near Newcastle that used to
supply Germany were naturally idle, and many of the lads from
these pits enlisted. Factories that supplied Russia were not busy
either, and Russian debts looked like bad debts. Some trades were
profiting by the war. Leicester was so busy making boots for the
English and French armies that it had to refuse an order from the
Greek army. Harness-makers had as much work as they could do at
Walsall. The factories for explosives at Elswick the same. Publicans
were flourishing though still ambitious; one public-house at
Manchester had these 'Imperial Ballads' printed on a placard:–

> 'What plucks your courage up each day;
> What washes all your cares away?
> What word do you most often say?
> Why, Imperial!'

the reference being to a drink of that name. But these successes were
extraordinary. Already it was said at Newcastle that shop-
assistants were serving for longer hours at reduced pay. Men
in motorcar works were on short time. A photographer at Manchester had to resort to this advertisement:–

> 'Gone to the front!
> A beautiful enlargement of any photo of our
> brave comrades may be had at a discount of
> 25 per cent.'

Where relief was being given, a queue of women stood along a wall in the sun.

For the women the sun was too hot, but not for the corn, the clover-hay, the apples, of this great summer, nor for the recruits sleeping out. The sun gilded and regilded the gingerbread. Everybody that could, made an effort to rise to the occasion of the weather. The parks and the public gardens were thronged. The public-houses overflowed, often with but a single soldier as an excuse. Bands played in the streets – at Newcastle bagpipes – to quicken recruiting. A crowd listened to a band at Birmingham outside the theatre before going in to hear Mr Lewis Waller recite 'Kipling and Shakespeare,' and the first remark to break the ensuing silence was, 'It's by far the best band in Birmingham, by far.' Street meetings having no connection with the war were held. Men in the Bull Ring at Birmingham one afternoon argued furiously on faith and works, quoting Scripture amid eager onlookers. At the top of Oldham Street, Manchester, two knots of men on a Sunday evening debated what would or would not happen under Socialism, while one in the centre of a looser knot shouted, 'Oh, my friends, God wants all of you.' The war, in fact, was the one subject that was not debated in public. A man breaking this rule was branded a Socialist. For instance, near the statue of James Watt at Birmingham a man had got into an argument about the provision for soldiers' wives. Moistening dry lips with dry tongue, he declared that the working class made fifty times the sacrifice of the upper class. He met nothing but opposition, and perhaps only persevered because he was wedged tight among his enemies and could not for ever keep his eyes downcast. At length a vigorous elderly man in a grey suit stepped in with fists clenched, said he was a working man himself, and laid it down that every one's business was to fight, to sink class, and to avoid quarrelling. His wife, smiling behind him, told the heretic that he ought to be ashamed. Someone chipped in, saying that as a matter of fact many wives were better off with their one-and-twopence than when the men were working. 'God help them before!' ejaculated the solitary man. Then another said he was going himself, and would go if his wife was penniless. 'Hear, hear!' said several; and others muttered, 'These here Socialists.' Of course, class feeling did exist. A workman in Birmingham hoped that not too many of the well-to-do would go to the front, because they were needed to give employment and to control it. The rich and the working-class, said a Coventry man, were doing their duty, but not the middle class – he called it the 'second class' – 'these young fellows who are neither man nor girl, and think about their socks all day.'

The war was not debated, but every one was bound to turn into it as into a main road of conversation, bound also to turn out of it. It could not be avoided. The newspapers issued edition after edition without reason. Pavement artists were strong on admirals, generals, and ships. Portraits of General French and Admiral Jellicoe adorned the entrances to picture palaces. Someone had chalked on a pavement at Manchester: 'See no sports. Fight the good fight.' Young men going to work by train began talking about the Russians. One interjected that he *was* glad to receive his salary in full at the end of the month. Another looked up from his paper saying, 'Kitchener's getting his second hundred thousand.' A Socialist was quoted as having said that 'we might as well be exploited by Germans as by British.' Gradually they drifted into stories about public men, into indecent stories about anybody, until running into a fog at Birmingham one exclaimed: 'It's a bombardment. We must be careful what we do and say to-day. It's a warning.' Older men going out to the Peak for Sunday, zigzagged from fishing yarns to 'uncreditable' tales told by a German in the Secret Service, on to the moorland appetite that makes you eat three-quarters of a pound of ham at a meal, and back again to 'I haven't had a day off except Sunday since the war began.' 'You durstn't.' The street roar of Newcastle or Sheffield was compounded of hoofs, boots, wheels, gongs, a thousand voices interwoven and one shouting, 'Fourth edition,' one whispering, 'If Turkey . . .'

Conversations definitely on the subject of the war, fed on the abstract diet which the Press provided, were much of a muchness. A man began reading: 'This bloke says the rapidity of the German advance on Paris fairly stupefied the French,' or he reminded his friend that 'this war has often been predicted in this very place.' A man interrupted his game of dominoes to say: 'I thought before now we were going to cut the German communications.' A man stands silent for a long time among his mates, and suddenly blurts out: 'What I want to know is, are these bombs' (he means mines) 'made of iron?' A favourite opening was, 'There's some great move coming.' The end of a conversation about the retreat was: 'The English have always been cool, calm, and collected.'

All kinds of abstract legends were current, as that the Germans were cowards, that the Kaiser was mad; but not many concrete ones. There was the Russian legend. Then there was a tale earlier in the war that British wounded were arriving at Grimsby, and the town was like a shambles. One man actually in Grimsby, answering an inquiry on the telephone, said that this was so; but another was able to deny it on good evidence.

One of the legends was that England was careless and slack. In the levelling of this charge I think there was a certain fondness as well as indignation. Men liked to think that we could play bowls and win a battle in the same day. 'England is too good-hearted,' said a man at Swindon. He came into the bar asking for 'Down where the water-lilies grow' on the gramophone, and, being disappointed, he sighed and began to speak of his 'month of misery'; for he had three sons and five nephews, or, as he sometimes put it, five sons and three nephews, at the front. 'The English are too good-hearted. Here, look 'ee. If any damned foreigner comes into this bar we give him a penny as soon as if he was an Englishman. Now I thinks and studies a lot. You recollect the manœuvres at Faringdon? Well, there was all nations there, Germans, Italians, Russians, French, Egyptians, and I don't know what – fifteen nations. Do you think they wasn't taking notes? Of course they were. And the Kaiser – the mad bull – didn't he come over and kiss King Edward, and wouldn't he as soon have knocked him down?' There was a man at Birmingham who began by talking about the Russians and Ostend, two millions of them, he believed. Oh, yes, they had certainly come down through England by night. He thought the Russians would repay the Germans for their atrocities. Nor do I think he minded. Yet he drew satisfaction from the faith that the English themselves would not retaliate. No, he said, the English are 'easy.' A Sheffield man who was advocating the bloodiest treatment for the Kaiser said that, 'If English soldiers fired at the Red Cross, Lord Kitchener would blow their brains out, he would.' Men were bloody-minded, to judge by their talk. They would have had no patience with the gentle person who had his favourite horse shot to save it from the battlefield. More intelligible to them would have been the gentleman of Cromwell's time who sent orders to have the sucking foals slaughtered that the mares might become chargers.

Such men had a strong, simple idea of a perfidious barbaric Germany. 'They have been preparing for this war ever since old Queen Vic died, and before that. I'd turn all the Germans out of England, same as they would turn us out.' 'I wouldn't; I would shoot the lot of them.' 'These nationalized Germans – you don't know what they are up to. Double-faced, they're all double-faced. They're savages, killing children and old men. I'd like to get at the Kaiser. I wouldn't kill him. I'd just turn him loose . . .' 'I wouldn't. If I could get at him, I'd . . . and choke him with them.' Thus spoke two workmen in Coventry. An old woman at Swindon – one of thousands – wanted to 'get at the Kaiser.' Everywhere men were drinking health – with a wink and 'You know what I mean' – to the Kaiser or the 'King of Proosher.' A very sober workman of fifty in Newcastle who was working short time simply did not know what epithets to give the man, and had to relapse on 'that tinker' (with much expression). Almost the only judicious reference to him that I heard was: 'Either the Kaiser is mad or he has found a new explosive.' People varied a little more in their attitude towards the German nation. 'They have got to be swept out of Europe,' said a man at Sheffield. A gentle old man was going to Harrogate with 'nerves run down' and 'distorted views,' and he had got it into his head that he had eaten a German sausage. The man with *The British Weekly* was consoling him: 'Oh, you may depend upon it, it did not come from Germany. There's nothing coming from there now. They make a great quantity at Leeds. They don't call it German sausage either.' A Tyneside Scot, after pronouncing the Kaiser mad to make war on 'all nations,' said: 'The Germans are a rotten lot. They won't stand and fight like any other nation. They keep moving all the time.' Others regarded the German army as a sort of ridiculous bully and coward, with this one grace, that it would probably shoot the Kaiser. A few praised German strategy and organization. One youth at Manchester even ventured to think 'they must be a fine race of soldiers.' A man at Sheffield held up a pair of German nail-scissors, lamenting that now he could not buy anything so neat at fourpence-halfpenny. A man at Manchester was asking: 'Where shall we get our gas mantles?' It was a Coventry man who went so far as to say that the German people were as good as ourselves and not so very different. 'They don't want war. It's not the Kaiser either. It's the aristocracy. Still, the Kaiser must not come here, like other deposed monarchs.'

This man, like every one else, was sure of victory. Some expected Paris to fall, but . . . They only laughed at any doubter. Most held the opinion that in retiring on Paris the Allies were leading the enemy into a trap. They did not stomach the idea of English soldiers retiring and retiring, and they imagined it must be deliberate. Open boasting had gone out of fashion, unless the man is a boaster who says on a black day that an Englishman is equal to five Germans. Patriotism took subtler forms. It was reported that one of the new Territorials weighed nineteen stone. 'Oh, but he will soon lose four or five stone, don't you fear. It's a healthy life, a grand life.' 'What I most rejoice at,' said a man at Swindon, 'is that we did not want the war.' Scores said something like it. It was 'the greatest war of all time,' said all sorts of people. In Sheffield a solitary pessimist was content to think it the ruin of Europe, a great sudden movement in 'evolution.' The dirtiest man in Sheffield, with the most rasping voice, talking among his mates on a Saturday afternoon about rights of way, dukes, corporations, trespassing, and poaching, jerked out the remark: 'The capitalist is forking out now to save his own property.' A printer in the same town said: 'We are not soldiers or politicians; we are workmen. We have our trades, it is not for us to fight. That is another trade: let the soldiers fight. That is what I used to say; but it won't do now. All I can say is that I don't feel like fighting, myself. There is a great deal of loyalty everywhere, and I hope we shall win.'

Peace was not much talked about. A man at Swindon was figuring a reconstruction of Europe after the war. 'Why,' he asked, 'why shouldn't all the countries be bound together like the United States? There are a lot of nationalities over there, and they agree very well, I fancy.' Probably many were using the same phrases as the Birmingham chess-player: 'The pity of it, when you think of all the education in England and Germany. *We* don't go out into the street and fight if we have a difference. It sets a bad example to the nation.' 'It's man's nature to fight.' 'It isn't mine.' 'Your move.'

Only one eloquent militarist did I hear, a Manchester Irishman. He, too, declared it man's nature to fight. From Cain and Abel, having demolished and labelled as un-Christian the suggestion that we were descended from monkeys, he branched out to the animals. 'It's the same everywhere,' he said. 'They must hit out. Until they have hit out, they don't know themselves. To hit out is a man's very life and nature, the best he can do, his greatest pleasure, what he was made for. Most of us have to obey the law, if we can. But the soldier is a hired law-breaker and murderer, and we must let him enjoy himself sometimes. Don't you go pitying the poor soldier. Poor soldier! This is the time he has been waiting for. He is in a passion, and nothing hurts him. Sudden death is a glorious thing.'

This was not a soldier. He was a workman, a looker-on, one of the thousand loitering workers and unemployed who stare at the hundred recruits between the statues of Watt and Edward the Seventh at Birmingham, and in squares or by-streets all over the country. The soldier has another style. A crippled pensioner at Birmingham said simply that if he was fit they would not have to call him twice; then he gossiped of the Burmah war, of catching and killing your own mutton before eating it, of an immortally tough bullock, of having a foot cut off by a Dacoit, of how far better off to-day's soldier is with his bacon and jam and tea for breakfast. A soldier's father at Swindon just said his son was glad to go, but wished it had been with Buller. These were men who would not be hurt till they were struck, and I do not know how much then. The Irishman was not one to squander himself on a battlefield; his duty to his country was to preserve his tongue without having to hold it. But he was a patriot.

Probably there are two kinds of patriot; one that can talk or write, and one that cannot; though I suspect that even the talkers and writers often come down in the end to 'I do not understand. I love.' It must happen more than once or twice that a man who can say why he ought to fight for his country fails to enlist. The very phrase, 'to fight for one's country,' is a shade too poetical and conscious for any but non-combatants. A man enlists for some inexplicable reason which he may translate into simple, conventional terms. If he has thought a good deal about it, he has made a jump at some point, beyond the reach of his thought. The articulate and the inarticulate are united in the ranks at this moment by the power to make that jump and come to the extreme decision. I heard a mother trying to persuade – pretending she was trying to persuade – a young man against enlisting. She said: 'I would not risk my life for anybody. It isn't yours, for one thing. Think of Mary. I would sooner go to America . . .' She found a hundred things to say, few of them quite genuine, since it was her desire to overpower him, not to express herself. In argument he was overpowered. His reasons he could not give. Nevertheless, if he passed the doctor he was going; if the doctor rejected him, he rather hoped some girl would taunt him – she would have to produce a champion to justify her. Had the eleven or twelve thousand recruits from Birmingham written down their reasons, I dare say they would not have been worth much more than the pen, ink, and paper. That is, assuming they included no poets, and I do not see that they were more likely to prove poets than the men, women, and children who made haste to send in their verses to the papers. Out of the crowd at Newcastle the dissatisfied one spoke best. If any at Coventry or elsewhere were kept waiting so long outside the recruiting office that they changed their minds and went away, they might speak better still. Some men of spirit may have kept back to spite their interfering persuaders. Why, the lowest slut in the town, fetching her beer at eleven-thirty, would look after a procession of recruits and say: 'So they ought to. Lord! look what a lot of fellows hang about the corners. They ought to fight for their country.'

There was really no monotony of type among these recruits, though the great majority wore dark clothes and caps, had pale faces tending to leanness, and stood somewhere about five foot seven. It was only the beginning, some thought, of a wide awakening to a sense of the danger and the responsibility. Clean and dirty – some of them, that is, straight from the factory – of all ages and features, they were pouring in. Some might be loafers, far more were workers. I heard that of one batch of two hundred and fifty at Newcastle, not one was leaving less than two pounds a week. Here and there a tanned farm labourer with lighter-coloured, often brownish, clothes, chequered the pale-faced dark company. The streets never lacked a body of them or a tail disappearing. Their tents, their squads drilling this way and that, occupied the great bare Town Moor above Newcastle. The town was like a vast fair where men were changing hands instead of cattle. The ordinary racket of tramcar and crowd was drowned by brass instruments, bagpipes, drums and tin boxes beaten by small boys, men in fifties and in hundreds rounding a corner to the tune

of 'It's a long, long way to Tipperary.' Thousands stood to watch
them. With crowds on the kerb-stones, with other crowds going
up and down and across, with men squatting forward on the
pavement, it was best to have no object but to go in and out. The
recruits were the constant, not the only attraction. The newest
ones marching assumed as military a stiff uprightness as possible.
The older ones in uniform were slacker. Some stood at corners
talking to girls; others went in and out of 'pubs' attended by
civilians; more and more slouched, or staggered, or were heavy-
eyed with alcohol. Everyone was talking, but the only words
intelligible were 'Four o'clock winner' and 'It's a long, long way to
Tipperary.' At nightfall the boys who beat the drums and tins
began to carry around an effigy and to sing 'The Kaiser, the
Kaiser,' or

> And when we go to war
> We'll put him in a jar,
> And he'll never see his daddy any more.

Companies of recruits were still appearing. Perhaps their faces
were drawn and shining with drink, fatigue, and excitement, but
they remained cheerful even when a young officer with a dry lean
face and no expression said 'Good night' without expression and
rode off. His was the one expressionless, dead calm face in the
city, the one that seemed to have business of its own, until I
crossed the river and saw the women on the doorsteps of the steep
slum, the children on pavement and in gutter. They were not
excited by the fever in Clayton Street and Market Street, any more
than by St Mary's bells banging away high above slum and river,
or by the preacher at the top of Church Street bellowing about 'the
blessed blood of Jesus Christ.' In an almost empty tavern a quiet
old man was treating a lad in a new uniform, and giving him
advice: 'Eat as much as you can, and have a contented mind.' It
was a fine warm evening. But what could the great crowd do to
spend its excitement? As a crowd, nothing. In a short time it was
doubled. For at nine o'clock the public-houses had to be emptied
and shut. The burly bell of St Nicholas tolled nine over thousands
with nothing to do. Those who had not taken time by the forelock
and drunk as much as they would normally have done by eleven,
stood about aimlessly. A man took his stand in Bigg Market and
sang for money. It was not what people wanted. Several youths

together at a short distance and tried to bawl down the singer. Even that was not what people wanted. Even the temperance man was only half pleased when he reflected that what he had long agitated for in vain had been done by one stroke of the military pen. There was nothing to be done but to go to bed and wait for the morning papers.

In the Crowd at Goodwood

When three or four races had been run, the crowd of poorer and of non-sporting on-lookers spread once more over the course, but as few pretty women and gay dresses remained in the select enclosures, the crowd turned away, and the course became almost empty. Some lay on the slopes below and ate or smoked; below them small bands of early-goers and late-comers were mounting or descending the paths of the hillsides. Beyond them, and above the tree-hidden village and railway station, the land rose again into many rounds of bald or beech-capped hill, and beyond these into a level ridge that was all one oak wood. Here the barley was in stooks; there the oats were obliterated by poppies. Under one dark edge of beechwood a broad field was lemon-coloured with charlock. Above all was a cloudy and windy sky, now and then permitting gleams out of the blue to give a summer sound to the broil of continually tossing branches in the beechwoods of the hills, and the elm clusters by farm and wayside.

The earth, like the sky, seemed to have nothing to do with the flimsy white grandstand on the hilltop, the long white rails lining the curved course, and the gay crowd and the grey crowd. The only difference to the earth was that the grass and furze of the near slopes were decked abundantly with paper of several hues, and that the paths of the neighbourhood were trampled into mire and extended to the width of a wide road.

The greater numbers of both crowds were on the other side of the course, where drink, food, betting and amusements were to be had, with a dark background of stately and innumerable beeches, the 'birdless woods.' There were long rows of motor-cars, carts, and bookmakers' stands; behind them a row of booths for eating and drinking and games of some skill and more luck; and behind these again the caravans and low tents of the gipsies and other nomads; then the road and the high wall of the 'birdless woods,' noisy with the wind and yet looking silent.

Now in the interval the bookmaker, 'Joe' or 'Charlie,' could heave his vast bulk out of the cart and arrive somehow upright upon the ground below with garments still unburst by the quaking volume of flesh which they contained. In solitude, but not in silence, he licked up two plates of salmon with much vinegar. Now the dark sportsman, with frowning face, bulging eyes, and square blue jaws, stood munching bread and lobster, converting it, with even more determination than content, into frowning face, bulging eyes, and square blue jaws. Some one had given oranges to the bare-legged band who had been tumbling about, swearing, cheerfully quarrelling and backing the jockey with the red cap and black shirt, etc., and they ate the peel whilst watching the lobster-eater without too much envy. He in his turn had half an eye upon a gipsy woman of enormous bulk. She was certainly as much a 'sitting' as a 'religious' or 'laughing' animal. She sat alone, among the horses, in a deep yellow blouse, many-coloured gaudy shawl, black skirt, and high-feathered black hat. Without stirring anything but an eye, she watched the young bony-faced women from neighbouring tents — their brown faces newly washed, their black hair combed and evenly parted, their eyes bright as with a little quicksilver, and their lips smiling, as they bent down, holding buckets at a pump worked by the menfolk.

The spectators flowed in streams and masses alongside the tents of the gipsies, who were washing, cooking, eating, talking, or educating the young, exactly as if they were surrounded, not by a crowd, but by four walls of a house. Their horses were not more unconcerned, though they were more still, with patient bended necks. Stillest of all were the hounds, curled up, and silent and asleep, all but their eyes and ears. Sometimes the crowd formed an island to allow two knowing little barefooted boys to box, or a ponderous, ill-featured couple to dance, all beaming with alcohol and mutual affection. The gipsies and other showmen were blessed with strange contentment. For example, at the end of the row of stalls and coconut-shies a man was standing in charge of a great low table. Clients were to spin the indicator and thus just possibly win one of the coconuts or plates of shell-fish upon the table. He was a burly man, as broad as he was long, with a face like leather, and stiff black hair and moustache, and no roof to his mouth. He invited clients by a powerful monotonous cry of 'Come along. You can't all win. You can't all win' – which was a very accurate statement. As he ended the cry he stooped, and with great ease won a plate of shell-fish. This he refused to eat, having won it only to encourage others. He then repeated his cry of 'Come along. You can't all win. You can't all win.' Powerful as was his voice, his deformity made him almost unintelligible, and for this or some other reason – as, for example, the philosophic accuracy of his thought, if not his speech – no one answered his call. Yet he also had this strange content, and obviously no fear of to-morrow, death, or anything else. He was no ghost. But the crowd was ghostly. The nomads, working and idling, were real enough, but not so the main crowd, eating, drinking, smoking, betting, or looking on. It was a childless crowd, and there were few women. Laughter was not infrequent, but no smiles could be seen. The visitors were not at ease: collected from everywhere, and massed together, they had yet nothing in common but internal solitude and external pursuit of pleasure. Separated from their homes in Lambeth, Redhill, or Portsmouth, they seemed to have lost their identity. Their immortal souls had taken holiday, scattered about perchance like the paper on the gorse of the hillside. They were nothing but bodies, dark suits and bowler hats. The man with no roof to his mouth was not a ghost, but I can make no such assertion about any of the multitude, of which I was one.

The most native and natural to the place of all these thousands were the four white 'minstrels' and one blacked bone-man, who appeared in this interval for the first time. The white duck suits (with purple collars and cuffs) and straw hats seemed a kind of undress in which they had been surprised; and they matched the trivial white grandstand and temporary buildings, and might have been born and brought up there. The sight of them made me think of the summery white woodwork in December, and the minstrels encamped in it alone amidst the wind, rain and frost of the high solitary downs. Even on that day, whenever the sun was in the cloud, the wind was chill. It was chill as the minstrels came out, wiping their lips from the meanest of the refreshment booths. None of them was young, and none was fat. Two had not dyed their grey hair. All were clean-shaven and had regular features, colourless, hard actor faces and grey eyes. The eldest, a venerable sharp-faced boy of fifty, was limping. They remained silent and in single file as they put away the ends of their cigarettes, and climbed the steep bank up to the course, stooped in a brisk-looking style under the rails, and crossed over to a place within two yards of an enclosure. There they formed a line, still in silence; but after a brief glance at one another they plucked their banjos while the bone-man grinned a flashing grin, shaking his black college cap, so that the red tassel fell towards his nose.

Suddenly they began to play and sing. As they did so, even the venerable 'father' of the company began also to sway and rise and fall from heel to toe with a jauntiness to match the tune. The few men and women still strolling in the enclosure now strolled vaguely towards the minstrels, and one or two even stopped by the iron railings and stared at them in silence. One beautiful, fair, tall woman, of not quite forty, the only woman in the enclosure, and her daughter of about eleven, both in white and green, came up and watched them smilingly, her head thrown in a sort of kindly haughtiness back under her yellow parasol. Others came and went, but these two stayed. They smiled out of perfect health and good nature, but partly also in pity for the singers, and in scornful amusement at the song.

The four minstrels, known among themselves and to some seaside crowds as 'The Bonny Bachelors,' were singing the joys of watering-places, of summer holidays spent in drinking copiously and walking out with 'lots of girls.' The five verses brought before the mind this vision. A crescent of tall, gaunt boarding-houses and hotels following the line of a bay from an old castle at one end to an abrupt cliff at the other. Half-way between the castle and cliff a pier, painted white, and running far out into the sea on countless long thin legs. A promenade, the whole length of the crescent, having a stone parapet and a wide stone pavement continuously trodden by holiday-makers. Here and there two or three young men dawdle up and down with light canes and cigarettes, and make eyes at bunches of girls slightly below them in class. Out at the pier end a band plays jerky, frivolous music. A few sails dot the bay. A white motor-boat throbs fussily out to sea. On the green rocks below the castle end of the parapet a lonely man is casting a fishing-line far into the still water. The sea is clear blue in the hot, perfect weather. With the aid of brandy and soda-water – of some

blearing of the eyes and much dull spending of the spirit of youth –
the glare of the sun and the blue sky, the long dim outline of the
high coast, the glittering sea, the heather and sea air, and the loud
music, the glances, neat forms and happy movements of girls,
mingle in the minds of the young men into a half-delirious and
half-dreamy hope, so that they seem to be walking in a world like
that of a musical opera, of wickedness, gay, expensive and
without ending, where all the women were as beautiful as that one
in the enclosure at Goodwood, and all the old men as frivolous as
the grey-haired minstrel.

The song had a jaunty tune, composed, as it was meant to be
sung and heard, in a state of incomplete intoxication. It combined
languor and jauntiness to a miracle. It was continually tending to
perish of languor and continually rescued by jauntiness. It
expressed, with a perfect understanding of popular opinion, the
gaiety of bachelors and emancipated husbands.

The beautiful fair lady and her pretty daughter stood and
smiled at the middle-aged minstrels singing the dull, saucy chorus
again and again. The happiness and beauty of these two in the
light of the sun was so full that everything partook of them. If they
heard the skylarks singing above the birdless woods they did
not discriminate between that music and this of the 'Bonny
Bachelors.' Each gave them an equal opportunity for happiness,
and a fresh excuse for a smile.

The fifth verse was sung with all the determination of the first,
and the toes of the most aged minstrel seemed not to tire of rising
and falling to the tune. While the chorus was still being repeated
the blacked bone-man took off his college cap and made as if to
ask the listeners for rewards. Immediately, all within the
enclosure, except the mother and daughter, gave some more or
less consummate intimation of having just then something else to
do, and they stalked off as slowly as was compatible with safety
before their charity was undeniably besought. The beautiful lady
did not move away, but even came a little nearer, right to the
railings, and smiled and said a few words which gave her
happiness, while she and her daughter put something into the
college cap. Everyone else on the course as well as in the enclosure
had escaped the appeal. Nevertheless, after an interval spent in
silence while the bone-man was away, up again went the purple
cuffs to the banjos, and up went the heels of the cricket shoes, and

the tune was repeated. Still the lady smiled, either at the minstrels or at her daughter. Only after the third verse, and without any sign of weariness, but smiling and gently giving a bow, which the bone-man returned with prodigious courtesy, she moved away with the sunshine. The crowd was now thick about them, and there were too many coming and going for the bone-man to fill his cap; those that stood still were looking at the beautiful two departing, not at the minstrels. They made an end only just in time to leave the course with the crowd before the next race. In slow, silent procession, still looking the only natives, the soiled white and purple and the misfitting black of the 'Bonny Bachelors' were distributed in the crowd, to re-light their half-cigarettes, to watch the moment's inhuman fury and beauty of the horses passing in the race, and, when it was over, to return and hope to see their patronesses again. When the eldest of them appeared to be about to consult a bookmaker, some one in the crowd flung the jeer: 'Think of your wife and family'; but he joined in silence as before the jauntily bobbing row of the 'Bonny Bachelors' playing the old tune.

The Friend of the Blackbird

For the whole of one year, whenever my daily walks led me down a certain old lane that used to be full of sun and forgetfulness, I was sure not to have it to myself. It was no longer used as a road, the farm it had served once being covered up in ivy and nettle; and as a footpath it was not a short cut to anywhere. Until that year I had met no one there. I have not met anyone there since. He was nearly always in the same place, just where the first bend in the lane shut out the road. At first, I thought he looked unusually out of place, with his new, stiff clothes, tall grey hat, polished ebony walking-stick, and movements angular and precise. I was not glad to see him — an invalid, I supposed — in a place which I once believed to be my own, and could not regard as a thoroughfare.

One day he stopped me by asking the name of a flower which he pointed out tenderly and politely with his glossy stick. As he spoke he turned his eyes towards me, though hardly upon me, so that I seemed to be bathed in their light, which had a cold brightness and purity as of newly melted frost, and a blissfulness also which was so intense as to be unearthly. Clearly he was one who saw invisible things. Feeling that he was not looking at me I could observe his eyes closely, and they were indifferent to my curiosity. They were moistly bright, of a clear grey, and almost circular, the lids being unnoticeable under the gentle arches of thick, light-brown eyebrows; their expression was of childlike earnestness and simplicity, tinged with surprise that might almost have been fear. His face was square, and the delicate skin, drawn tightly over prominent bones, was nearly all concealed by the short brown hair on cheeks, lips, and chin. Through the hair showed a pair of lips matching the eyes — full, moist, shapely, and soft, of an unblemished innocence. He was short, squarely but lightly made.

His voice was in keeping with eyes and lips; it was deep, slow, and soft almost to a breaking point.

I saw him many times before we spoke more than a few words again. As I passed he used to cast upon me that bright, unchanging glance without any kindliness in its gentleness, and seemed to feel rather than to see that I was on that common plane where everybody knows what you mean because you mean nothing in particular. In reply I could only look upon him with curiosity that was quickly overcome by discomfort, by awe, and even a kind of dread. Beauty, genius, or happiness, each in its own way, compels awe akin to fear, in the detached beholder. This man had happiness. Never before or since have I seen happiness so shining. Where at first I had blindly seen only his external incongruity with the untended hawthorns and virgin grass, I came to see perfect fitness. He was entirely at home there. In my memory the intensity of his happiness is all the more wondrous because of the pain of his end not much more than a year after I saw him first.

He knew himself that he was to die soon.

He was the son of a farmer among the mountains. When he had to go to school at eight or nine years old, it was in a town within sight of the ridges, but thirty miles away. In the town he had grown up. He was there when his father died, and except on the day of the funeral he never revisited his home. Tired of school, he left of his own accord and became a collier. For six days out of seven he washed only his lips clean, and that with ale. At the end of the sixth he washed the whole of his face, that he might kiss a maid. He fell in love. But the maid died, and at her funeral he dropped, fainting, into the grave. From that day he began to read all night. He seldom saw the sun, except on Sundays, and then only through the windows of his bedroom where he worked, or of his chapel. He began to preach, and in a few years was thought fit to be a minister. His furious pieties in the pulpit won him at first a congregation that would travel many mountain leagues on horse-back or on foot to hear him. But out of the pulpit he was a different man. He was silent and morose. He would take no part in festivals, in music, in politics, in judgments of erring man or woman. They thought him proud; they muttered that they would not go on paying a man to mount up into the clouds for one day in the week, and when he had recovered from a long illness, he found he must go to a small house in the hills to serve two chapels many miles apart. He had loved God over-much. But he did not cease from loving. God hid Himself from this worshipper, but he knelt and smiled as if God had loved him. He thought of no one else; there was none but Him and of Him he thought as winter changed to spring, and spring to summer, and summer to winter, as roads glide into one another. He did not look down to behold the earth and sea, nor up to the sky. There was nothing for him but God, and the two little grey chapels far from man, on the great moors.

Once again he fell ill and in his delirium the truth passed before his eyes – that he had loved God overmuch and His creatures too little. Sickness left him unable to walk any more from chapel to chapel over the cloudy hills. He had to teach little children in a hamlet so poor that they were glad of him. There he lived alone, except for the children and the birds that inhabit the lean oaks of the stony copses, the alders along the brooks, the fern upon the lone crag that filled half of his northern sky. Since his illness he had forgotten about God, and remembered only the misery of his creatures. But the children and the birds cheered and taught him. On this earth he learned that it was a man's part to love the earth and its children. There would be plenty of time left in eternity for loving God. We do not demand, he reflected, that the maidservant lighting a fire at dawn should think about the sun, or that the soldier loading his rifle should think about his king; and so an earthly man need not greatly be troubled about anything but his fellow-men and animals, companions of the brief lifetime that is as a meadow in one of the folds of the mountain of eternity. In those old days, he thought, when the Lord went over Jordan with the children of Israel, men were as children, and He walked with them, but now He has ascended and we see Him not until we also shall have gone up, we know not whither. Nor did his thought perish when another sickness overthrew him and left him one hand trembling as if it were no longer his own. The children presented him with the ebony stick, and he left them to die. In the meantime he had taken to this lane.

Sometimes he brought a book out with him, and when he did, it was a book of travel or natural history. He had an inexhaustible desire to know about everything that lives on the earth, both near and far. He had learned the songs of many birds, and spoke of them familiarly with admiration and delight. The immensity and variety of Nature, as he found himself, or read of it in the gorgeous records of travellers, were a source of continual satisfaction; he had never dreamed of them before. Everywhere he found beauty, personality, and differences without end. The old simplicity and horror of the world conceived as the abode of evil man and a dissatisfied, incompatible Deity were forgotten. He could speak of God without emotion. After reading a book in which a liberal and gentle soul created a liberal and gentle Deity, and showed the necessity for his own adherence to the religion of his fathers, his only comment was: 'It is a good book . . . a good God, but not a very great God after all . . . What does that thrush say? We must consider him. But so far they do not seem to know very much about him, except his skeleton and his diet. There must be one God for both of us. We can afford to wait. So can He.' But that was only a casual, light-hearted expression of the creed that was coming to him under the sky. He turned away to look at a blackcap singing every minute high up in golden-green blossom against the blue sky, where the sun and the south-west wind ruled over large, eager grey clouds with edges of gleaming white. The little dead-leaf coloured bird quivered all over; his throat swelled in bubble after bubble; his lifted black head was turned from side to side as he sang; and he moved slowly among the blossom.

The high, quick, dewy notes filled the paralytic with a thin, exquisite pleasure, as if his soul had climbed upon the line of his vision and crept into the singing bird. 'All these things are mine. They are me. And that is not all: I am them. We are one. We are organs and instruments of one another.' He did not forget the trees – 'those tethered dreamers, standing on one leg like Indian mystics.' With them also he felt the same community, as though more rarely and in a way not to be spoken except by putting out his hand to touch their bark and leaves. The animals, too, were more remote than the birds, and reminded him too often of men's careless sins of cruelty. He did not preach kindness to animals, but pitied those men who had not yet awakened to the need of kindness, as if they must be suffering for the lack as much as the animals. He could not tell why men kept birds in cages to sing. Their freedom in living and dying was lovely to him. Every creature, including man, is best in freedom, he said, looking up at the white clouds coursing in the freedom that was from ever-lasting to everlasting. He sighed with regret, mingled with apology, as animals slipped away out of sight. Then he was glad to hear the blackbird and thrush again, the sweet, lively talking of the thrush and the pure melody of the blackbird. They were his favourites. He could talk of the different blackbirds he had known, and their places in town or wild, and describe their differences. With a little laugh, because he remembered the days before he had such thoughts, he said plainly that they had souls and lived, as we do, after death, though he did not know, nor perhaps did they, what life it might be. Only, there was one thing in the blackbird that he could not enjoy – probably, he admitted, because he could not understand; and that was the laughing, discordant notes that often concluded his song, especially in the late spring. This distressed him, partly because it was not musically in keeping with the song, and partly because the bird seemed to be laughing at himself. He had been reading Byron, and it reminded him of the way the poet sometimes wound up a stanza with a cynic phrase; and he could not enjoy this in bird or poet. Those birds were children of the sun, he said to himself. Before, if not above, all birds and all creatures, he loved the sun. The only time when he mentioned again the little grey chapel that stood highest among the mountains was to conjecture that it was built near the site of a temple for sun-worship. There were large upright stones in an adjoining field that were said to have formed part of a sun temple; and he liked to remember that. It was the God, not of the old stones, but of the chapel, that descended upon him in his last illness.

For weeks he lay sick and wild with dreams of the night and fears of the day. He raged and accused himself of unpardonable heresies, and defiance alternated with remorse. He was placid only while he whistled over and over again with unearthly sweetness and clearness, a fragment of one of the mountain songs of the blackbird, heard far away in the wild lands. It was a fantastic whim, for Whatever overpowered him in that friendless death-chamber, amid snow and silence, to wrest such blasting discords out of an instrument that had seemed in the lane to know only natural joy and tranquillity. 'The little God,' he said, in one of his latest moments of relief, 'the little God torments me.' And again: 'But I go to the Great One. It is well.'

Friend of the blackbird, is it well?

A Sportsman's Tale

(1909?)

My friend would be content with nothing but a day's rough shooting.

He had just come home after several years in South Africa, and, having spent the first few days in London with his family, he had taken the train down to Mayse to see me. He had not changed except that his skin was toasted to a nicety, and his moustache bleached as pale as a toothbrush. On the evening of his arrival we drank whisky together because we had done so on the evening of his departure ten years before. In an attempt to make nothing of those years he told many of the same stories. He had little to say about South Africa. It was, he said, a marvellously gold country for brown boots, on account of its long dry season. Speaking of the natives, the Boers, and the condition of affairs, he said that the English newspapers of a shade of politics different from those with which he left his native land were entirely misinformed or wilfully mendacious. We fell to recalling our schooldays, as we always used to do. We had spent the best ten years of life together and after that saw one another about twice a year, and at each of these meetings we revived the same things and grew sleepy over them and the drink and the long dark cigars that look so well sticking out of his handsome face and agreed so poorly with me. No shadow had ever fallen upon our friendship. We were two entirely different natures – he was a cricketer, a sportsman, a dancer, and could jump over spiked railings as high as his shoulder. Now and then he would look puzzled, or I would be impatient, but we yawned and smiled, filled our pipes, and recalled the story of the cat and the baker.

Most of those ten years which had bound us together were spent out of doors. Our friendship had begun on a paper chase from our school in a suburb of London when he was twelve and I was ten. We found ourselves left alone after running and walking through a sunny October morning, because he had gone off alone on a false scent and because I ran badly. We had never been in that lane of larches before. It was the first time we had got into a piece of pure country out of London on foot. We had been in the country by long railway journeys to seaside resorts or the native places of our parents. But this was different. We had no idea that

London died in this way into the wild. The sun shone. Rooks cawed on oak trees standing in undulating pastures at the edge of a long wood. Moorhens hooted on a hidden water behind the larches. We came to a small grey inn at the end of a row of old cottage gardens all full of the darkest dahlias, and my new companion bought enough bread and cheese for us both. We walked on without thinking either of home or of the chase and ate slowly but in large mouthfuls. Gradually the half green road was lined with horse-chestnuts, the fresh fruit and empty pods lay bright in the glittering grass, and as we ate we stooped continually and put the biggest into our pockets. 'What's your name?' he asked suddenly, musing and not looking at me, and pleased and not at all surprised I told him 'John Hughes'. At which he said merely

> 'John! John! John!
> With the big boots on'.

I knew his name well enough, for was he not the younger brother of the best runner in the school? Harold Born. And so we became friends. It was nightfall when he had got into the trail again and began to retrace it. I was worn out and would have given up but for my pride in the long run and the pleasure of feeling that he did not mind my hanging on to his arm . . . Again and again we revisited that lane of larches and the long oak wood, and took moorhen's eggs in spring and chestnuts in autumn. For some years I at least had a strong but vague and untried belief that the place had been forgotten and was known only to us, so solitary was it and so peculiarly bright the sun and green the grass and lazy the cawing of the rooks, and sweet the singing of the missel thrushes in the little round islands of wood amidst the ploughland – those islands which, when we advanced together to another school used always to come up in my memory with the words of an old Greek poet about Circe, daughter of Hyperion, who bore three sons to Odysseus, the strong and blameless Agrios and Latmos and Teligonos, and these 'very far off in the holy isles ruled over all the glorious Tyrrhenians'. When we had not visited the place for some weeks it used to appear from time to time as extraordinarily beautiful, and though I knew that when I next went that way with Harold I should find it, I did not really believe that it existed – for others – when I was away from it.

From that year onward we two went through most of the stages into which the ordinary man's love of Nature is divided. First the wild unconscious play when we hardly distinguished between the open fields and the neighbourhood of towns except that we preferred the fields. Then, very soon, the hunting stage when we deliberately played at savages. Then the time of collecting eggs, flowers and insects, of stuffing birds and animals. And not long before we left school, the poetical stage when we read poetry out of doors, or rather I did, while he listened. There was not a poet's emotion which we did not heartily believe ourselves to share, evoked by the poem but not imitated from it. What had come to the poets in their most serene or passionate moments we glided into as easily as we gathered flowers for Maud or Blanche or Mabel, as we lay in the grass with our eyes divided between the books, the land and the clouds. Yet even in those days I nearly laughed – only it was not permissible in those awful rites to laugh – to see Harold with his handsome heavy face reciting from 'The Revolt of Islam' with a grave, puzzled expression discernible under the rapture. His feeling for Nature was unassumed and profound, I am sure. At school and generally with people, except at games, he looked rather stupid, but in the fields he wore a blessed confident look which was a mark of grace. Yet I think none of the modern poets had expressed his feeling exactly. It was too simple and old for that, and he could not have said what it was himself. It was the feeling perhaps which Homer left unexpressed. In my nimbler fashion, however, I led him on with delicious and impassioned unreality through the moods of Theocritus, Spenser, Marvell, Gray, Blake, Wordsworth, Shelley, Coleridge and Keats; he assenting good humouredly, only half willing and yet more serious than I at heart, I on the other hand overdoing many parts. He drew a line only when I used to discuss the Greek mythology and valiantly import the gods and goddesses and nymphs into our groves. Poetry was very well, but these figures in firm cold marble stood in no conceivable relation to any truth known to him. And in this matter he did not hesitate to laugh as heartily as in the classroom when the master was absent . . .

On that evening of his return I reminded him of this and he laughed again. He said he no longer read poetry. The volumes I had persuaded him to buy were in their old places in the bedroom at his father's house, scented with dead flowers and with the camphor of butterfly cases. He had looked at them the night before and torn out a flyleaf on which he had written some heinous Shelleyan rhymes of his own. He recalled them in his honest way, at once diffident and bluff – 'O bounteous universal Pan' . . . and many other O's – 'And let me not do any deed That sins against thy gentle creed' – 'Teach me to honour all I can The things that are afraid of man.' In Africa, he said, you learned how low is the value set on the lives of animals, natives and Boers. He had gone back to the hunting stage and his voice was full of enthusiasm when he proposed that we should make a day of it with our guns and the spaniel Dash, and be up at day-break on the following morning. And so he went to bed. But I must needs turn up one of the books we had owned together and read

> Where is the throng, the tumult of the race?
> The bugles that so joyfully were blown?
> – This Chase it looks not like an earthly Chase;
> Sir Walter and the Hart are left alone . .

So well was the experience remembered that the words were tedious, and I shut the book.

We were out early the next day on one of those October mornings when we seem to taste all the stored richness of the Spring, Summer and Autumn days that have gone by, and we forget utterly that the next day or the next will let in Winter. The air was full of mist which unveiled for a moment and then veiled again the ridges of distant stony hills, hard and angular as a lean cow's back, and a hem of blue sky above them; and sometimes hid the treetops of the near wooded hills and everything above them. The mild silver sun and the insinuating mist played together, the sun loving to find out one elder leaf diaphanous and wine-coloured among the green, or, while the mist possessed all but the whole wood, wooing the solitary green ash at its edge. Then the mist would seem to die away altogether into the sky; the ivy bloom hummed with bees and wasps and flies, and the dead leaves began to smell hot and sweet; the coloured woods on forgotten hills stole out into sight as if borne along by the wind that scared the mist, and we fell silent altogether, I because I could not talk and he because he supposed I would not. Again the scalloped capes of white vapour found themselves again upon the hills, even to the grassy feet of their woods; and only a pond in all the land would retain a visible memory of the sun; the trees dripped; the dark thickets glittered with dewdrops on thousands of cobwebs.

Harold was delighted. This, he said, was England pure and simple. Really, you know, he continued, when you have lived in a country like this you cannot treat the friendliest of foreigners as one of yourselves; it is no use pretending. They can do a lot of things we can't, I admit. Pictures, buildings, dresses and so on. But they have not got a country in the way we have – I mean nothing like this, just outside your door, that makes you feel just as you did when you ran out of school on a half holiday and began kicking a football about. That is not quite it, either . . . His face was puzzled and he was half angry with me for being the cause of his trying to explain what he did not wish to explain, when Bang! he fired at the first rabbit and it bounced up with the leap of its life and fell dead. His face now emerged out of the mist that was descending over it, and he was at ease again. He hummed an old mournful air which he had always hummed when he was pleased right through. He looked at me, and just to say something, asked: 'What are the words of that song, you know?' 'You were humming the end of "Poor Old Horse"' I said. 'O yes!

"Likewise my poor old bones that have carried you many a
                                                        mile
Over brooks and ditches, gates and bridges, likewise many a
                                                        stile,
Poor old horse, poor old horse."'

Funny thing' he went on, 'that they should have a tune like that about an old horse, and supposed to be spoken by the beast. When I hum it it always makes me think of the last time I rowed in my college boat. We did well, but it was my last time . . . funny thing, music. I should say that musicians that make tunes don't know what their music means.' He fired again, this time at a wood pigeon that was wavering in its flight as it neared the copse and took thought on what bough it should choose for a perch. It continued to rush forward and fell sharply against a tree just inside the copse, breaking its beak. A thrush that had been singing flew desperately away, and the silence was complete. My spaniel was old and hung behind, taking every least excuse to lie down in the warm short southward sloping turf among the rabbit holes. The country was as quiet as a church, and every time Harold fired at pigeon, rabbit or hare, it struck me as odd that a man could smash the silence so easily. I had not carried a gun for years and should not have fired that day if I had not been afraid of Harold's amusement and also willing to show him that I could still drop a flying bird at fifty yards in a clean manner. 'Beautiful' he cried with genuine pleasure as a pigeon fell. Winding about round spinneys and down thick hedges we forgot one another and became absorbed in our different ways. The sun had sucked up the dew, and the dead leaves were dry and quietly rustling. Harold looked marvellously content with his way of greeting the great mother from whom he had been absent so many years. As for me I saw a hundred things that might have made a man happy and loved them and yet was not happy with thinking of a poem I had re-read the night before, and especially the end where the poet calls Pan

> Strange ministrant of undescribed sounds,
> That come a-swooning over hollow grounds,
> And wither drearily on barren moors . . .

I was impatient with myself at thinking that after all these years I had never troubled to understand the poem written by that young man at Oxford. To thrill with the words and a throng of clouded images, recollections and half relevant digressions as I sat in an arm chair was not to understand them. Living in a city at the end of the nineteenth century, I had been at no pains to abandon the conditions of such a life in search of what was clearly before the mind of that young man as he mused on the son of Mercury and Dryope or, as some say, of Penelope. Mine had been the usual fault of readers of poetry – to think that it was a flutter of words about things within a man's easy experience, an exaggeration of ordinary matters, or else a mere invention, a pretence pardonable because venerable in antiquity.

As I walked, lagging farther and farther behind my companion, I thought I was getting rid of this fault, at least so far as the song addressed to Pan was concerned. Once I sat under some beeches and saw Harold disappear and leave empty a long narrow winding valley whose smoothly rounded sides were clothed in tall ash trees, low underwood, and its bed with grass. Yet not empty! I was quite certain that over and above the trees and the grass, and the singing thrush, over and above the visible form and colour and all things of which an inventory could be made by a close observer, there was something else, and something which there was a power within me specially fitted to perceive, could it but be called up out of the dungeon I had made for it by all the carelessness of my past life. I sat and watched the feathered ash leaves fall slantwise through the still air and the beech leaves fall down straight. Many lay at my feet crumpled and rustling as they curled up crisp in the heat. Those left on the beeches, and they were many, were so richly coloured that they seemed to roast and crackle in the sun. At the dome of the sky there were deep blue valleys winding among white clouds just as the green valley below me wound among the gorgeous trees. In the south the sun was a dazzling disc of glass.

But where was that 'strange ministrant of undescribed sounds', the nymph-lover, the 'dread opener of the mysterious doors leading to universal knowledge'? My curious credulous eye saw the beginnings of giant shapes in the root work of the trees, in branches whose twistings mingled fantastically, in a rock bearded with moss that jutted out from the wood's edge; but I was not to be put off with some goat-legged hairy creature standing upright and with horns upon a head like a man's head.

I looked up at the blue through my hands, fascinated by the line of indigo following the outline of the flesh, and by the fine hair-like beams with which my gold ring was bristling. I closed my eyes and let the sunlight pierce the eyelids with a glitter of pearl. So long as I kept them closed I felt as if a hurry of myriad feet and wings were encircling me round about, but when I opened them I saw only the tremendous stillness of the earth, saw the silence and the stillness which had emerged from mere negations into a positive expression of hidden life. The arch of sky which also was very still, a low tender sky, was at one with the earth, and suggested those old gods who were lords of the breath of life, gentle and mighty, who swayed thunder and rain in the heavens and at the same time cared for forest, garden and flock on earth, who might be represented by a statue with a head and shoulders of celestial beauty rising above a trunk and limbs of heavier and rugged mould, upon feet imperfectly emerging from the unhewn rock, an Apollo above, a Pan below. Peaceful as was the valley and the hollow sky I was conscious of an element of terror lurking within those genial, rich woods and the mild pastures rising beyond.

Even Silvanus was said to have cried out in a loud voice, from a forest hard by a battle which he had watched, acclaiming the victors.

When Harold came into sight again on a sloping field under a high wood, he looked ghostly small and weak as if he were passing into the palace cavern of such a god, whose power it surely was that made this figure of a man, up there in the pale grass, so flitting and vague. He turned out of sight round a corner of the wood.

The invisible presence was not enough. It was all about me: I felt myself being absorbed by it as one is by a crowd in a moment of great fear or suspense. My need was deep for some visible thing to which I could bow the knee or lift eyes of trust or expectation. If this surrounding power would take form I could recover and pack together my own identity, which was fast escaping, and perhaps lay it at the feet of the god.

Hardly was I shaken out of this condition by the report of another shot from Harold's gun; but his voice followed with a medley of bellowing cries that might satisfy the very heartiest lover of echoes feeling at ease with himself on such a day — hunting cries, imitations of a horn, repetitions of my name as a mere excuse for a musical rolling shout of a kind I had not heard for ten years. And before each cry and doubled and tripled echo sped all affrighted portions of the great power — scurrying away in all directions like rabbits in a hollow field when someone appears suddenly at the gateway. I jumped up, only half glad to be released, and rejoined Harold.

We were now on a high piece of rough common. In front of us the mist was still clinging to the hills like a memory, like a wraith of the old race that left its bones under the cairns on top. The splashes of light were bold and large on the golden trees below the mist. Round us was dewy furze, grey green, and fragrant bracken, and brambles ramping this way and that, and on the short turf some ivory fungi, a few harebells, and the warm blue flowers of the least scabious. We gathered a few blackberries. A robin sang an intent song with a melancholy which I could see no reason for, yet welcome and very sweet. A few grey fieldfares scattered away from us with wintry cries. The air was still and perfectly warm. It was out of this bracken that Harold's next rabbit broke and never reached the opposite gorse which was all it thought of when it began. Before it leapt in the air as if shaken violently I had been following its movement, forgetting my companion, with a kind of belief that it was the last of the scurrying multitude, fragments of the divinity, which his shouts had put to flight a few minutes ago; and involuntarily I gave a slight cry and said 'life parted from life' and then 'it has failed' more loudly so that he heard and with his jolly voice retorted 'Dead for a ducat . . . Let's have lunch; if I only had the patience to wait for it I could eat all I have shot . . . well, with a little help from you'. He picked up the rabbit and was silent.

So there with our backs to a dead gorse bush that was as warm as a fruit wall, we sat down and ate our lunch. Suddenly, after laying a sound foundation of sandwiches Harold said:

'I almost wish I hadn't shot that last rabbit; I am not superstitious, but I will tell you why. A man I saw a lot of in the Transvaal – quite the finest shot I ever knew – a Scot – a man, you may say, who shot with his eyes and merely made sure with his trigger – used to drop his rifle now and then when he had actually covered a buck or whatever it was, just saying, "No, that's forbidden", and let it go. After a time I asked him about it. After looking rather surly he told me when he was a boy he was out one day in Argyllshire shooting with a man who taught him the art. This was a mountain man, stern and religious, who lived with his grandmother, a reputed witch – a real ancient Briton, I imagine. Well, this man was discovering birds by magic in little bits of woody and oven bake ground, as if he had put them there himself and made them fly up just at the right moment. He would say "There!" and sure enough out of the earth went up just what he was looking for. They made a good bag and Angus was getting excited, when the man said "There!" again; but as soon as the bird rose he caught Angus by the arm and said "No. I made a mistake. That is forbidden". He told me that he believed even if the man had not touched him he would not have fired, as he felt something . . . something weird. It was odd, but after that he had a return of the same feeling from time to time and would as soon have gone against it as have shot his grandmother (which was his teacher's phrase). But I never felt it myself until now. Angus used to say: "Some of these creatures don't belong to us, but . . . and I know it at once when I see one." He was a queer chap, a pro-Boer although he lived there, – so thick headed he was and did not see ordinary things . . . These dates lined with almonds are excellent.'

Nevertheless, Harold applied himself in an altogether enviable manner to the lunch, and I also was hungry. It was almost too warm. We finished our pipes on a gate nearby, not talking much as we caught the full stretch of landscape before us, the mist now no longer to be seen but its ghost surviving to soften hill and wood and in half hiding everything visible to reveal the invisible. Harold knocked the ashes out of his pipe in a decided manner as if to recall himself to himself and proposed to return to a wood he had hurried over in the morning. I had not finished my pipe and said I would wait a little. He strode away with that splendid step that singled him out in foreign cities and country places as a conqueror. I slipped down off the gate and went back to the gorse and half leaned upon my elbow on the warm turf. Harold's gun did not once disturb me, yet at first as I lay with my dead pipe I kept turning round as if something were near and yet not in the least expecting to see anything when I had turned. This feeling is perhaps peculiar to townsmen who are seldom long alone and are at all hours open to visits of one kind and another, besides being half aware of the coming and going about them in neighbouring rooms or houses or roads of that life which even when unheard makes a 'tingling silentness'. I know that some cannot quite comfortably support this vaguely expectant state in the remote country where reason tells them that it will be disappointed, and where even if they wish they may have to travel miles to see a man. But I am not much troubled in this way. On the contrary I have a fear lest there may be a man somewhere near who will be curious or want to talk. In a short time I was at ease, fearing no disturbance, and lying with my face to the cool eastern sky. The gorse, the grass, the fungi, the blackberries, the light dry soil itself, all warmed by the sun, gave out a pervading sweetness, which always has for me a profound homeliness like the smell of peat for one who was born where they burn peat fires. Gradually I got used to the scent and filled with it. I was bathed, but now quite pleasantly, in a sense of enfolding companionship all round me, and I closed my eyes in order to woo it more closely. How many times have I done this, setting aside an enchanting book with a hope to meet a deeper enchantment, only to fall asleep! And sure enough sleep came, and in my sleep I dreamed.

I dreamed that I was riding with Harold and that we galloped until I lost him in a wood that seemed everlasting when suddenly it ended in high precipices under foot, and steep narrow clefts between them, and below the precipices lay the sea; and because the descent down the clefts was very steep I tied my horse to the last oak and descended one of them until I came to the strip of orange sand bordering the calm sea. Looking now to the right and the left I could see no ascent for return, but only a long wall of granite precipice all but perpendicular. It was not such a wall as I had imagined when I stood at the edge with my horse. It was pierced by tiers of enormous arches in rows apparently without end. They were raised on pillars capable of supporting the earth and its mountains, as indeed they seemed to do. When I went nearer, I saw that those pillars, and all the lofty archwork as of a gigantic dovecot whose doves were the fabled rocs, were made not of weathered stone, but of the roots of the forest which I had left. While I went slowly along the sand I looked between the arches and saw labyrinthine corridors surmounted by similar arches and supported by similar columns. The multitude of these columns made a forest lighted with a clear cold light, and it was paved with orange sand. I entered and my footsteps were the first to dint that pavement, I could see nothing alive in all the spaces before and above me. No sooner had I lost the light of the sun than I felt it to be impossible to turn back. My feet so moved that I rather floated than walked. 'This' I said to myself 'is the grave,' but then I smelt again that homely scent of the warm earth and perceived that I was no longer alone. I was passing with a movement that needed neither feet nor wings through a misty host of creatures whom I could distinguish as men and women, beasts and birds. They were nothing but eyes, that flashed out, like flowers seen at twilight seeming to hang suspended without stalks, and disappeared and gave way to others in the mist. Nor did I look for more than eyes, but I thought that they looked askance at me for my solidity. As I moved onward they gave way and closed behind me with a light whispering of slender voices like a wilderness of reeds when a solitary man creeps through them over a fen at dawn. Some of the eyes troubled me with uncertainty; for either they were yellow and fierce as a falcon's and yet known to me for a man's, or they were wild and sorrowful and yet an animal's. One and all fled from me after they had gazed upon me into that dense innumerable thicket of eyes. When at last all had left me I saw that the pillars had become taller and farther apart like a forest of beeches and chestnuts. The sky was formed by the foliage meeting overhead, a green sky as of beaten metal. So tall were the trees that larks soared and sang but never touched that sky. And in the avenue where I walked I recognized the two rows of chestnuts where I had walked as a boy. Like that childish country this also had its own sun. There was the same light on the grass. On either side between the trees I saw the same fields and in the midst of them the copses of old which still continually sent forth fountains of thrushes' songs. But it was not permitted to turn aside and I was soon past these places I had known and beholding broad happy fields and fortunate glades which also I recognized: not that I had ever trodden them, but that they were unquestionably those which Virgil had described; this was the ampler air and this the light of a sun shining for them alone. Here, I knew, I cannot say how, the poet had seen the heroes of Troy and the poet priest in sweeping raiment, born in the golden years, feasting, singing, upon the river meadows, beautiful and majestic, and with them their beautiful horses; and here had stood their chariots. But I saw them not, and heard not their singing. Instead of Ilus and Assaraius and Dardanus, founders of Troy, stood the mammoth and the mastodon, huge and mild and at ease. There pastured, not the warhorse, but the delicate stag and many herds and flocks divided after their kind, and hares and rabbits leaped amongst them as they fed. The groves rang with the music, not of poet's harp and the paean of heroes, but of blackbird and nightingale. The sunlight, warm and blissful and serene, dwelt over tree and grass and pasturing flocks and singing birds, visibly blessing them. High up in the green heavens sang what seemed great white birds whose melody was sweetest of all, high and full and unpolluted; but one fell suddenly out of the branches at my feet, stained with crimson and motionless. I looked round and saw no cause, but a voice whispered, 'Have not your poets told you that a skylark wounded on the wing doth make a cherub cease to sing?' I thought to say that we on earth did not take our poets literally, but there was no ear in which to speak and I went on once more. Nothing disturbed me or those fortunate fields. I was able to taste with no pang save of extreme pleasure the beauty of the crystal air and of the trees and their branches carving it with proud and exquisite forms, of the grass burning amidst the boles with a myriad flames of cool emerald that were never consumed, and the undying flowers of purple and white and gold. So clear was the singing of the birds that it could almost be seen making perfect forms that slowly died into the soft wind. Very black was the black feather and very scarlet in that pure air, and the golden petals shone as if each flower had burnt its way out like a star through the sky, and all the ground seemed hollow under my feet. All things appeared to me like the earth when it is fairest in May, in youth, at the most perfect moment of youth, and yet not quite the same: it was as if my eyes were bathed in fairy dew so that they saw everything and the souls of all, and I were an omnipresent spirit hovering over the life about me with full delight. The inhabitants took no heed of me. They ran, they flew, they reclined, they perched and they sang. The birds soared to the green sky, and some, I thought, descended out of it and flew always in one direction.

I noticed that there was a broken stream of birds and beasts moving continually the same way, and that I had taken this path: I continued to do so. Sometimes the trees opened wide apart and ceased altogether for a wide space, though always on one hand or the other could be seen a line or group of trees having the effect of a temple. Over these open spaces a roof of silver mist took the place of the green ceiling of leaves. The land here was smooth, but moulded with an infinite variety of hollowed vale and heaved upland as of heavenly Downs. Great rivers ran through the land, with islands of lustrous grass and of trees. On the higher land I passed their sources, lakes which were as blue and deep as the sky above the earth. Birds floated upon them and animals grazed at their edges or stood and looked over, and among the beasts there were a few men, of great stature, shaggy and silent.

One of the hills to which I was now being led was higher than the rest, and I thought as I approached that it was the wall of this country. The birds whose course I was following alighted from time to time on the trees far up its flanks. The trees were now gathered once more into a grove, and here the birds were silent. I should have said it was evening, so still and solemn was this ultimate grove, had not the air been as lucid as before. The arriving birds were flitting from tree to tree onward along the grove. In front of me rose a round lesser hill clothed in straight lofty trees of many different kinds whose clear stems row above row, resembled the pipes of a majestic organ; and round about this the gathering flocks were slowly eddying. At one edge of this round hill I saw what seemed a steep rock like one of those rocks which take on the likeness of a giant at sunset in a wild land. Equally still, surrounding it and dwarfed by it, lay a circle of enormous crag-like beasts, mastodons, elephants and others which I had never seen, or read of, or dreamed, though the human fancy is so strange in its capacity that I at once accepted them, in my growing awe, as living things. Behind this mighty circle were the lesser animals, giraffes and lions, and great horned cattle, elks and mooses, and a few of the tall men I had seen beside the lakes; and these in their turn half concealed row behind row, without number, of the other beasts and from the wolf to the hare. So large and dark and multitudinous was this circle that it was like one of the assemblies of ashen clouds waiting above the grave of the set sun, or promontories and lesser cliffs and uncouth rocks bent round a gulf of the sea, in the midst of which towers a dark isle – as the giant-like rocks or rock-like giant towered in the midst of the conclave before me. And just as sea birds rise from such an isle and cloud it with wheeling pinions so these birds encircling the central rocks hid it half from my sight. Birds of every kind were mingled in that dreamy motion of many plumes. And they were woven harmoniously so that the solemn oaring of the heron, the nervous reflective flight of the wood pigeon, the hurtling of the wildfowl, the darting of the kingfisher, the gliding of the swallow, the undulating of the little birds, all made one tremendous coloured flood.

The thought was irresistible that those motionless beasts and swaying birds were united in worship of the strange figure in the midst, and I felt a threat in the immense power before me. I wished to turn away and to watch it at a distance, but I could not, and I heard the voice that had spoken before saying 'This is great Pan'. I looked and fancied that I could make out among the wings two horns like leafless and branchless trunks of oak, and even the dark gleam of two eyes which might have been springs of water in the rock. If any other voice than that in my ear was speaking it was wrapped up in the murmur of the worshipping wings.

Certainly the god did not acknowledge my solitary arrival. He had been in this underworld almost since crows were black, and though he knew much about men, it was not often that (he) saw one such as I. So spoke the invisible voice admonishing me. When the god descended here man had not long appeared in the upper world. Here he was not admitted, or only one or two at long intervals were allowed to take the shape of bird or beast. Most of these were poets, but not all poets came hither. And what are those who are not poets, I asked, and I learned that they were of many kinds, and often such as were despised by other men. The voice refused to tell me who they were, because it would throw men into despair, since they cannot live on truth and yet are discontented with anything else. For the most part men, when they die, disappear into the wandering air. They do so much on earth that they are weary and they are incapable of ease. But, said I, these are the Happy Fields of which the great poets have told us; where then are the heroes of old. Most, I learned, are dead and dust, turned to flowers and grass to feed cows and birds and bees which were before men and will survive them. Achilles, indeed, among the heroes, was here, brought down for his love of horses, but unrecognized now in equine form. Men were the god's dream, and they in turn dreamed him, but they were an error, and became a nightmare, and their creator fled down to the underworld to escape from them. They cut themselves off from their kind, from the rest of the animals. They never wearied of persecuting those others of whom many disappeared from the earth and were safe only in the pastures under the world. Men retain nothing of the animals except the belief that they are never to die. They would have perished long ago were they not replenished from time to time by offending spirits of birds and beasts. Once they also worshipped with the rest, and of those were the men scattered in the circles of beasts round about the god, but they became proud and forgot the god of all and disdained these happy fields and could worship only an incarnation of man. What could men do here? They could not be content to sing and feast with these myriads, so they are turned into flowers and into the wandering clouds and the winds, and so their hot spirits are calmed and cooled and humbled and taught to forget, while those other creatures pass from one world to another as out of one field into the next and are content to know no difference, save that here there are few men. Rapt by that unceasing motion of adoration I could have stood for ever as still as the quiet beasts, but the thought came over me to kneel upon the grass, and as I knelt I tasted the scent again of the autumn grass, and burst into tears, falling face downward upon the earth and lying there listening to the wings. So soft and deep and warm and sweet scented was the grass that I forgot the god. Never, I think, would I have wished to raise my head out of that deep grass, when suddenly a loud violent noise shattered the peace and the music. I half rose up, my hand still buried in the warm fur of the earth, and my brain unconsciously struggling into the world. But my wet eyes were swiftly aware of Harold coming towards me, his gun in one hand, in the other a dead hare.